Readers love Gayleen Froese

Lightning Strike Blues

"This is a refreshing 'take' on the superhero trope.... The story is exciting with plenty of mystery and angst."

—Paranormal Romance Guild

The Man Who Lost His Pen

"These types of stories are very difficult to pull off in a novel, but Froese did not disappoint! Every single character and movement and set piece has a purpose, and seeing it all through Ben's detective eye is fascinating."

—Emily's Hurricane

The Girl Whose Luck Ran Out

"Definitely recommended for those who like to follow mysteries, enjoy engaging characters, and second chance romances."

—Nat Kennedy Books

"I can't wait to read the next book in the series. I believe once more people hear about this book, Gayleen Froese will have a hit on her hands."

—Gina Rae Mitchell

By GAYLEEN FROESE

BEN AMES CASE FILES
The Girl Whose Luck Ran Out
The Man Who Lost His Pen

DISCHORD
Lightning Strike Blues

SEVEN LEAGUES
The Dominion

Published by DSP PUBLICATIONS
www.dsppublications.com

the dominion

gayleen froese

DSP PUBLICATIONS

Published by

DSP PUBLICATIONS

8219 Woodville Hwy #1245
Woodville, FL 32362 USA
http://www.dsppublications.com/

The Dominion
© 2024 Gayleen Froese

Cover Art
© 2024 Kris Norris
https://krisnorris.com
coverrequest@krisnorris.com
Cover content is for illustrative purposes only and any person depicted on the cover is a model.

Trade Paperback ISBN: 978-1-64108-538-0
Digital ISBN: 978-1-64108-537-3
Trade Paperback published March 2024
v. 1.0

Printed in the United States of America
∞
This paper meets the requirements of
ANSI/NISO Z39.48-1992 (Permanence of Paper).

To the Edmonton 3 Day cast and crew. It seems like only yesterday that we were harassing Todd Babiak and flashing the Tim Hortons morning drive-through line.

Acknowledgments

THANKS AS always to the awesome people at Dreamspinner, and to Laird Ryan States for helping with everything. I've already shouted out the 3 Day people, but special thanks to Pam Hyntka for the encouragement and support while standing over a garbage can at two a.m. (and in all the years since). This book wouldn't exist without Tate Young and you.

the dominion

gayleen froese

Prologue

Foreword

I HOPE you're not waiting for *Seven Leagues Over the Dominion* to come out. If you are, you'll be waiting a long time, and you can blame my editor. Or maybe you can blame me, for bringing an uninvited guest to lunch.

I was meeting my editor for a nice business lunch three months after my trip to the Dominion. We were both enthusiastic about a Seven Leagues book covering the most magical place on Earth. At a certain point, if you're writing adventure travel guides, there's no excuse not to go there. The local crime lord will rip your heart from your chest, werewolves can legally eat you, and they had to rebuild City Hall because a dragon burned it down. It's incredibly dangerous, more so than any war-torn republic or 8,000-metre mountaintop. No tourist should ever go there. That's why it was unmissable for me.

She was looking forward to hearing about my trip and to helping me decide what parts I should write about. The Seven Leagues books are pretty strictly structured, with sections about travel to and from the destination, travel within the destination, where to stay, what to eat, how to avoid trouble with the law… all the information you'll need to go places you shouldn't. I know the formula because I created the formula. I'd even written some of the book before our meeting, knowing what would need to be there.

Still, there's room to focus on what's special about a destination, such as the Dominion's lively college scene, or its hallucinogenic wastelands. That's the sort of thing we discuss when we get together.

That day I thought it would be a good idea to bring my photographer along. Karsten Roth was new to the Seven Leagues series, and he was a hell of a catch since his photos had been on the covers of everything from *National Geographic* to *The Cryptid*. I guarantee you've seen his work. You probably don't recognize his name, and you certainly wouldn't recognize his face because he likes it that way. My editor was a fan, and even she couldn't have picked him out of a police line.

She was thrilled to meet him. I told her that would wear off fast, and Karsten hit my arm with his camera bag.

He was polite and dour and funny. He brought her flowers and said he was in awe that she could put up with me. She was charmed.

She insisted we both tell her everything, every detail about our trip, and we stayed so long that we ate dinner at that table too. Over dessert, she declared that *Seven Leagues Over the Dominion* could wait.

I was shocked to say the least. She'd spent hours enraptured by our story. Why wouldn't she want the book?

It turned out she wanted a different book. She wanted a travel memoir, not an adventure guide, about me and Karsten and what happened to us in the Dominion. She wanted both of us to tell the story, not just me. I didn't write that kind of book, and Karsten didn't write at all, not professionally, but that didn't matter. She'd hire a memory extractor, one of the best. All memoirs were created that way these days, she said.

Karsten was horrified at first. Everyone gets their minds read all the time—by customs agents and cops and bored telepaths standing next to us on the subway— but memory extraction is more intensive than any of that, and Karsten is a private guy. He refused, first in his proper Oxford English and then in his more colourful German. Miri, my editor, patted his arm and said it was fine. He didn't have to do it. She'd rather have his perspective and his version of events, but the book could be done without it. Being the evil genius she is, Miri had no doubt guessed what his reaction would be. There was no way he was going to let me tell the story of our trip without his input. He said I was a scoundrel and a fantasist and some word that was long, German, and probably slang, since I didn't recognize it. My version of anything required a second opinion.

Also, though he didn't say it to Miri, there were things that had happened between us that even his sophisticated European sensibility might not want spelled out for everyone to read. If he wasn't part of the book's creation, he'd have no say in what did or didn't wind up on the page. The truth is, I wouldn't have embarrassed him. But he didn't need to know that right then.

As for me, I had mixed feelings. I'd gone to the Dominion planning to write a certain kind of book. I wasn't sure I wanted to change things up.

But the evil genius reminded me that I'd grown up on memoirs of travel and adventure. She said I'd had the real thing in the Dominion—mysterious deaths, a cunning villain, a monster the size of a city block… even my own near demise. It would be a shame to squeeze a story that big around the edges of a travel guide. Besides, we could still do the travel guide, and then I'd have the chance to get two slots on the bestseller lists.

In case that wasn't enough, she waited until Karsten had wandered off to the washroom, then leaned forward and said, "You can find out what he really thought of you right from when you met."

I told her Karsten didn't exactly leave people in the dark regarding his opinion of them. But you'll notice I did the book anyway.

—Innis Stuart, writing from Dawson City, Yukon Territory, Canada

Introduction: A History of Memory

AROUND THE mid-1960s, when most North Americans had become comfortable with magic, some people got the idea that it was ridiculous to have limitations.

Old-fashioned, even. If you'd ever been carrying groceries and wished you had a third arm, you didn't have to just wish for it anymore. You could hire someone to make it happen. Why drag a scuba tank around to explore the ocean? Why study for exams when you could pay to never forget anything you'd seen, heard, or done? It was an exciting time in which it seemed as if we'd all be able to be anything we wanted, provided we had the money. Why not?

Today, we know why not. There were the spells that went wrong and the shady operators who would give you a third arm and then leave town before you discovered you'd be growing an arm a week from then on. More importantly, though, there were things we found we could not change.

Take memory for example. We should have known we wouldn't be happy remembering everything. We should have known because there were people in the world before magic who could. They hadn't purchased a spell or potion. They'd simply been born with hoarding brains. You could ask these people what they had eaten for breakfast on a specific day thirty years earlier and they would tell you without hesitation. It's tough to verify an ordinary breakfast that's thirty years gone, so the subjects—as these people were known—would be asked about the weather on a certain day or the newspaper headlines. They were never wrong.

They were also unhappy. They felt rootless and detached. Without momentum. They were haunted by a million small things.

Eventually, the people in the '60s and '70s who bought perfect memories came to feel the same way. It seems there are things we are not built, in psychology or temperament, to be.

These days if you want to remember everything about a part of your life, you pay for a memory extraction instead. The best extractors in the business will find everything you remember and everything you'd forgotten about for a week or a month or, if you can afford it, a year. No one I know of offers more than a year. It's too much effort, too much magic, and too much information.

The police were the first to use this service. It was unheard of at first, so it was legal everywhere. Then it was challenged in court after court and became illegal in most places. Then it was necessary in solving a few downright devilish cases, and people started thinking it wasn't such a bad idea. Now you'll find it used in most places that allow any magic at all.

If something is used for one thing, people will find a way to use it for a hundred. If you're well-off and living in a place where magic is used casually, you may even have bought an extraction yourself. Maybe you wanted to present your child with the story of her birth or preserve your wedding day. Everyone has photos and video of these events, but a good memory extractor creates something more personal. It's your perspective—your memory, your thoughts, in your voice— translated to text. The first extractions read like witness statements, and it was said they'd never replace writing for thoughtful evocation and grace of prose. But the process has developed over the past few decades, and now memory extracts are indistinguishable from the sort of literary works and memoirs that were written two hundred years ago.

Except, of course, that they are accurate. They are coloured by what the subject saw and noticed and by the subject's way of thinking about these things. They reflect misunderstanding and obliviousness. But they reflect these things honestly and without prejudice.

I would be lying if I said I didn't feel a romantic pull toward the image of a lone man at his journal or keyboard, trying to capture his memories of travel and adventure before they flew away. Those are the books I read as a boy living on Canada's boundless prairie. I would read on the porch at my grandmother's farm, then set the book down, look at the horizon, and itch to go there. I had the idea I would write about what I found.

And I do. I write my Seven Leagues books alone at a keyboard, wrestling with memory and sometimes getting it wrong. Sometimes getting it wrong on purpose because, let's face it, adventure travel should be an adventure, in life and on the page.

This book, though, has all the adventure it needs without any help from my imagination. It's about the Dominion and Karsten and me and what happened to us and why and how we're still alive. I didn't want it to be a mistake or a lie.

What you are about to read, ladies and gentlemen of the jury, is the whole truth and nothing but the truth. So help me.

—Innis Stuart

Excerpt from *Seven Leagues Over the Dominion*

"The Dominion is a hell of an idea, and if I ever want to live in an idea, maybe I'll move there."
—Connor Avery, President, One Tir

FAE LEADER Connor Avery was using his famous backhand when he called the Dominion a hell of an idea. The city is said by some to be a hell on earth, full of spectres and monsters of every description. Certainly the Dominion's notorious Scree Quarter is a place to, as Keats wrote, "haunt thy days and chill thy dreaming nights," but there's a lot more to the Dominion—as the thousands of tourists who visit each year will attest.

Formed in 1965, the Dominion was a response to the growing trend of magic regulation around the world. It had been nearly twenty years since the varied forms of magic had sprung from nowhere to become as common as science, and it had taken almost that long for most governments to come up with coherent responses to the new world disorder. When they finally did so, the pendulum, in the opinions of many, overswung. Today, magic is banned in a number of nations and in at least a few regions of nearly every country on Earth. Places where it is allowed impose strict regulations on its use. Where does this leave creatures who are inherently fantastic? Often they're forced to reside in regions or neighbourhoods set aside for them. As you might expect, these usually aren't the most desirable parts of town.

The Dominion was conceived as a response to all of this. A block of Canadian and American land along the Pacific Northwest, including the cross-border Dominion City, was offered as a free space where all comers would, in theory, be welcomed, and those whose personal habits were unwelcome elsewhere could finally be themselves.

Despite what Mr. Avery may have to say about the place, there's no question that the idea of the Dominion was timely and compelling in the increasingly restrictive climate of the early '60s. It seemed sincerely intended as a sop to those who felt alienated and unwanted elsewhere, though critics have since claimed that it was intended to draw undesirables from across North America to one place where, as trillynoid activist Raymond Knot has said, "we can have at each other and leave the normal folks alone."

Whatever it was intended to be, the Dominion stands today as an experiment with mixed results. Werewolves and vampires run wild while less bloodthirsty locals defend themselves by any means necessary—all with the blessing of the Dominion's libertine legal system, in which self-defence is sacrosanct. The murder rate is so high that local newspapers report each night's events as a kind of box score. Death by accident is commonplace, and nearly one hundred tourists each year do not return home. If it can't be said for certain that they've all met with a dark fate, it's only because about half of their bodies are never found.

Yet it has its charms, drawing the curious who want to have mystical experiences not easily available outside the city's domed force field. The Dominion's many body modification shops and psychic transformation facilities attract those who wish to become curiosities in their own right. It can't be denied that a trip to the Dominion can change you, whether you want it to or not. Dollar for dollar, no vacation will give you more unique moments to remember or more incredible stories to dine out on.

Though the territory belongs, jointly, to the United States and Canada, the Dominion really is a country unto itself. When you enter, you give up any expectation of personal security aside from what you can provide for yourself. You give up the law as you've come to understand it, including the laws of physics as Einstein described them—except, perhaps, in the sense that his theory of relativity can be described as "what goes around comes around."

Welcome to the Dominion. It's a hell of an idea.

Chapter One

Night, June 14
Innis Stuart

I HAD been on the plane for hours by the time it reached Frankfurt. I was traveling from Tibet, where I'd been on another wild Yeti chase. I've been on a dozen of them, and I'll probably be on a dozen more before I wise up and give up.

When my longtime compatriot Jake Adler called and invited me to visit him in the Dominion, I was reluctant to return to Canada. Nothing against Canada. It's the most boring country in the world, and I say that with love. No one shoots at me there. No one tries to transmogrify me. I can always get a decent cup of Earl Grey and a doughnut. There's a reason it's my permanent home.

My issue was with the Dominion itself. I write about the world's less trammeled places, where no sane tourist would go. While there's no question that the Dominion is a singular experience, it's also a tourist trap. In a sense I could just as well have decided to write about Hawai'i. That way I could have spent time on the beach.

What changed my mind, aside from the opportunity to visit with an old friend, was that though the Dominion is full of supposedly sane tourists, it really isn't a place any sane tourist should go—no more so than an active war zone or Transylvania. But there it is, right in North America. It's easy to get to. The infrastructure is more or less intact. Nearly everyone speaks English, and American and Canadian dollars are accepted everywhere. Logistically, it's even less of a pain in the ass than a trip to Cancun. All of which is deceptive, because it convinces people that pretty much anyone can—and should—set foot there.

My intention in starting the Seven Leagues travel series was to arm people with the information they'd need when taking a trip that could be the last of their lives. With that in mind, bringing Seven Leagues to the Dominion wasn't merely a viable option—it was a responsibility.

I was repeating this to myself as my photographer came up the aisle of the plane, easily identifiable by his battered Domke camera bag and slightly pissed-off expression. I'd never worked with Karsten Roth before, but he had a reputation for being a sour-souled cuss. Funny in an acerbic way, and a phenomenal photographer, but not a ray of sunshine peeking through the clouds.

Apart from its expression, his face was far from off-putting. He was one of those chalky Europeans with fine features, sky-blue eyes and blond hair so light that it seemed out of place on anyone who wasn't a toddler. If I'd seen him in a bar, I might have tried a line on him. Considering the look on his face and that we were going to be working together, I decided to give the pass a pass.

He nodded at me, apparently recognizing me from an author's photo or my website. Without a word of greeting, he threw his gear into the overhead bin and dropped into the seat beside me.

"Did you change planes?" he said.

"Is that how you say hello auf Deutsch?" I asked.

"It's small talk," he replied. "I don't really care."

"I changed in Ankara," I informed him, feeling oddly satisfied to be providing information he didn't want. "We'll change again in Toronto. I'm surprised we're not going over the Pole."

He snorted, and his thin mouth curved a little.

"No one would go over the Pole these days," he said. "Three planes disappeared there this spring. The third was looking for the first two."

"It's probably Santa Claus."

He gave me a sideways glance, as if he were curious but absolutely not going to admit it. That white-blond hair was working against him, because his eyes were clearly visible behind the fringe of his bangs.

"Very funny," he said.

"I was just thinking, supernatural creatures thought to inhabit the North Pole...."

"Has no one told you, Innis, that there is no Santa Claus?"

I shrugged.

"The Turn was before my time, I'll grant you, but they used to say there weren't vampires or unicorns either. I guess, though, along those lines, it would be a little funny if Santa turned out to be a mass murderer."

"Yes, very funny," Karsten said again.

Something about his tone, the Muscadet dryness of it, made me smile.

"I figured vampires turned out to be pretty much as advertised. You know, until datura. It'd be weird if Santa wasn't jolly."

"Perhaps it is the Krampus," Karsten suggested. "Perhaps he is not merely a racist myth."

"Hey! I think you're joking," I said, "but you might have something there. Sinterklaas, Woden... there's a threatening vibe to the whole deal, if you read the old myths."

Karsten gave me a derisive look. It was, to my surprise, slightly wounding. "You saw that horror movie, didn't you? From this Christmas, with the evil Santa Claus sleeping underground. I take it these things capture your imagination."

I didn't know where he was going with that, though I did have a feeling I wouldn't like the destination. I decided to return to a happier point in our conversation.

"Three planes in a year. Shit."

"I would think you'd know such," Karsten said. "World traveler."

He spoke English like every other well-educated German I'd met, with a convincing British accent and a dead giveaway in how his sentences were built.

"Haven't flown out of Europe in a while," I said. "I'm glad you were able to get away for this."

"The Dominion," he said. "Everyone has to go once."

I managed not to wince.

"That's the popular view," I allowed. "Anyway. I thought you'd be busy. I hear your dance card's pretty full."

He shrugged. "I had been wanting to work with you. And why are you laughing?"

I kept on laughing for a minute or so. I was punchy, yes, but it really was pretty damned funny.

"Oh my God. And that's how you greet me. How do you talk to people you haven't been wanting to work with?" I asked finally.

He didn't smile. "I don't."

I had no answer for that, because it was likely true. Before I could think of anything else to say to him, he pulled his phone from his pocket, popped earbuds in, and shut his eyes. The flight attendant would be by any second to tell him to put his phone away until takeoff. I tossed my jacket over his head, hoping she'd think he was taking a nap under there. It was the least I could do for someone who'd greeted me so warmly.

He didn't move, which was a good sign as far as the job went. It was rare for someone not to move when you surprised them. In a photographer, that kind of steadiness resulted in great shots—until the intrepid bastards took one between the eyes because they didn't have the first clue when to duck.

As long as he managed to stay alive until this trip was over, he'd probably work out pretty well.

There was no shortage of photographers who wanted to work with me since publication in a Seven Leagues book was excellent exposure, and better still, Monomyth Publishing picked up the tab for travel, accommodations, and bribes. This time I'd picked Karsten, in part because he could enter the Dominion, which was a qualification not everyone could boast. While the city claimed to open its gates to everyone, it actually had unusually strict rules when it came to issuing visas. Anything from being virulently anti-magic on your website to advocating travel restrictions for magical beings was enough to get you banned for life. Rumour had it one sorry bastard had been banned because he'd written something unpleasant about witches on a bathroom wall and been caught on a security camera. How the Dominion got access to such information was a mystery, but a minor one in the scheme of all the mysteries of that place.

Mainly, though, I had picked Karsten because he was a mystery in his own right. He was known as the man on the spot for unnatural disasters. His big break had come during a South Pacific tsunami caused by sea serpents battling off the southwestern coast of Borneo. He'd been in the area shooting venomous birds and had captured remarkable images of the destruction hours before anyone else arrived on the scene. Years later, as the team photographer for the Seven Shamans, Seven Summits tour, he'd been on the eastern slope of the Vinson Massif when it lifted its skirts and marched across the arid waste of Antarctica. Both times, he'd walked away with award-winning photos and, reportedly, not a scratch on him.

He was, unquestionably, best known for his tour-de-force in Tunguska. Alone among the world's photographers, he had run a gauntlet of interwoven trees and tigers the size of elephants to reach the spot where the 1908 explosion was miraculously undoing itself. Trees righted themselves and grew leaves for the first time in nearly a century. The earth pitched and swelled, and Lake Cheko reared up and poured its water away into the ground at what had been its southern shore.

Hundreds of photographers and journalists, upon learning of what satellites and clairvoyants were picking up, tried without success to make it to the scene. Some stopped and turned away with the conviction that the land didn't want them there. Others put the lie to that conviction by becoming lost in that land where, presumably, they still rest today. Karsten Roth alone captured it all. To this day, he has been unwilling to tell anyone how he got into the Tunguska region. There was something special about the guy, no question, but what was it? Clairvoyance? Precognition? Or something genuinely strange?

Possibly he refused to speak to all those curious reporters and magicians and scientists because he had no intention of working with them. Maybe he'd tell me later.

I doubted it, but it didn't matter. A good mystery was something I'd always enjoyed.

Karsten Roth

I HAD thought for some time that Innis Stuart was not what he pretended to be. In his Seven Leagues books, he presented himself as the fearless explorer. He who went where others did not dare. It was possible he had not dared to visit such places either. Here is what I had learned:

He had been born in Canada, in Brandon, Manitoba. It was not, I believed, a place of excitement. His parents had been geologists, and he did travel with them. One story he told of his youth was that he went to a place in the north of Manitoba called Churchill. This was an odd town on the shore of Hudson's Bay. Churchill was known for being the home of a few thousand people and also of many polar bears that came to visit for half the year. Innis had said in his books that he had met one of these bears when he was only seven years old and that he had bravely faced this animal down with a stick and a loud voice. The terrified bear, as he told it, ran away.

There are not many people in Churchill. I had made perhaps a dozen phone calls to local hotels and restaurants before finding someone who had been there when Innis Stuart met a polar bear. It was true that he was only seven years old and that the bear was frightened away, but it wasn't due to Innis's voice. Instead a local man with a shotgun convinced the bear to take its leave. Innis, I was told, had been crying. Any small boy would. I didn't hold this against him. It was only that the true story was not as he had told it.

He had said that he went to Lakehead University in Thunder Bay, Ontario. I had confirmed this. He had a bachelor of science degree in geology, and as he said in his books, it had been this education that had first taken him around the world, in the employ of mining companies. I had traced his footsteps, as it were. He had been in North Africa and in the Middle East and in Central Asia. He had been, as he had said, on the island of Aeaea, south of Italy. He said that he went there because he had been asked to find a strange ore that was supposed to lie in its hills, one that looked like diamond and flowed like mercury.

This may have been true, but I doubted his story of finding a group of highly intelligent wild boars while on the island. He said he had sent them to Italy for further study, but I was not able to find records of their transport, arrival, or receipt.

I did know that our host in the Dominion, one Jacob Adler, had been on the island of Aeaea at this time, a member of the Canadian peacekeeping force that had been occupying the territory while Albania and Italy argued its rightful dispensation. He and Innis had been seen together, and it was said they'd had the manner of old friends.

The name of the Seven Leagues books came from the seven-league boots that Innis claimed he discovered in Bulgaria and used several times when in one scrape or another. To walk seven leagues in a single step would have been useful indeed. So useful that I did not believe he would have given these boots, had they been his, to a stranger in need of a rapid exit from Turkmenistan. Yet this is what he claimed, and so he could not be asked to produce the magical shoes.

I can say that he was not in Mongolia when he claimed to have lost three companions to the Mongolian death worms of the Gobi. He had been in the country, yes, looking for copper, but the area in which the worms lived had been plagued by dust storms the entire time, making travel to that region impossible. Innis had not been there when he said he had, which led me to believe he had never been there at all.

His Wikipedia entry has been edited repeatedly, but the editor has somehow managed to elude Wikiscan, and so it's impossible to tell who made the edits or what has been changed.

I believed some things to be true. He had been in Transylvania as the land was returned to the vampires. He was able to enter countries where no visitors were permitted. I knew this because he had been seen in them and because I knew people who had worked with him there.

These friends said there was something wrong about Innis. One had said to me, "He has never been in jail." Even if he had only been half the places he said he has been, he would surely have been arrested at some time. Yet everyone who has been his photographer or porter said Innis Stuart had only to say a word or two and the police left him. Moreover, the police did not leave with coins in their hands.

He was impossible.

I would only be in the Dominion for a few days. I did not know how much I could learn in that time. I also did not know why I cared so much about this or why I had come so far to investigate, but I had gone places on instinct in the past, and it had always been the correct thing to do. I was content to know only that there was something to be uncovered. As with the stones beneath Lake Cheko, I would do what I could to tip the bowl and pour the water away.

Evening, June 14
Innis Stuart

EVEN UNDER a full moon, the Dominion glowed as we approached. Now, I know that every tour guide mentions this and most of the things you see in every tour guide are overhyped. Trust me, the lights of the Merrows under the Pacific are an exception. Ghostly and striking, they are truly one of the world's most remarkable sights.

The Dominion is densely populated, both on land and beneath the water, but the population remains manageable in spite of its geographical constraints. This is due in part to the murder rate, as well as the tendency for couples to leave the city before starting families. Simply put, the Dominion is no place to be an infant—or a virgin for that matter. I'm not convinced that virgin sacrifice is as magically useful as it's purported to be, but a lot of people do believe it, and if you're the virgin in question, it only takes one believer to make for a very bad night.

On a more pleasant note, though, the city manages to comfortably house its people by allowing the use of what's known as "nonspace." Many buildings are considerably larger inside than outside. Certainly this space has to come from somewhere, but it's probably not our universe, so Canada and the US have agreed that it isn't our universe's problem. If someone from another dimension wants the space back, the assumption is they'll come and let us know.

I nudged Karsten, who had come out from under my jacket long enough to change flights in Toronto and then gone back into hibernation, this time with a small tablet concealed beneath my coat. He pulled my jacket down, causing his hair to stand on end as though he were touching a static ball in a science center. My smirk must have tipped him off because he scowled, pulled a water bottle from his backpack, and wet his unruly hair down. He glanced out the window.

"Larger than I thought."

"The Merrows really extends the space," I said. "It looks smaller in the daytime, because you don't see the lights under the ocean."

He looked from the window to me.

"I thought you said you had not been here before."

"I haven't," I said. "But I've flown over it. Never at night. It's probably twice the size we're seeing anyway."

He nodded. "Nonspace, yes? They described it well, I thought, on *Doctor Who*."

I didn't even try to hold back the smirk that time. "On *Doctor Who*?"

"The TARDIS," he explained, "is the ship. You have seen the program?"

"I guess. I know what the TARDIS is."

"It is larger inside than outside."

True enough. And prescient of the show's early writers, because nonspace hadn't existed back then... or if it had existed, we normal folk hadn't known about it.

"And how was that supposed to work?" I asked.

Karsten reached into his pack and took out a pair of gloves. He placed one on my lap and held his arm out so the other was in the aisle of the plane.

"One looks larger than the other."

I nodded. The flight attendant was watching him as well. Curious about what he was doing, maybe. Or maybe just wondering what the passenger in 17C looked like when he wasn't hiding under a jacket.

"If you folded the space between them, you could put one inside the other. And yet we know they are both the same size."

I shook my head. "I know I'm tired, but I don't think that's helpful."

He shrugged. "It is all perspective. Will your friend be meeting us when we land?"

"He'd better," I said. "It's a full moon. I wouldn't travel alone in this town on a good night, but with a full moon? A million dollars wouldn't entice me."

"We need a troll," he said.

I raised my eyebrows. "Do we?"

"There was an Old Norse poet," he said, "who said, 'They call me troll; Gnawer of the Moon.'"

"Giant of the Gale-blasts," I answered. "Curse of the rain-hall."

For the first time since I'd met him, he gave me a real smile. "Swallower of the loaf of heaven," he said. "What is a troll but that?"

"Contentious," I told him. "In my experience. Anyway, yeah, I'm sure Jake will be there. I'm paying him to provide security for us. Anyone who visits the Dominion without arranging for security is nuts."

"You could have stopped at anyone who visits the Dominion," he offered.

I smiled, made a fist, and tapped the side of his hand. "Truth."

Karsten Roth

I THOUGHT at first that we were flying into a cloud. The moonlight was no longer coming in the windows. The plane was rocked. Innis said, "What the hell," and I realized then that it could not be a cloud. How could we have seen the city with a cloud below us?

The pilot said, "Just a little turbulence." Innis laughed, loud and long. It must have been nerves.

"My sweet ass," Innis said.

Other passengers looked at him. Most did not seem unsettled.

The woman in the seat across from us was black-eyed. Not bruised, but with eyes that were entirely black. Looking about the cabin, it was possible to say there is a troll. There, fae. But, for the most, the people around us were simply strange in ways I could feel but not isolate and describe.

They were not tourists. My liaison at Monomyth had told me that we, as outsiders, had required special permission to fly in on the night of a full moon. I could assume, then, that everyone else on the plane was coming home.

"Birds," Innis said. He sounded pleased. I eyed him. "That was birds. Those were birds? They were birds. My God... there must have been hundreds of 'em. Couldn't tell what kind."

"Nothing supernatural," I said.

His eyes widened. "Well, what do you want to call supernatural these days? I hate that word. Anyway. Did I tell you there are only four flights into the Dominion a day? All commercial. No private planes."

The plane banked for the landing, and my stomach went opposite it. I shut my eyes. I felt my water bottle being pressed into my hands and took a sip.

"There you go," Innis said. "They have so much air traffic, with the flying beasties and the telekinetic flyers, that they can only clear the skies four times a day. If your plane is late, it gets turned... whoa. Speaking of turns, that was tight. Turned away. You wind up in Seattle."

There had been the customary applause when the plane landed in Toronto, but not here. We landed smoothly, though. My stomach was grateful.

As the plane slowed by fractions and we waited, Innis went on with his lecture. He seemed accustomed to holding forth. At least he had a smooth and pleasant voice and interesting things to say.

"If you're not a resident here, you pretty much have to fly in. Or there's a ferry from the States. No ground customs. No shapeshifting into a flying form. No teleportation."

I shook my head. "There is never teleportation for me."

"Me either," Innis said.

He looked, for a moment, human in a way he had not before. This is not to say that he was a troll or a merman. Instead he was too smooth, too at ease and ready with an inoffensive laugh. Glib, I think, is the word. He had been glib, but now he seemed sincere.

"I used to port sometimes, but I had a buddy who was porting from New York to Jakarta a couple of years ago and he never showed up."

"That happens one hundred and eight times per year," I said. "On average. Those are the incidents that are reported. There must be more."

Innis raised an eyebrow. "Statistically one of the safer ways to travel," he said, "but that's leaving out the whole 'there may be a fate worse than death' factor. Here's the thing—the place where my buddy was supposed to show up, they had a rain of frogs. And you want to hear something worse? People on the ground said the ones who survived the landing looked as if they were operating as a group, making some kind of formation. Like maybe they were trying to spell something."

My stomach went sideways again. "Enough," I told him.

"Yeah," he said.

We unbuckled our seat belts and began to gather our belongings. I could see on any flight who the real travelers were. We did not even wait for the seat belt lights to go out before we got our packs and prepared to leave the plane. We'd long ago stopped being so obedient as that.

The layout was efficient at the Dominion airport, and we did not have to walk forever. Perhaps it made use of nonspace. We had no checked luggage, as also befit real travelers, and we were ready within moments to clear customs.

"We had to do this in Toronto," I said.

Innis nodded. "You're not exactly in Canada anymore. I mean, you are, but... look, it's just a formality. They don't much care what you try to bring into the Dominion. They're much more interested in what you try to smuggle out."

"I will try to leave with my life," I said.

He laughed. "I think that can be arranged."

Chapter Two

Evening, June 14
Innis Stuart

THOUGH MOST people talked up the wild weirdness of the Dominion, there was another aspect to the city that was as well known among those who had been there: the strangling bureaucracy. Forms were required to do nearly anything more complicated than tying your shoes, and most residents carried what were known as R&Rs—Rights and Responsibilities cards—that outlined what they would and would not be allowed to get away with. It was not, strictly speaking, true that the town was lawless. It was better to say that the law was so complex and conditional that most residents chose to act as though it didn't exist.

As we were, strictly speaking, landing in a country that was both Canada and the US (or more accurately, neither), we would be expected to clear customs. I told Karsten it was just a formality. I didn't tell him that formalities in the Dominion could often take days to resolve and that the endless demands for forms you had never heard of and could not possibly obtain were enough to leave the most patient of travelers in tears. It had been a long flight, and I didn't think his morale could take the hit.

A weary-looking attendant with glittering pink skin and obviously dyed blond hair stepped into our path as we headed for the arrivals area.

"Paperwork," she said.

"I'm Innis Stuart," I told her, pulling out my photo identification. "My publisher has arranged everything. Monomyth Press."

She blinked. I saw two sets of eyelids move, one up and down and one across.

"You're not residents of the Dominion?"

Karsten shut his eyes. He clearly expected to be put right back on the plane. His pained expression was charming. I bit back the urge to say so. People who are cute when annoyed don't want to hear about it.

"No," I told the attendant. I gave her a smile, which was nearly always the right thing in a tricky situation. "But we got special permission to arrive during the full moon. It's all stamped and signed in triplicate."

Some said the Dominion was one of the last places on Earth to still be using carbon paper. Some said the city made some kind of magic out of that, as if it were a ritual that guaranteed the eternal life of red tape.

She looked at me. Her eyes flickered over Karsten for a second but came back to me when she saw that he was a million miles inside himself.

"Fine," she said, stepping aside. "Welcome to the Dominion."

Karsten's eyes popped open, and he stared, first at her, then at me. I grabbed his arm just below where I'd pinched it and got him moving before our new friend had a chance to change her mind.

"That was not what I had expected," he muttered.

"Don't question it when you catch a break," I told him.

"They didn't even search our bags."

"Shut up."

I hadn't seen Jake Adler in donkey's ears—by which I mean a long time and not actual donkey's ears, because these days you never know—but there was no mistaking the guy. He was a little over six and a half feet tall, with thick black hair and extremely pale blue eyes. At the right angle, in the right light, they almost lost their colour completely.

"I can't believe they let you out of prison," I shouted.

"I can't believe they let you out of assassin training camp," he shouted back. Others in the area, some of whom were sporting multiple faces or talons at the ends of their arms, backed away. Karsten was looking from one to the other of us as if desperately hoping we were kidding but not prepared to bet on it.

I gave Jake a hug, and he returned it in that awkward, half-arm's-length way of his. He always seemed concerned that his hugs could break a rib, and for all I knew, they could.

"Six years?" he asked me when we disengaged.

"At least," I said. "Jake, this is Karsten Roth, my photographer. Karsten, this is Jake Adler."

"Pleased to meet you," Karsten said with no sign of sincerity. He shook Jake's hand, and Jake nodded.

"Likewise. You gentlemen ready to hit the road? I'd like to get you both tucked away in your hotel before the witching hour."

He'd parked his Land Rover in what appeared to be a strict no-parking zone.

"Pretty brave," I commented. "I've heard it can take six months to get your car out of impound around here."

"Professional courtesy," he said. "I was a cop here for five years. Let's not stand around."

He didn't sound nervous, but he was all business, the way he was whenever he took a calculated risk. Karsten seemed to pick up on that, and his eyes were fully open for the first time since I'd met him. He didn't hesitate before climbing into the back of the vehicle.

"I'm amazed you still have her," I said as Jake and I settled into the front.

"Only vehicle I ever trusted," he said. "I don't bag drive her and she's not a bitch to me. Better than I've come to expect from any other ladies."

I left that alone. Jake Adler holding forth on the topic of women wasn't anything I needed to hear after a day that had already been far too long. We drove in silence for ten minutes or so, leaving the airport and heading into the Dominion's

Pines Quarter, the closest thing the city had to suburbia. The houses had been built in the late '50s, a last-ditch attempt to keep residents who were fleeing the new strangeness of the Dominion's soil.

"So normal," Karsten murmured.

"Looks deceive," Jake said. "Especially around here. That whole tract on our left was one of the worst hallucination zones before the Dominion went to the weirdos. It's calmed down since then."

Part of the reason for choosing this particular region for the Dominion experiment had been the land's inherent strangeness. From the mid-fifties on, it had been difficult for anyone without their own knack for magic to stand the place. Spirits were everywhere; the city's very layout was inconstant, and certain neighbourhoods were known for creating convincing hallucinations—or visions, depending on who you asked. Unlike in other hallucination zones around the world, it didn't seem to matter what mental baggage you brought in with you. You saw what the land wanted you to see.

"The city honestly thought a few rows of shiny new bungalows would convince people to stay?" I asked.

Jake shook his head. "I don't know what they thought. I know some people figured they could tap the power the way they do in China. But it runs wild."

It was true. No one had successfully managed to turn the Dominion's inherent power into anything that could be packed for transport or poured into the middle of a Twinkie.

"We're coming up on the Heart," Jake added.

The Heart was a large patch of land in the center of the Dominion, an almost perfect square that had been laid out with the help of scrying surveyors. It surrounded the cross where the city's two rivers, the east-west Empire and the north-south Howe, met.

"We have to cross into the East Hills Quarter," Jake told us, "then I'll take you across to the Old Quarter. You'll be staying downtown."

"There's no diagonal bridge?" Karsten asked.

"Not a usable one," Jake said. "There's an island in the middle of the rivers' intersection, and you'd have to go over it to cross the river that way. That's not going to happen."

"Why not?" Karsten said. "It should not be logistically difficult."

"That island is a bad place," Jake said.

Karsten was silent, probably waiting for him to elaborate. I knew better. Jake's tone said the topic was closed.

As we neared the bridge to the East Hills, an ornate grey stone structure with fake gas lamps along the sides, a field of white caught my eye, and I turned my head to see a park covered in white roses.

"Roserood Park," Jake said to my unasked question. "The roses grow wild. There's a piece of the park in each quarter. The bandshell is in the Old Quarter. Nothing going on there tonight, though."

I leaned back and looked over the bridge at the stone buildings of Dominion City University. A turreted building slightly to one side bore the sign "Rubedo College."

"One of my cousins studied there," Karsten said.

"Magician?" Jake asked, his voice tight.

"He thought so," Karsten said. "It did not turn out that way."

I smiled and watched the college until we turned toward the bridge to the Old Quarter. Rubedo accepted nearly three hundred aspiring magical practitioners each year, but only a hundred made the cut for graduation.

"Some people say it's a cash grab," I said. "Bring 'em in, get their tuition, then tell them they can't spell."

Jake snorted. "Wouldn't surprise me. That's City Hall on our left."

It was an unassuming building, concrete and glass, a contrast to the '20s art deco evident in the rest of the Old Quarter.

"Was it rebuilt?" I asked.

"In 1976," Jake said. "There was a fire. We have a lot of fires."

"I'm not seeing much action," I said, "considering the moon. I thought this was supposed to be a wild ride."

"The city has a Full Moon Night In program," Jake said. "They shut down transit, hike the parking rates, give bars and restaurants incentives to close. And there are free movie downloads for households. Little carrot in with the stick. You still wouldn't want to be in the Scree tonight."

"I'll take your word for it," I assured him. "I may be an adventurer, but I like to live to write about it."

Jake carelessly raised one shoulder and let it fall. "Some people love it. It's like the running of the bulls. That's one reason non-residents aren't allowed in when the moon's full. And then you've got the people who want to bag a werecreature. The bullets will be flying in the Scree tonight."

We drove on in silence. I listened for gunfire, but there was nothing. It might have been blocked by the thick trees of Roserood. We went north, through Chinatown, and I saw people on the streets for the first time. Two men and a dragon were sitting outside a dark café, the men breathing in the smoke that drifted from the dragon's nose.

"Stop," Karsten said from the back. I could hear him going through his camera bag.

"They're out there most nights," Jake told him. "Get your shot another time."

Nonetheless, I heard the window roll down and the camera click as we proceeded along the narrow street, Jake driving more carefully than was usual for him. Probably worried about what he might hit.

We pulled up in the loading zone of the Pickman Hotel, which the tour books called the finest and most secure hotel in the Dominion. It was also supposed to be haunted, but that could be said of pretty much any place in town.

"Pack up and get inside," Jake instructed. "Shake a leg."

From the corner of my eye, I could see Karsten looking as if he wanted to say something. I shook my head, and to my great relief, he kept whatever it was inside.

Karsten Roth

IT WAS my job to get photographs, so of course I attempted to photograph the famous Pickman Hotel. My shots were blurred because a hand was placed upon my back and a shove pushed me through the doors. It was ridiculous. There was no one on the street.

I photographed the lobby instead. It was grand and elegant, like those in my favourite hotels at home in Berlin. There were giants in one corner, reading the newspaper in oversized armchairs. Giants loved high-ceilinged places and also, in my experience, had a feel for elegance.

There was a shrill woman at the desk, complaining that her room had not come as advertised.

"It says right here, 'haunted room.' I specifically picked a haunted room."

The man behind the desk rolled his eyes. He made a show of it.

"Ma'am… what do you want me to say? We have ghosts. We do not have trained seals. They don't rattle chains for sardines."

"I paid extra!" she snapped, waving a sheet of crumpled paper. Her tone became more nasal with each word.

"You paid extra for the possibility of a haunting," the clerk said. He sighed, and his broad body moved up and down with it. "That's not a guarantee. It says that on your little printout too. It's like whale watching. What is it with me and marine mammals?"

Innis went to stand behind the woman. He kept a few feet back. It was clear he was next in line, but there was enough room in front of him that he was unlikely to be hit if she decided to swing her arms like an angry toddler. He was not a stupid man, this Innis Stuart.

"I'll report you!"

"Report my balls," the clerk said. He had the voice of a man who had been tired for a century, though his face was that of a man in his twenties. The woman looked as though her eyes might fly from her head and attack him, like round green wasps.

"What is your name, you rude bastard?"

"Casper," he told her. "Go back to your room. I'll throw on a sheet, let myself in, and say 'wooooo' in your ear."

"I am going to another hotel."

The man's shoulders slumped and his head hung.

"Don't do that, ma'am."

"Oh, you're sorry now? Well, it's too late!"

"I'm not sorry," he said. Now he looked at her again. "It's a full moon. Please do not go out there. I'll comp your stay."

The woman slapped her crumpled paper on the desk.

"You'll comp it anyway, you rude bastard! I'm not paying!"

"We have your credit card number and psychic imprint on file," he said. "If I say you're paying, you're paying. Look. Lady. As much as I'd love to bid you a fond farewell, it would not be responsible of me to let you leave. I'm saying this for your own good, because being annoying should not be a capital offence. Not even in this town."

She straightened her back and rose to no more than five foot three.

"You can't stop me!"

The man behind the desk was at least six feet tall and nearly half as wide. He stared at her and said nothing.

"I'll call the police!"

"Great," he said. "Me too. Wanna see who can call fastest? Winner gets a free night at the Pickman."

"I'll see you in court!" she said and was nearly magisterial in this final line. She turned, her wedge heels scuffing the floor, and marched out the front doors.

"I'll see you in the Bell Toll," the man muttered after she had gone. Behind him, the brown-and-gold patterned wallpaper buckled, swelled, and took the form of a man.

"You want me to go after her?" a muffled voice asked. Papered lips formed the words.

"Nah," the man at the desk said. "She's a grown-up. It's her choice. Without free will, where would we be?" He smiled at Innis. "Welcome to the Pickman, sir. How can I help you?"

Innis Stuart

I WASN'T surprised when the Pickman's night auditor told me he had no reservation for myself, for Karsten, for Monomyth, or for Jake. Some said the city's mischievous spirits deleted computer records and moved files around. Others said the city's workforce was always half-gibbering and therefore unreliable.

I suspected both contributed to the problem, but more than that, there was an imbalance in power always seeking to right itself. For every freedom that was granted under the city's dome, a restriction reared its head. You could see auras, maybe, or read minds, but you couldn't have the room you reserved a month ago.

"I know mistakes can happen," I told the night auditor. "You might not have us in your system. But you've got to have some rooms on reserve, right? I don't mind paying extra."

He smiled tightly. "No need to grease my palm, sir."

"I wasn't offering to," I said. "I thought I'd try paying extra to the hotel."

His smile loosened. "That won't be necessary either. We can probably accommodate you. It's not a full house tonight."

"Glad to hear it."

I was happier than I could say, because I'd been on one plane or another for around twenty-four hours and none of my sleep had been restful.

He was as good as his word and, within minutes, Karsten and I had keys in our hands.

"All right," Jake said. "You're safely tucked in, so I'm out. What time do you want me here tomorrow?"

I looked at Karsten. "Ten? You and I can meet in the bar at nine, for breakfast."

He frowned. "For certain there is a restaurant. A café."

"An adventurer always chooses the bar," I told him. "Jake?"

"You learn more in the bar," Jake agreed. "And the menu is usually the same. I have another job for another client tonight, so...."

"Go," I said. "Thank you. See you tomorrow."

He nodded and went. Karsten put his camera away. He was staring intently at a painting between the elevators, an abstract rectangle with jagged lines that seemed to vibrate. A sign below it read, "Warning: Do Not Look Directly At Painting."

I put a hand on his shoulder and gave him a shake. "C'mon. Bedtime."

"It said something," he said. "The painting said something."

"Yeah, no doubt," I said. "But it probably wasn't worth listening to. Let's go."

Excerpt from *Seven Leagues Over North America: Pacific Northwest*

"Seriously, folks. I got nothing against the Dominion. It's a great place to raise your kids. From the dead."
—*comedian Sammy Nino, on his I Thought I'd Die North American tour*

IN SOME respects, the Dominion is sitting on prime real estate. It embraces miles of oceanfront land, all of it craggy enough to be picturesque but not wild enough to discourage boat traffic. Indeed, it has been a successful port for many more years than it has been a sanctuary for strangeness. A great deal of Canadian and American trade with the Far East has traditionally come through Dominion City, especially since the docks were built up in the latter part of the nineteenth century.

The city has also long been a tourist destination. Through most of its history, visitors have come mainly from North America and have enjoyed the ease of traveling across the Canada/U.S. border within the town. During Prohibition, the city drew countless bon vivants who enjoyed catching a show on the dry side, then taking a cab to the increasingly famous—some said notorious—nightclubs on the north side of town.

In later years, as laws shifted and the price and availability of goods varied, visitors' reasons for border hopping changed. There were always reasons to visit the other side.

By the early 1940s, the town had become a draw similar to Niagara Falls. It was a trip to two countries for the price and trouble of one, with a lively but reasonably safe nightlife and a few natural sights worth seeing. While Dominion City had nothing as unusual as the Horseshoe Falls, it did have the pleasant combination of mountains, ocean, and old-growth forests.

It also had a reputation as a good city for a young family. It wasn't a place for people with ambition—those people still went east, or down the coast to Los Angeles. For those who just wanted steady work, an affordable home, and a place for the kids to find seashells, though, Dominion City was nearly perfect. It had grown steadily throughout the '30s and '40s, even through the Depression, and was poised to become one of Canada's largest urban centers.

The city's bright, if pedestrian, future changed rapidly when the magic arrived. It's difficult to quantify the effect the change had on different locations. It was a confusing time, and many events were either misunderstood or kept secret. However, it is known that Dominion City and its surrounding areas had a remarkably high transformation rate—nearly fifteen percent across the population.

Even more unusual was the fact that unlike other magical hot spots, Dominion City wasn't a legendary home of magic. It wasn't Ireland or Transylvania. The indigenous peoples of the area had been no more spiritually active than those in other parts of Canada and the United States. Everywhere else in the world that magic had come on strong, there had been a sort of aptness to it. Generally, dragons were where the maps had suggested they would be. But no mapmaker had ever written that over North America's northwest coast, and there had been no reason to think this place would become more magical than any other ordinary town.

Yet over a period of no more than a few months, people found that friends, neighbours, the man at the newsstand—even their relatives or themselves—had changed. Some had picked up magical talents, others curses. Some bore little resemblance physically to what they had been. Some had changed on the inside.

Of course this was going on around the globe, and everyone who lived through the Turn has stories to tell. It's worth remembering, though, that this level of change was rare. Most communities faced transformation rates of one percent at most.

It's often said that societies suffer extreme psychological damage when they lose ten percent of their populations. While the change induced by the Turn was rarely fatal in itself, it did represent a kind of death to many people at the time. It was the death of who they thought they were and of what they thought their city would become. It was a period of mourning for expectations, hopes, and the belief that some things were predictable.

Alongside this symbolic loss, Dominion City suffered physical casualties. There were the usual post-change suicides and a number of so-called mercy killings. There were also clashes involving werewolves, vampires, and other predators that led to deaths among the transformed and banal alike. Add to this simple accidents of the "I was cleaning my teeth and they went off" variety, and the Dominion's death toll quickly became uncomfortably high, even for the times.

Still, the exodus from Dominion City did not begin immediately. In retrospect we can say that the city was hit harder than most places on Earth. At the time, though, confusion reigned worldwide. The city's residents didn't know if life would be any safer or saner elsewhere.

The construction of the Pine Quarter's inexpensive bungalows also convinced some residents to stay for a time. Suburbia was a new and appealing concept, and real estate agents pitched the Pines as a quiet, safe community. In some respects it was. That depended, however, on what was happening in the area's vast—and at that time unmarked—hallucination zones.

For those who unknowingly crossed the street into a hit of ethereal acid, the consequences were far worse than merely sitting and staring at the grass in breathless wonder. They were downright ugly. Still, the Pine Quarter's community leagues were determined to make a go of it by locating the zones and putting up warning signs. Residents volunteered for this project, as well as for neighbourhood watch programs. For a brief time, it seemed as if Dominion City's blossoming suburb might be almost liveable.

What convinced nearly one-third of the city's population to abandon hard-won homes and move elsewhere was not the emergence of magic, but instead a geographical event. For the sake of convenience, most people refer to it as an earthquake, though a look at before and after aerial photographs gives the impression of something much more directed and deliberate. The Howe and Empire rivers, which had previously met in a lazy X, now formed a nearly perfect cross. The place where they met, which had been open water, now contained a small island that, unlike land disgorged by a typical quake, bore a rich garden of trees, brush, and in particular, the roses for which that land is now named. The island is rumoured to be bare these days, but the roses remain in the land surrounding the rivers' junction.

Most damage from the relocating rivers was done to the city's second quadrant, commonly known as the Scree. It's probably fair to say that the area has never completely recovered.

It was shortly thereafter, as people pocketed their insurance money or simply cut their losses and headed out of town, that a smaller flow of people began to move into Dominion City. These were the first of the world's magical entrepreneurs–some would say opportunists–who were convinced that magic must be good for something and that there was money to be made in tapping it. What's more, abandoned land and houses were everywhere. Once the area's magic was under control, those resources could be exploited as well.

While this plan was always morally questionable, it wasn't illogical. Not on the face of it. To this day there are people who believe that the Dominion is a gold mine—or perhaps more appropriately, a uranium mine. Boundless power just waiting for someone clever enough to package and sell it.

So far no one has been clever enough. Whatever runs through the land under and around the Dominion has resisted all attempts to shape and tame it. As the Dominion's first mayor, Abbie Strunk, said in his inaugural speech, "I'm not going to kid myself that I run this city. Anyone who tells himself he runs the Dominion is asking the front desk for a nasty wake-up call."

A few years ago, students at the Dominion's Rubedo College conducted an investigation of magical energy in and around the city. They didn't focus on the underlying magical lines that have been of interest to so many speculators over the years. Instead they looked at the residual energy of Dominion City's painful transition into the magical age. So many deaths. So much psychic and physical damage. Did a kind of poison remain in the area, influencing the Dominion's future?

Their results were inconclusive, muddied by the power overlaying the place, but they found reason for concern. Maybe the Scree is as violent and unhappy as it is today because of the economic damage of the past, or because every city has its downtrodden areas, and in the Dominion, that is the Scree. But we've learned a lot about residual magic over the last few decades, and we'd be irresponsible not to consider the possibility that there is something more.

For anyone who's curious as to why the Canadian and American governments would give over so much prime, if spooky, real estate to the creation of the Dominion, this is the most plausible answer: the land is not as good as it looks. It's a beautiful house built over an ancient burial ground, and the buyer should beware.

Chapter Three

Morning, June 15
Karsten Roth

THE SIGN above the bar said Hounfor. It was French, I thought, but not a kind I knew.

"It's voodoo," Innis said. He clapped me on the shoulder. I was proud that I did not jump.

So it was not enough that I would have breakfast in a bar, or that breakfast would in all probability be oily and rank. More than this, I had to eat in a Wodu bar.

"It is not too late to find the restaurant," I told Innis. He laughed and went inside.

The bar was dark enough that it might still have been in the middle of the night. Perhaps time stood still in there. Stranger things happened in the Dominion, I was told.

Innis chose a seat at the bar next to a thin Black man with snow-white curls. The man nodded at Innis. Innis offered him a hand. Always so confident that everyone wanted to be his friend. The conviviality of his manner almost convinced one that this was true. And it did not hurt, of course, that he was handsome. I was irritated by him, but not blind.

"Innis Stuart," he said.

"Danny Wedo," the man said. He sounded very old, far older than he looked.

"You here on business or pleasure?" Innis asked. I felt myself turning red. Could he have found anything more embarrassing to say?

"Pleasure," Danny said. "Always pleasure. My wife is the hostess here."

Drums beat from the speakers behind the bar. A man was singing about burning up, burning up. His voice sounded like the door to a haunted house swinging open by itself.

"Then you must know what's good here," Innis said.

Danny smiled. So peaceful, that smile. "Everything."

"I don't think I'm hungry enough for that," Innis said. He lifted his hand for the bartender. The bartender rounded the corner with creaking and rustling. They were made in part of leaves and dark, knotted wood. I had seen a similar person in Tobago many years earlier.

"What can I get you?"

The voice was warm and smooth, like good rum.

"Eggs Benedict, if you make that," Innis said. "And coffee. Make the spoon stand up. Karsten?"

"Coffee and a croissant will be adequate," I said.

"We can do that," the bartender said. "Danny, you having your usual?"

"Of course, of course," Danny said. "Thank you."

"Is the bartender your wife?" Innis asked.

Danny laughed. His head tipped back to let the sound out. "No, not that one. You'll see my wife tonight, if you're here."

"Maybe," Innis said. "We're here for a few days anyway."

"Good, good," Danny said. His eyes became unfocused. He stared into the bottles behind the bar.

Innis turned to me. "See? There's nothing wrong with breakfast in the bar. Quieter… better service…."

"I am here on your nickel," I told him. "You will have things your way."

He smiled. It was, it seemed, difficult to offend this man. "Not gonna give an inch, are you? Can you pass me that newspaper?"

I glanced to my left and saw a copy of the *Dominion City Phoenix*. I passed it to Innis, saw another copy beneath it, and took that one for myself. The headline was what my British journalist friends would have called "a grabber."

275-Year- Old Police Officer Still Permanently Dead; Witnesses Sought

The story was of a police officer named Aloysius Harper, whose body parts had been found across the Dominion on seven consecutive nights. When they were found, the parts were said to have shown some life. A few days later, they withered and seemed to die what the newspaper called "an irrevocable demise." Most of his body was found by the police or residents or dogs. His lungs and larynx were not located.

A coworker told reporters that Aloysius had recited a particular spell each night in order to stay alive. Though this was not common knowledge, it was assumed that the murderer must have known. Else why would the lungs and the voice box be gone?

The murder had happened six months earlier, and the police were still hunting for anyone who had seen anything, had any clues. The message was that time could pass, years perhaps, but they would not forget or leave it alone.

"Incredible," Innis said.

I set my paper down. "I suppose, but isn't it what we should expect here? Spells and dismemberment?"

"I don't mean that murder," he said. "I mean the contrast between that murder and… look, flip your paper over and check out the bottom half of the page."

I did so and saw what the desk clerk had meant when he spoke of the Bell Toll. Those words were printed at the top of a list that ran to twenty names or more. Murdered. Dead by misadventure. Missing, presumed dead. All in a single night.

This information took up less than half the space of the story above. I looked at Innis and saw shrewdness where there had been mindless good humour only a few moments before. He was more observant than he would have others believe.

"I would be put out," I said, "if I had been found dead and this were all they had to say about it."

"Meanwhile, a cop who's been dead half a year gets a whole half page. And the top half of the front page, no less. Hell, I have nothing but respect for cops in this town, but it still seems a little uneven."

"Perhaps all of these people will haunt the newspaper office," I suggested.

Innis smiled. "Perhaps. Life surely is cheap around here."

"Too many people," I said. "Not enough room."

"Always world enough and time," Danny said. I was startled. Somehow I had forgotten he was there. "Ah. Our breakfasts arrive."

My croissant looked surprisingly fresh. Beside it was a pot of dark jam that smelled of summer in a dark forest. Innis's eggs were soft. The yolks bled into the hollandaise. It was possible this bar was not the disaster I had expected.

"Delightful as always," Danny said. The plate in front of him bore a single boiled egg, peeled, resting on a dusting of white flour. He picked up the egg with long fingers and ate it. This was a delicate operation. It took six bites or more.

"Admit it," Innis said. His mouth was full of egg and sauce. "You were wrong."

"You are disgusting," I said.

He smiled wide to show me his meal. "Thank you."

Innis Stuart

JAKE WAS prompt. I'd known he would be. You didn't spend all that time in the military without learning the importance of being where you said you'd be, when you said you'd be there. He took a seat next to Karsten.

"Where to?" he asked.

Forgetting I was on a bar stool, I tried to lean back in my chair and barely caught myself before tipping over. Karsten smiled. Jake just looked at me, impassive. Waiting.

"I was hoping you would tell us," I said. "It's your town."

"Don't give me that honour," he warned. "Well. You're going to want to see the Scree. That means talking to Manya."

"Whoya?" I asked.

Jake's face remained set and blank. I wondered what might have happened the night before to put him in a mood this black.

"Manya. She has no last name that anyone knows of. The Scree is her territory. Not officially, but... you know how it is."

I did. Gangsters, warlords... call them what you would, any dangerous town worth its salt had at least one petty dictator. When resources were slim and violence was high, I had seen cities secretly support these people in ruling their chosen fiefdoms, if only to impose some kind of order where gory chaos had reigned before.

"Okay," I said. "Let's meet Manya."

We piled into the Land Rover. Karsten, having apparently learned his lesson the night before, had his camera at the ready and his windows rolled down within seconds of getting into the back seat.

"I would roll those up," Jake said, "before we hit the bridge."

"I'm here to take photographs," Karsten said.

Jake narrowed his eyes. "And I'm here to keep both of you alive. Roll up the windows or we're not going anywhere."

We sat in silence for at least a minute before Karsten gave up and closed the window. I had to admit, he had a work ethic.

"Keep them closed," Jake said. "I will know."

I didn't look at the back seat, but I could feel Karsten rolling his eyes.

The bridge to the Scree ran north–south over the Empire River. The change in scenery was almost immediate, beginning as soon as we left the Heart.

The Scree itself had always been forbidding land, as the name implied. It was rocky, rough, difficult to build on, and unwelcoming to plants. It had once been home to a neighbourhood of the type that's romantically called "poor, but honest." Now it was poorer, and about as dishonest as you could get.

The small bungalows and narrow two-storeys had lost most of their paint to the salt air and more than a few windows to years of strife. Junk, too weathered and bent to identify, overflowed the tilting garages and spilled across weedy yards. It was rare to see a door without a sigil scrawled across it or prayer strips tacked above.

"Can we stop?" Karsten asked. His voice was strained with the effort to sound polite. "I'd like to take a photograph."

Jake sighed. "Make it fast."

Karsten was so fast that I nearly missed what he was capturing with his camera. It was graffiti on the crackled grey wall of an abandoned gas station, a call and response. "TANSTAAFL," one message read. "There ain't no such thing as a free lunch." Below it, "You are the free lunch. —Solomon Short"

"Good eye," I said as he got back in the car.

He grunted. "It's what I do."

Because God forbid he might admit he was happy I'd praised him. He was, though. The corners of his mouth had quirked into the distant relative of a smile. I told myself that I was on the job, that I had no reason to feel as if I'd just had a shot of whiskey, and that I had more important things to look at than my photographer's lips.

Today the streets were full of people. None of them seemed happy to be up and about. They were sitting on crumbling porches and wandering the sidewalks. People with split clothes were sprawled in doorways and parks, and I realized they must be the werecreatures, sleeping it off. The people in the Scree were in worse repair than the buildings, raw and broken and sticky with blood.

"Discount body modification," Jake said, "and paranormal warfare. It takes a toll. That's Manya's house on the right."

Manya's humble abode took up an entire city block and rose three storeys. Jacweitz Organ Factory was painted on the redbrick along the north side. I assumed the windows were not the originals since they were all intricate stained-glass designs with dark green leaves and thick brown stalks winding through each tall and narrow rectangle. It was impossible to see inside the building, and I doubted much light was able to get through.

Jake pulled into a space near the front door with a smoothness that said he'd parked there many times. If Karsten's expression was anything to go by, he'd noted it too and wasn't impressed. For my part, I couldn't hold it against a man that he was consorting with villains or thieves. I'd lived in some pretty sketchy places, and I knew eventually you came around to doing whatever you had to do to be an effective force in your town. Sometimes that meant taking up unpleasant allies.

Jake nodded at the thick grey security guards, seven feet tall, flanking the frosted glass and steel doors. Karsten looked at me, and I patted his shoulder, which converted the look into a glare. Annoying him was dangerously fun, and I told myself to cut back on it. I didn't want to be alone on this job, taking pictures myself. It was a pain in the ass to do that while collecting information and interviewing people. Besides, Karsten had fans, and I was hoping they'd buy the book.

The guards waved us inside one of the most remarkable buildings I had seen, at least as a private home. It had been opened to the roof. Sunlight came from a rich blue skylight and poured through the dark green light from the side windows on its way down. The floor was wood, long walnut planks, but from the quality of the light and the vastness of the room, I could have sworn I was on a moss path in an old-growth forest. There were doors in the far wall, which indicated that there must be something behind them, but still it seemed as if the entire city block was encompassed by that one open space.

Then the building's owner stepped from the shadows, and I forgot about the building entirely. Beside me, Karsten tensed. I couldn't be certain, but I suspected it had crossed his mind to run.

The woman was at least eight feet tall, which explained her love of high ceilings. She was smiling, showing off her metal teeth. Her elegant hands ended in talons.

"I'm Manya," she said. "You must be Mr. Stuart. Jacob told me he might bring you by."

I stepped forward with my hand out. By the time I realized that her hand would likely shred mine, it was too late to pull it back. Luckily, she stepped around me and shook her head.

"You will excuse me. I never shake hands. Will you join me for tea?"

"Yeah," Jake said. "Thank you. If you're not busy."

"I always have time for new friends."

She threw that over her shoulder as she walked with surprising grace toward a set of red velvet couches to our left. The couches surrounded a glass-topped table set on carved wooden fish, forest green and curved toward each other in a bow.

"Tea," she said to the air.

We sat. Karsten took the spot nearest the door, which I was starting to think was his usual choice.

"Your table is beautiful," he said.

I was surprised enough to jump a little.

"Thank you." Her smile was more disturbing when it was broader. "They are taimen. Do you know them?"

He tilted his head. "Russian? Central Asian, at least."

"Yes. Siberia and Mongolia both have the good fortune to be home to taimen. There has always been something of magic in them, since long before the Earth turned. It's said a taimen was once found by a group of starving hunters, trapped in the ice of the Amur River. Throughout the winter, they cut chunks of flesh from his body and ate them. When the ice melted in spring, the taimen woke and swam away."

"No shit," Jake said.

He said it congenially, but it was discordant and not something I'd have expected from him. If Manya noticed, she didn't tip her hand. She waved at something over my head, and I turned to see another of those tall grey guards coming our way with a tea tray in his hands. He set it on the table as delicately as the best French waiter in the world, then slipped into the dark again.

The tray was also carved wood. I gave it once- and twice-overs since it wasn't a typical tea tray. It featured an unusual seven-pointed shape furrowed into thick stained birch. The teapot and cups were balanced on the raised wood.

"Some men become offended when I pour the tea," Manya told us, "so you may pour your own."

We did. Jake and I did anyway. Karsten politely declined. It was green tea. As we sipped in silence, the room darkened. I glanced up, saw dark bodies on the skylight, and got a weird little shiver from that before realizing they were birds. Just birds having a meeting. Manya glanced up at them, then smiled at Karsten as if the birds were a joke they were sharing. He appeared puzzled and chose to give the arm of his chair his full attention.

"I understand," Manya said finally, "that you are a writer of travelogues, Mr. Stuart. I imagine you are here because you would like to write about the Scree."

"I think a story about the Dominion would be incomplete without it," I said.

She smiled over the rim of her china cup. How she managed not to break it against her teeth was a mystery.

"I agree," she said. "I would prefer that I not be the subject of discussion, directly or indirectly. But you may ask your questions and take your photographs." She nodded at Karsten and he gave her a wan smile. "You may travel in this quarter without undue concern, at least for the next few days."

"Thank you," I said. I stopped there, because I had what I wanted. Anything further I might say could only screw things up.

"We shouldn't take up any more of your time," Jake said.

Manya looked at him. There was something odd about her expression, but I couldn't put my finger on what it was.

"We all have places to be," she said. "Be well. I'm sure I'll see you soon."

Afternoon, June 15
Karsten Roth

IT WAS not a bad day. I have always enjoyed taking photographs of unselfconscious places and people. Innis asked question after question of the residents, and they looked at him and barely noticed me. I have also always enjoyed going unnoticed.

There were no chances I could see to catch Innis in a lie, but I was confident such opportunities would come if I remained quiet and patient.

I wandered apart from him for a while, and it was in this way that I found Jake by himself, leaving an alleyway, blood on his shirt and his hands. He was wiping his hands on his shirttails before tucking them back into his pants. He did not seem surprised or unsurprised to see me. He did not seem anything at all.

"A job," he said simply. "I work in private security."

I nodded. "Innis told me. I'm sure it's nothing you can discuss."

"Right," he said.

A goat walked past us. Its splayed hooves nearly stepped on my boots. I was startled and moved away.

"Real adventurous type, hey?" Jake said. He laughed. It was a disagreeable sound.

"It surprised me," I told him. "Is it normal to have goats in the city in this country?"

"You mean Canada," Jake asked, "or the Dominion? We didn't have them back in Brandon, but this place isn't the same. Thought you'd have figured that out by now."

Brandon.

"In Manitoba?" I asked.

Jake slapped my back. His hand was huge, and unlike when Innis did such things, it hurt. I did my best to keep this from him.

"Right you are. How's a guy from Germany know something like that?"

I nearly said that I knew it because of Innis, because it was his home, but I did not want to say so to Jake. He might have wondered why I was so interested in the history of his friend.

"A superior educational system," I said instead.

"Uh-huh," Jake said. "Anyway, they like their goats in the Scree. They use 'em for rituals. And the goats eat the garbage."

From the look of the street we were on, it seemed they could have used more, or hungrier, goats.

I was trying to think of a casual way I could ask Jake about Innis. How did you meet, I could say, perhaps. Have you known each other long? Before I could decide what to say, Jake grabbed my arm and turned me back the way I'd come.

"Come on," he said. "You shouldn't be off by yourself."

There was nothing I could say. I was, I felt, lower in the pecking order than this man.

Innis was happy with his interviews. He rattled on all the way to the hotel about the black market and the cost of housing in the Dominion and the horrible things people in the Scree believed about how supernaturals were treated in the outside world.

"They think all the paranormals are in camps," he said. "Or dead. You'd almost think someone was spreading these rumours with a purpose. Keep people from moving out of the Dominion, maybe."

"You could speculate all day," Jake said.

"I'm certain that you could," I agreed.

Innis smiled. "Getting a little sick of the sound of my voice?"

"I'm learning to tune it out," I said.

He raised his index finger as if I'd brought up a fine philosophical point.

"Excellent plan. Speaking of which, Jake, what's our game plan now? Any suggestions?"

Jake nodded. "If you want to see the East Hills, we could hit a university bar. You might want to have dinner, catch a few z's. I'll come back at nine."

"That works," Innis said.

This was the way of being a photographer on someone else's project. No one asked if anything worked for me. But I didn't pay the bills either.

Dinner was in the bar again. It was busier than it had been in the morning. We took a table this time. A small cloth bag hung from the lamp above us. It was patchwork, red and blue scraps of leather. Innis saw it and smiled.

"I see they've got their mojo working," he said.

"It's juju," a voice said from the table beside ours. I looked over and saw Danny Wedo, our breakfast companion. He was eating a plate of fettuccine and sipping at a glass of milk. "Nothing but good."

"Is your wife here?" Innis asked.

Danny shook his head. "Not until later. Will you be here later?"

"'Fraid not," Innis said. "Tomorrow, maybe."

"She will be here then too," Danny said serenely.

"Must be nice to be him," Innis said to me quietly.

He was studying the drink menu propped up on the table. Rum and rum and rum. For a change, rum with rum.

"I might be every bit as happy," I said, "if I had alcohol forever at my elbow."

Innis grinned. A waitress came to our table, filled our coffee cups, and stood before us with her hands on her hips. She had red hair piled high on her head and a white apron over her short blue dress. She seemed to have arrived from Alice's Restaurant.

"No menu," she said. "Just to let you know. We've got jambalaya, if that suits you."

"What if it does not?" I asked.

She shrugged. "We've still got it."

Innis laughed. "It suits me. Karsten, if you don't like—"

"I was only wondering," I said. "That will be fine."

When she had gone, I leaned back against the leather seat. "Your friend had blood on his hands today," I said.

Innis pinched the bridge of his nose. "Just because he associates with someone who's in a questionable line of work...."

"No," I said. "I mean that his hands were covered in blood, and he wiped this on his shirttails. It was on his shirt as well, but he had closed his jacket by the time you saw him again. He is probably burning his shirt as we sit here."

Innis opened his mouth, and I waited. His fingers tapped on the fork in front of him. His shoulders shifted.

"Well," he said, "he does a lot of projects for people. It's none of our business."

"Do you think his projects include murdering people in alleyways?" I asked this politely. Innis shut his eyes.

"It's none of our business," he repeated. "So tell me. How are you liking the Dominion so far?"

"It is not a nice place to visit," I said. "And I would not want to live here."

Innis flicked the tines of his fork with the tips of his fingers.

"I think it's pretty dull so far, to be honest with you. The Scree wasn't any worse than a lot of places I've seen. It's inner city."

"Manya was unusual," I said.

Innis raised his eyebrows. "That is true. Nice house too."

I drank coffee. It was bitter and strong, just as I liked it.

"Did you see a bedroom? A bathroom?"

"I saw some doors," he said. "Of course, we don't know that she needs either a bedroom or a bathroom. For all we know, she hangs upside down from the ceiling to sleep and eats the souls of the dying."

"We should not assume anything," I agreed. "I think it must be difficult, when you are that tall, to use a washroom in a hotel or restaurant."

Innis waved a hand at an oversized booth that was a few feet away from us. "I understand they have different classes of room size here too. Anything from three feet to ten feet, they've got you covered. Did you go into that convenience store this afternoon? Or was that just me and Jake?"

"I must have been somewhere else."

"Huh," Innis said. "You shouldn't go off like that. Anyway, they had three washrooms for different sizes."

The waitress arrived with our food. "If you want anything else," she said, "just holler."

"I thought you did not have anything else," I said.

"That may be," she said, "but there's no law stopping you from hollering."

She turned on red stiletto heels and swayed toward the bar. Innis watched her go. I waited until she was well gone before going on with the conversation.

"Alive and dead are small distinctions as well," I said. "Did you see the zombies?"

"They don't like to be called that," Innis said. "It's… daturized vampires? Something like that." He laughed. "I don't know. I call 'em zombies too. But I wouldn't say it too loud."

"They would happily have drained me when they were well," I said. "Why should I owe them something now that they have caught the zombie virus? Are there any true vampires left in the Dominion, do you think?"

"I think most of them cleared out once the datura flu started going around. But there could be a few. I guess some of them are immune."

"They took such pride in their appearance," I said. "Forever young and beautiful. Look at them now."

Innis shook his head. He had his shrewd expression again, this time giving the impression he was seeing into me. "And pride goeth before a fall?"

"History will tell you so."

I tried the jambalaya and found it excellent. It seemed in this place you could simply order and trust that it would be to your taste.

"Yours are a dour people," he said. "Never mind the Scots. You Germans are depressing as hell."

"It's good your travel has broadened you," I said. "so that you no longer stereotype other nations and peoples."

He laughed so loudly that others turned to look. "I'm much worse now than I was before I hit the road."

We spoke of inconsequential things for the rest of the meal, when we spoke at all. It was not angry or uncomfortable. I was, to my surprise, quite comfortable with him after this one day. We were simply weary.

"Jake was right to suggest a nap," Innis said.

"Likely true," I said. "Will we meet downstairs at nine?"

"Barring disaster," Innis said casually, as if it were a comment of habit with him. "I'll see you at nine."

Chapter Four

Innis Stuart

I DIDN'T doubt the wisdom of Jake's advice, but I've never been a big fan of naps. A person doesn't find out much when they're asleep, not unless they're some kind of psychic. And from what I hear, it's nearly impossible to tell the difference between a dream and a vision.

It wasn't as if I was going to sleep anyway. I had too many questions spinning in my head. All day, as I'd wandered the Scree and talked to the Dominion's underclass, the cop's murder had been in the back of my mind. I couldn't figure out why it was such a big deal.

Not that I was insensitive to the murder of police officers, or murder in general. But the geist of the Dominion, so to speak, seemed to be more callous than that of the average town. I couldn't imagine any murder capturing their imagination for a week, let alone six months.

It told me there was something about the Dominion that I didn't understand, and understanding the Dominion, in as far as that was possible, was part of my job. I picked up the phone, dialed information, and told the machine on the other end that I wanted the number for the *Dominion City Phoenix*.

I barely had time to register my shock that I hadn't had to repeat myself a dozen times before a second machine informed me that I had reached the switchboard of the *Phoenix* and office hours were over. I wasn't concerned. If the person I was looking for was still on the crime beat, there was no way she'd have gone home.

The mailbox gave me her extension. Donna Hartley, 332. Her weary voice greeted me after three rings.

"Crime."

"What about it?" I asked.

She laughed. "Innis Stuart, you walking disaster area. I heard you were in town."

"I notice you didn't try to call me," I said. "You have my cell number."

"Nuh-uh. I burned your card in a cleansing fire."

Not true. Reporters never let go of a good contact, and I was downright excellent.

"Can I buy you a cup of coffee?" I asked.

Donna sighed. "I'm sure you can afford it. You're probably still getting paid too much. But I'm slammed here. Why don't you just tell me what you want?"

"To talk to an old fr—"

"Friend?" Donna anticipated. "Shoot the shit, Innis? For the unbridled hell of it?"

"Maybe I want something," I admitted.

"Close your eyes," she said. "Forget the coffee. We'll meet up elsewise."

I would have preferred coffee. I shut my eyes and heard Donna humming down the line. Crooning, more like. The sound always set my teeth on edge. My stomach went south without me, and then I was standing in a library. A bookworm's paradise, several stories tall with mahogany everywhere. The lights were dim, the skylight showing a night sky, and Donna was the only other person in sight.

She looked the same as she ever did. About five-five, with straight hair in a sleek and practical dark brown bob. She wasn't a pretty lady, but there was an admirably solid quality to her, even in these little trips to her psyche. She came across as someone you could trust.

Mostly, she was.

"You think well of yourself," she said, looking me up and down.

Apparently, how I appeared inside her head had something to do with how I appeared to myself. Which was, as far as I knew, how I looked period.

"I didn't think you covered old news," I told her, and she snorted.

"I try not to. What brings you to the Dominion? I thought you considered this place a tourist trap."

"Sometimes literally," I agreed. "Listen, Donna… speaking of old news… what's up with Aloysius Harper?"

That surprised her. She half sat on the edge of a heavy table, displacing a leather-bound dictionary. I wondered what I'd find if I opened it. Maybe all the words Donna knew. Maybe just "Fuck off, Innis," all the way down every page.

"You going into true crime?" she asked.

"God, no," I said. "I saw your byline on an article about him. Front page, above the fold. Very nice."

"Oh, I see. You're here to show support for my career."

She wasn't as annoyed as she sounded. No reporter who'd had the front page that morning could be talked into a seriously bad mood.

"Look," I told her, "I'm simply trying to get a sense of this place, and my sense so far tells me there's no way anyone should still care about a six-month-old murder. Even if it was a cop."

"We're not heartless," she said in the tone someone from Billings would use while pointing to the local orchestra and insisting, "We're not hicks."

"Never thought you were," I soothed. "But this is a town that moves on. So why not this time?"

She shrugged. "You want the news that's not fit to print?"

"As usual," I told her.

Then I jumped at the sound of a cart being wheeled somewhere on the floors above us.

"Just the janitor," Donna said.

I didn't ask why she needed a janitor inside her own head. I didn't want to know.

"Was there something special about this cop?" I asked instead. "More than the usual Dominion kind of special?"

"In a way," she said. "You heard he was nearly three hundred years old. That means he was kicking around for a lot of years before the Turn. People've said he was a vampire or a magician or fucking Merlin himself, you know, pretty much anything you can think of. But no one actually knew."

"Did anyone ask Officer Harper?" I asked.

"Detective Harper," she corrected. It seemed automatic. Then she smiled. "Al. He was a good guy, to tell the truth. I interviewed him a few times. He used to say he was an old alchemist who made something useful once. But if he was telling the truth about his age, alchemy was pretty well passé by the time he was old enough to practice it. I think he was joking, kind of riffing on the elixir of life business. Most of his friends seem to agree."

"And he had some kind of ritual," I said.

"Yeah. See, that should narrow down the suspects, because he only told a few people about it. People at work, mostly. This is the Dominion, though, so you've got a psychic on every street corner."

I raised an eyebrow. "Can you hire them by the hour?"

She slapped my arm. I was surprised when it stung a little. Apparently pinching myself would not wake me up.

"Not actually on street corners," she said. "We're not the home of the psychic escort. I'm just saying it's common. So maybe someone read it off him."

"So they made sure he couldn't say the magic words," I said, "and that's what did him in."

Donna looked annoyed and disgusted, as if she'd poured curdled milk on her cereal and not realized it until she saw the lumps.

"Oh, worse than that," she said. "Whoever did it cut him to pieces and left him all over town. Still alive. Except the head. That didn't show up until he was good and dead. It took him seven days to die, Innis. His head was somewhere, attached to nothing, no windpipe, still alive, thinking about how he couldn't say the words and there was jack shit he could do about it. What do you think he thought about? He couldn't even mark the time. Was he hoping for some last-minute save? Or was he hoping seven days would go by already? It must have seemed like a very, very long time."

My stomach felt funny again, and I thought maybe she was sending me back and I'd see the insides of my eyelids in a moment. Instead it seemed my stomach was trying to get away from the image of Detective Harper's last week. Lucky stomach, having an escape route.

"So the cops are taking this hard?" I asked.

She narrowed her eyes. "Jesus, Innis. What do you think?"

I thought that despite its reputation the Dominion seemed to have a pale to get beyond. But I wasn't quite dumb enough to say it.

"Someone went too far," I said, more diplomatically. "Do they have any decent suspects?"

"What do you think?" she shot back. "The only people who saw anything say Harper, on his last day intact, left an East Hill doughnut shop in the company of someone. And the appearance of this mysterious someone? Male or female? Big or small? The witnesses cannot, for some reason, recall. Typical Dominion bullshit. Someone found a way to cover themselves, and there was no one around who could see through it."

"So the cops have nothing."

Donna gave me a half smile. "Did I say that? I think they have a suspect. But who? I have nothing."

"No arrests," I said. "In six months."

"You know what I think?" Donna stood and stepped closer to me, as if she were afraid of being overhead. By the janitor, maybe. "I think this is bigger than a cop murder. Those body parts around town… I plotted them out. It wasn't random. It was a symbol. Nothing I've been able to identify, but there's a definite pattern. I bet it was part of a ritual. There've been other missing pieces, here and there. Bits and pieces out of zombies and werethings and… you name it. Someone took a change purse—you know what a change purse is?"

"A purse with change in it?" I ventured.

She laughed. "It's that extra organ werewolves have—scientists figure it's how they transform. Anyway, there's a black market in some of this shit, and people take their trophies, but… I don't know. Call it instinct. Somebody's up to something, and it might be something big."

"Ooh," I said. "You sound like a reporter in the movies when you talk that way." I smiled to show I was teasing, and she had the grace to smile back.

"Yeah, yeah. Like you're not given to nights at the opera. While you're in town, if you find out anything along those lines, let me know. You know you owe me."

I knew I did. I had from way back.

"Deal, my lady," I told her and offered a hand to shake.

She turned her back on me instead, walked to a nearby column, and flipped a light switch.

I saw bright lines in the dark. Blood vessels. I opened my eyes and hung up the phone. That never got any less weird.

Karsten Roth

I WAS flipping through the television channels, searching for CNN. Someone knocked on my door. Innis, I thought, and so I opened it without peering through the viewer.

"Hey," Jake said. "Can I talk to you for a minute?"

Was it nine already? I glanced at my watch. Strange to wear a watch, but ordinary phones were not reliable here, even with the EVP filters sold in every airport. For knowing the time, a watch was simplest and recommended to tourists. Those who lived here would spend, when they could, on phones that cut through interference from other worlds and times.

Hours to go before nine. So why was Jake at the hotel? Without thinking, I looked at his hands. They were red. He had scrubbed them, perhaps under water much too hot for his skin. It was somehow worse than the blood.

"Can we not speak later?" I asked. "At nine o'clock?"

"I just want a minute," he told me. "Privately."

It was madness to think he might murder me. What reason would he have? I'd seen nothing, really. What reason did I even have to believe him dangerous? And did I not want to learn more about Innis, who this man had known for many years?

I stepped away from the door. He followed me inside. He pulled the door shut behind him and I looked—again without thinking—to see how far from me the hotel phone was. I believe he saw this. I was not as subtle as I should have been.

"I get the feeling you're uncomfortable about this afternoon," he said. "With the blood."

"As you said," I told him, "it was your business."

"Yeah, I know," he said. "But you got skittish. I don't like that. Skittish people do funny things."

Like getting the next plane home, I thought and did not say.

"I quite understand," I assured him. I would not have blamed him if he did not believe me, the way my voice shook.

"I had a client," he said, "who needed me to get something back for him from a not very nice man. To be honest with you, my client's not so nice himself. But that's the way it goes sometimes."

He did not sound troubled by this.

"You used to be a police officer," I said. "Is it difficult, now, to work for these not-nice clients?"

Jake had a way of laughing that did not suggest anything was funny to him.

"You're a kid," he said. "Maybe it never occurred to you that sometimes niceness is a luxury, even if you're a cop. Hell. No matter who you are."

The first thing in my mind was that I was not a kid. Jake might have thought me twenty or twenty-one. Many did. I decided my additional years were not important enough to mention.

"I'm sure the Dominion is not a simple place," I told him.

He smiled and it seemed a real smile, as if he liked that. But not as if he liked me. "You can say that again."

He was hunched a bit. He was tall enough that perhaps he hit his head on things. Lights and such. Something about his stance put me in mind of a werewolf

I had seen once, on a full moon. That werewolf had been in a cage some distance away. Jake was so near to me that I stood in his thick, wide shadow.

I remembered I had business with him.

"You and Innis seem to be great friends," I said.

Jake shrugged. "Known each other a long time."

"How long?" I asked.

"We were kids together in Manitoba," Jake said. "Innis didn't tell you this? He likes telling stories."

I returned his shrug. "Were there dragons in Manitoba?"

"I guess the good old days probably aren't exciting enough for Innis to talk about," Jake said with a laugh and a smile, but he did not seem pleased.

"But he could make them exciting," I said. "Couldn't he? He is a writer, after all."

Jake gave me a piercing look. It seemed more honest than the smile, and so I preferred it.

"You saying he makes stuff up? He probably does. Why not? He's not writing encyclopedias."

He was not, and I had even said so to myself. What does it matter? But something was not right with Innis Stuart, and I had a voice inside saying I was not to let it go.

"He offers advice," I said.

Jake snorted. "One thing you gotta learn in life is what advice to take. If Innis is weeding out some people who never learned that, it doesn't break my heart."

I could not imagine what would. I nodded to show I believed him. He took it to mean I agreed, I think, because he gave me his smile again.

"I'm glad we understand each other," he said. "I feel a lot better. How do you feel? Less skittish?"

"Absolutely," I agreed. "Yes. Not skittish at all."

"Glad to hear it," Jake said. "I'll let you get some shuteye now. See you in the lobby at nine."

"Lobby at nine," I echoed.

The hotel room door locked automatically, as most do. Still, I checked it after Jake had left.

Two times.

Then I lay down for the nap and was, I thought, still awake when I found myself back in Russia. Walking toward Lake Cheko, still full and bright with Siberian summer sun. Was it noon or midnight? The light did not suggest one or the other, but I thought, midnight. The witching hour, as the English say.

It was quiet. In a place the size of a small nation, perhaps fifteen thousand people lived. None of them stood precisely here.

I heard the sound of dried pine needles as I walked, and then I was still walking but heard nothing. I stopped and looked at my feet. The light changed. I gazed up, and there was the lake, all the water of the lake, rising as if it were being spilled into the sky.

It kept rising to be a wall. The edges curved. Whitewater swirled in the middle, and it appeared to be nothing so much as a giant mouth with water teeth and wide blue lips.

The mouth opened. I thought it might consume me, and I wondered, would I be torn apart or would I drown? And then it said, "Karsten."

It was the voice of a lake, thick and round. I had no voice. I nodded. It said, "My daughter owes you a boon."

My eyes opened and I was in my room, hours later, with the lake's spray on my face.

Excerpt from *Seven Leagues Over the Dominion*

"You've heard of 'Pack In, Pack Out'? The Dominion's more, 'Pack Up and Get Out.'"
—Cheryl Franz, *The Dominion for Teens*

IN A way, the transition from Dominion City to the Dominion simplified work for the area's border guards and customs agents. As a Canada/US border town, Dominion City had wrestled with day-to-day challenges. The town reaped benefits as well, but there's no denying that international borders present a serious logistical complication for communities.

Most cities that straddle borders actually don't. They rest on one side of the border, while a twin city sits on the other. Between them, there's a divider that's more than symbolic. Some physical barrier—almost always natural and usually a river—keeps the communities separate and limits the points of entry on either side.

In the case of Dominion City, there was no natural barrier. The Empire River would have done the job, but the 49th parallel was a few miles from its southern bank, and no one was prepared to move the river, move the parallel, or make an exception. The city needed something artificial to demarcate the boundary.

Dispute between the Canadian and U.S. governments over how to handle the border within the town lasted until 1915, when it was decided that a wall would be built through Dominion City, with three access points along existing roads. Garrett Kelly, writing in the *Dominion City Crier*, dubbed the wall the "Good Neighbour Wall," a play on Robert Frost's popular poem: "Mending Wall."

The Good Neighbour Wall took several months to construct and was lengthened over the years as Dominion City expanded eastward. The original wall was a brick structure, nearly seven feet in height, with a rounded top. It created traffic bottlenecks, which became more serious as traffic—particularly motor traffic—increased. Predictably, it did little to stop determined foot traffic. Scaling the wall was a frequent activity for some residents and a rite of passage for the city's young people.

From time to time, the Canadian or American government would raise a fuss about the amount of wall-jumping in Dominion City, and noise would be made about increasing security, but the reality was that no one was willing to spend the money required to adequately police the entire length of the wall. Technology, in the form of sensors and cameras, might eventually have made a difference, but we'll never know.

During the same earthshaking event that realigned the Empire and Howe rivers, the Good Neighbour Wall proved that it knew Frost's poem better than most people do.

Routinely, folks will quote the best-known line of the poem—"Good fences make good neighbours"—as proof that, well, good fences make good neighbours. The poem, however, begins, "Something there is that doesn't love a wall/That sends the frozen-ground-swell under it/And spills the upper boulders in the sun/ And makes gaps even two can pass abreast."

Something sent the frozen-ground-swell, and a hell of a lot more, under the Good Neighbour Wall that night. By morning, bricks were strewn for blocks on either side of the border, and two guards were in the hospital.

Would the Dominion ever have been formed if that wall had not come down? I believe it would have, in one way or another, but it might not have become the nearly autonomous city-state it is today. When the wall fell, it took with it the idea that the Dominion was a border town—at least one where the borders could be arbitrarily set.

When Dominion City and its environs became the Dominion, new borders were drawn up that described the reach of the place's high weirdness. Outside the borders, it was strangeness as usual. Inside, all bets were off. What had once been Canada or the United States could not have been less important.

Today, the Dominion disregards the national boundaries within it. Residents of the Dominion carry Dominion passports, though no other nation considers the Dominion to be a nation in its own right.

Dominion residents are the Schrödinger's cats of citizenry. They are neither Canadian nor American unless and until they declare themselves to be one or the other. They are, upon declaration of citizenship, free to move to one of those countries, though I'm told this rarely happens. There are few reported cases of Dominion residents getting into difficulty while traveling. Most simply don't travel. As for the rest, presumably there's little the outside world can do to faze them. When they require diplomatic services, which is rare, Dominion residents do not seem to show any particular preference between Canadian and American embassies. Whichever is closest will apparently do.

Canadians and Americans do receive preferential treatment from the Dominion in the sense that they can make unlimited visits, while citizens of other nations are restricted to six visits per year.

The Dominion sets its own regulations for travel, import, and export. It polices its own borders. It does not charge duty of any kind. Other nations, including Canada and the United States, have regulations surrounding importation of products from the Dominion. In theory these nations will charge duty on the Dominion's goods. In practice no one I've heard of has ever paid duty when leaving the Dominion, because no one has left with significantly more than they brought in.

Non-residents are only able to enter the Dominion by plane or boat. No private flights are allowed for non-residents, and commercial flights are limited due to the amount of non-mechanical flight in the area. There are daily flights from major Canadian and American hubs and regular flights from Frankfurt and Heathrow.

The Dominion's one airport is located on the former American side, southeast of the Pines. The former Canadian airport still exists, but is officially closed. There are rumours that the airport is actually still open. Who uses it, and what for, depends on the rumour. Ask around and you'll find many rumours to choose from.

Commercial boat travel into the Dominion is also highly restricted; still, while less popular than flying, this is another accepted way to enter the Dominion. Boats dock on the former Canadian side, above the Merrows since this is where the water is deepest. The American docks, part of the Scree, were always less attractive to large boats and are now primarily used at night for activities best conducted in the dark.

Ferries run from Seattle twice daily, making a wide curve out to sea as they pass the Scree docks before swinging back in to shore.

Cargo trains are allowed in, but are carefully scanned first. Trains run straight to the docks, then back to the border. They make no other stops.

Rumours about the tragic fates of train-hoppers caught at the border are as common as those about the Canadian airport, and probably as reliable. Still, I do not recommend trying to sneak into or out of the Dominion by this or any other route.

Entry by teleportation, or shapeshifting to a flying or unnoticeable form, is strictly forbidden for non-residents except in cases where the non-resident is seeking refugee status.

The Dominion has a force field of sorts that blocks non-resident traffic. It has come as an unwelcome surprise to drivers, flyers, and teleporters who were either unaware of its existence or convinced they could breach it. To my knowledge no one has yet managed to break the field. Certain vehicles are able to pass through the field and take passengers, usually tourists, to the Dominion's outlying, nonshielded areas. Licences for these vehicles are expensive and difficult to earn, so tourists are advised to book these cabs or buses well in advance.

Dominion residents are given implants after their first three months of residence and are thereafter able to go through the field at any time, provided they leave on foot or in an approved vehicle. I've heard from fairly reliable sources that the Dominion's government has a panic button that will disable the field in case of a citywide emergency, allowing tourists and new residents to head for the hills.

Given the mysterious goings-on in those hills, I'd say it would have to be a pretty dire emergency before you'd be better off without the force field.

As for the Good Neighbour Wall, you can still see the scar where it once divided Dominion City. Oddly, most of the buildings surrounding the wall were untouched by the event that destroyed the wall itself, and the gap between them now creates a narrow path where the wall once stood. Someone who cared to do so could walk along most of that path without impediment.

The bricks themselves are long gone, pocketed by residents and tourists as mementos of a simpler time. This doesn't stop countless vendors from selling "genuine Good Neighbour bricks" to new tourists each year. Since those bricks, like most items, are not permitted to leave the Dominion, it's likely some of those bricks have been sold a dozen times or more.

If you want souvenirs from the Dominion, take photographs—carefully. Some residents don't appreciate having their souls stolen by shutterbugs. Better yet, ask your friends to take photographs of their trips to the Dominion, while you stay safe at home.

Chapter Five

I DISCOVERED at nine that Karsten was as punctual as Jake. All three of us arrived in the lobby at the same moment. Jake was wearing a dark shirt and slacks that might as well have had Cop painted across them. I was doing my best in a T-shirt and jeans, but only Karsten really looked the part for a university bar. He was nearly thirty, I knew, but he could easily have passed for nineteen. It made me feel a little guilty for admiring the fit of his bar clothes.

Anyway, how old we did or didn't seem to be wasn't important. We weren't hoping to be undercover.

I asked Jake about the bar as we headed for the Land Rover. His lips tightened.

"It's typical East Hills."

We took the same bridge we'd taken on our arrival, this time heading east toward the university. In contrast to the night before, students were everywhere, spilling from the sidewalks to the street and back again, an undulating snake of laughing, half-naked children. They would have been sexy to me once. I felt old and relieved at the same time. Apparently it was only grown men who could pass for nineteen that were attractive to me and not real nineteen-year-olds. If I were an old man at fewer than four decades of life, at least I wasn't a dirty one.

Many of the students had animal features of one kind or another. Others wore masks or animal prints.

"Is it some kind of carnival?" I asked.

"No," Jake said. "It's a fad. The ones who got mods are going to be sorry in a year."

He pulled in beside a yellow line on the sidewalk, slapped a police ID sticker on the dash, and got out.

"I thought you said he had left the police," Karsten said to me.

"Oh, cut him some slack," I said. "If I had a Park Anywhere card from some old job, I'd probably hold on to it too."

Karsten chose one camera, a discreet digital, to carry into the bar. Apparently he wanted to blend in, and why not, since he had a hope in hell of managing it.

The bar went under the nauseating name of The Tippler and I couldn't really blame Karsten when he stopped a few feet from the door.

"No. There must be some other place."

"There are a hundred other places," Jake said, "but they're all this place. Quit whining."

Since he hadn't been instructed to stop glaring, Karsten kept that up, but he did push open the Tippler's front door. It looked like oak, but from the way it flew all the way open and into the back of a reveler, I guessed it was something much lighter with a veneer of either wood or illusion.

The things outside were the things inside. Young people in animal fashion of one kind or another, drinking and dancing. The tables were small, round, and high, circled by tall and skinny stools. I couldn't see a way to get comfortable, though a second glance showed that the table could be adjusted for height and the stools for both height and width.

I didn't see the same amount of exposed bone and bubbling skin here that I'd seen in the Scree. Apparently the body mod shops were better in this part of town. There were fewer fires too, from what I was told.

The music was techno, which wasn't my first choice for an evening's entertainment and probably wouldn't have been my first choice for sustained noise torture, were I ever offered such a choice. The room was too hot, as nearly all bars were—the better to sell drinks. The air was almost visible, heavy with a mix of herbs and attars that were probably all guaranteed by some sidewalk potion vendor to make their wearers irresistible. They served instead to make me hungry for Italian food.

The things I suffered for my work.

We had to sidestep into the bar to get past the people who hadn't made it past the foyer. Jake spotted an empty table, and we squeezed around it. I let Karsten take the seat facing the door, knowing that he probably wanted it. I did too. Facing the door with your back to the wall was always the best seat you could get.

I hadn't expected him to recognize the concession, but he surprised me with a quick grateful smile. For a second, I toyed with the idea of cutting Jake loose. Karsten and I would be fine on our own. Before I could follow up on that impulse, Jake spoke.

"I used to make a lot of arrests here. There was nothing I hated worse than coming to East Hills. I'd take the Scree any day. These kids have no sense of culpability. They always think you have no business picking them up."

"Why are you no longer with the police?" Karsten asked. I was impressed with the way he made it sound like harmless curiosity, as if he weren't fishing for an answer like "I dismembered someone in the break room, and they decided to let me go."

"I need a beer before I talk about that," Jake said.

Our server came by with a bewildering menu offering drinks that were named after well-known magical potions, drinks that claimed to *be* magical potions, and microbrews with names so precious they should have been set in rings and sold to the newly engaged. Karsten spotted a good German beer and recommended it, a suggestion that Jake and I gratefully took. The place had sweet potato fries, since that had been hip a few decades ago, and I ordered a basket for the table. Hip or not, I still liked them.

As we waited I watched the action over Jake's shoulder. A middle-aged woman with a stinger instead of a left hand was poking some kid in what people who've been shot in the ass like to call "the extreme upper thigh." He didn't look impressed, but whether it was because she was stinging him or because she was much too old for the bar was difficult to say.

Next to them, a man who was the right age but equally out of place in a dark blue suit was flirting with a fresh-faced redheaded girl. They linked arms and headed down a hallway at the back of the bar. It was lit only by the exit sign at the far end.

The beer arrived with surprising speed, and Jake took a healthy swig before saying, "It was the werewolf and the transmogrifier."

"Aw… my mom used to read me that story," I said.

Jake narrowed his eyes. "Shut up if you want to hear this. I'm only going to tell it once."

I raised my hands. "Do tell."

"It was about six months ago. I was juggling two cases. We had a guy named Brody, Ben Brody. Obvious werewolf. I mean, full moon, bam, the guy's a wolf. Get him good and mad, he might go lupine then too. He starts finding himself covered in blood the morning after full moons, and he figures it's time to get his R&R." He turned to Karsten. "That's a Rights and Responsibilities card. Every predatory paranormal in the Dominion carries one."

"I'm aware of this," Karsten said. "It sounds mad."

"You're tellin' me," Jake said. "So anyway this Brody guy goes to the John Dee Clinic for assessment and R&R assignment, and he gets rotated to this crazy vampire—this was after we'd lost about ninety percent of our vamps, either because they'd turned zombie or because they'd left town to duck the virus. The vamp's lonesome or some such fucking thing, so he decides Brody would make a good vampire. Rending flesh, sucking blood, six of one, half dozen of the other. Gives Brody a vampire R&R. So naturally we pick him up a few months later because he's got a limb hanging out of his mouth, which would not be a problem if he had the right R&R."

"Mad," Karsten repeated. He was staring at the side of his glass. "Murdering people should be illegal. Full stop."

"The Dominion says hunters have a right to hunt," Jake said. "You're aware that people are allowed to act in self-defence. And this includes proactive self-defence."

"Proactive self-defence," Karsten muttered. "You've all lost your minds."

The redhead was back now, minus her blue-suited friend. Within seconds of her arrival, a kid in a black trench and bottle-black hair was at her side.

"So Brody's sitting in our waiting room on this bullshit charge, and meanwhile I'm taking a deposition from this woman who spontaneously transmogrifies.

Which again would not be a problem, except she didn't report it when she applied for her driver's licence."

"Why would you have to report that?" I asked.

Jake looked at me as though I were possibly the stupidest man he'd ever met.

"We don't grant licences to spontaneous transmogrifiers any more than we grant them to uncontrolled teleporters or epileptics. She turned into a moth about a block from City Hall. Her car plowed into a building, killed some woman right at her desk."

"It's easy to see why people live here," Karsten said.

He had his camera out and was trying to take pictures on the sly. I pointed out the woman with the stinger as subtly as I could. She was dripping something from her stinger into the virulently blue girlie drink in her other hand.

The redhead and the trench were on their way down the hall.

"There's no law saying you have to like it," Jake informed him.

"There is no law at all in Deadwood," Karsten shot back.

I couldn't help laughing. "It's not quite that bad."

"It would be better if there were no laws here," Jake said. "Laws of nature or supernature. That's it. That poor Brody son of a bitch was cooling his heels at the station because he tried to do the right thing. The bitch, on the other hand, didn't think she was responsible for the accident. We looked into her history. She'd been working as a short-order cook. Burned that place to the ground when she turned into a snake and left something on the stove."

"How do you claim you're not responsible for something like that?" Karsten asked.

Jake shook his head. Over his shoulder I saw the trench-coat kid return alone from the hallway.

"She claimed her ex-boyfriend slapped a spell on her, and that's why she was shapeshifting. She said it was his fuckup, and she wasn't taking the blame."

"Irrelevant," Karsten said.

Behind him, the stinger woman was poking an ample young lady, who promptly turned and slapped her.

"You think so and I think so," Jake said, "but this piece of work disagreed."

"You have to feel for someone who's got a spell sitting on them," I said. "I thought you had treatment centers for that here."

"Sure we do, but you have to give your name and psychic imprint, and she didn't want to do that because she didn't want restrictions on her driver's licence and employment card. If you were right, buddy," he said, jabbing a finger in Karsten's direction, "and we had no law here, she would've been treated, and everything would have worked out."

"Interesting point," I said.

I wasn't giving his point my full attention, though, because the trench was taking an East Asian woman in a violet dress down the hall, and the sense of déjà vu was dizzying.

"I figured if I didn't believe in the law, I shouldn't be enforcing it. So I quit."

"Understood," I said. "By the way, I think something weird might be going on."

Then I wiped my face, because Karsten had been caught in mid-swallow and was projectile-laughing his beer across the room.

"What do you mean?" Jake asked.

"I'm not sure," I said. "Come on."

I led Jake and Karsten to the hallway. Getting there wasn't as tough as it looked, probably because Jake's cop vibes were parting the sea as we moved. The hall had a few doors leading off it, including four to washrooms of various types and sizes, but I was pretty sure I'd seen the couples go past all those doors to the exit.

We went out single file behind Jake, which was probably a bad idea as neither Karsten nor I could see past him and were unprepared when he stopped dead. After we'd finished slamming into him, disengaging, and stepping to the side, I saw what had caught his attention. Three bodies were lying on the ground, next to a Dumpster: The trench. Blue suit. The redhead. Beside them, the woman was smoothing her dress. She glanced up at Jake and smiled.

"Oops."

"I thought they put you away," Jake said.

She leaned against the Dumpster, which was liable to stain the dress. Not that this… person… had much reason to care how her clothes would look ten minutes down the line. Not if I was right about what she did.

"They think I died last week," she said. "It had to be you, didn't it, Adler?"

"Them's the breaks," Jake said, grabbing her arm, swinging her around, and clipping a pair of thin plastic cuffs around her wrists. The cuffs shuddered and gave off a soft whine as he fastened them. He side-eyed me.

"This here is a body snatcher," Jake said, confirming my suspicion. "She gets off on diving into new digs, and it looks like she's been on a spree here tonight. Of course, people drop dead once she abandons their bodies, but you don't consider that your problem, do you, sweetheart?"

"Can you just hand me to the cops and skip the lecture?" she pleaded.

Jake grinned at me. "She's pissed off because she had the bad luck to run into me of all people. Because I see her ugly face no matter who she's riding."

"No shit," I said, impressed. Jake's ability went further than I'd thought. "I know you see through illusions, shapeshifting, whatever—but that works on body snatchers too?"

"Happily for me," Jake said, "and unhappily for her, yes. Anyway, seems our evening has been cut short."

"No, it hasn't," I said. "You running her in?"

"Figured I would," he said. "Why?"

"Karsten and I would like to see the police station." I turned to Karsten, who was crouched beside the stack of bodies trying to get a decent shot. "Right?"

I thought I saw a lack of enthusiasm in his eyes, but his tone was pleasant enough as he said, "By all means."

Karsten Roth

THE FOURTEENTH precinct was smaller than I had expected for a city in which trolls were arrested on a regular basis. In fact many of the tall and wide were hunched together in the waiting room, testing the durability of its vinyl-and-steel couches.

Innis and I were left there while Jake helped his former colleagues process the body snatcher. I had gathered from things she had said as we drove that Jake had unusual eyes. He saw through illusions, and this was how the body snatcher had known he would recognize her.

As if he were a fool, Innis was attempting to interview our companions in the waiting room. They were reluctant to talk. I had considered photographing them until I overheard the booking of a man who had stabbed a vendor in the Old Quarter's Waite Market. The vendor had been taking aura photographs for sale to tourists. The stabber had apparently been attempting to take the camera away and retrieve his soul from its flash card.

I kept my head down instead, flipping through pamphlets. "Curses! Avoiding Magical Manipulation." "Protect Yourself From Identity Theft!" "Understanding Your R&R."

I gave that last one a close look. It began with talk of Arizona's Stupid Motorists Law, where drivers who went into a flooded area might be charged with the cost of their rescue.

"No matter which Rights and Responsibilities card you carry," it said, "your first responsibility is security. Do not let others borrow your R&R card. Do not let others borrow your body. Do not leave yourself open to psychic manipulation or attack. Always remember that, as a predatory paranormal, you can be held responsible for anything your body does. Don't leave it unprotected."

My eyes were still burning from something in the bar. I wanted to close them, but I too did not want to leave my body unprotected. Perhaps I should have felt safer, in a police station, but I was not comforted by the way they had greeted Jake on our arrival. The kindest way I could have described their attitude toward him would have been "deep suspicion"—which made no sense if he had quit for the reason he'd said.

On the wall across from me was a poster advertising the Full Moon Night In program. It suggested that the police were quick to shoot on nights when werecreatures were everywhere. Perhaps a night at home would be better than a night at the resurrectionist's. There was small type at the bottom of the poster that said resurrection was not covered by Medicare.

A voice beside me said something about resurrectionists. I turned my head and saw a thin, pale woman with shells where her fingernails should have been. They did not seem to be affectations glued in place. I suspected they grew from her hands.

"I beg your pardon?" I said.

"They used to be grave robbers," she explained. "That's what the word used to mean. Resurrectionists. They sold the bodies. To medical students. And artists."

I nodded. I knew it had been this way once, in England and many other places. I hadn't known the term. She moved nearer and whispered to me. Her breath smelled of seaweed on the beach, stranded and rotting.

"I hear they still sell to medical students sometimes."

"Ms. Crowdis."

A police officer with a clipboard was at the door to the room, looking at my new confidant. She smiled. Her teeth had saw edges, like those of a shark.

"Time to go," she said to me.

She went to the police officer and was led away, deeper into the building.

I agreed completely. However, Jake was nowhere in sight, and I did not think Innis would want to leave without him.

Innis Stuart

KARSTEN SEEMED to figure if he curled into a small enough ball, he could straight up disappear. He was hunched over a stack of pamphlets and cringing whenever anyone was insensitive enough to speak to him. I was surprised he wasn't taking pictures, but maybe he had a better survival instinct than the average photog. Or maybe he was worried that the cops would take his precious camera away.

For all the luck I was having getting people to talk to me, I might as well have been invisible myself. Some people got downright surly with me, even after I told them I was writing a book, not a newspaper article, and I didn't need their real names. No one wanted to share their thoughts about the Dominion's unusual justice system.

I took a seat next to an open door, thinking I'd have to come up with another approach if I wanted to get any material out of this crowd. I heard voices inside the next room and glanced over my shoulder to see two women in DCPD blues, splitting a Twix and drinking Cokes at a high, narrow table.

"...fucking nerve, showing his face around here," one was saying.

"Yeah," the other said, drawing out the word. "Come on. We don't know that."

I thought it was funny how their uniforms and identical chin-length haircuts made them look completely alike. It took me a moment to realize they actually were alike: identical twins. Apparently they didn't have any unresolved anger about being dressed the same as children.

"He bailed on the screen. Totally refused to do it."

The one who'd said that crumpled the Twix wrapper and threw it at the plastic garbage pail on the floor. She missed. Next she'd get up to drop it in the pail, and she might catch me watching when she did that. I turned around and shut my eyes. I always eavesdropped better when my eyes were shut.

"A lot of people don't like having their minds scanned." I assumed it was the other one who had said that. "I don't like it either. I'd like to see them get rid of it. Does that make me guilty of something?"

I heard footsteps going from the table to the garbage pail and back.

"Oh, come on. He did the screen every year, the whole time he was here. All of a sudden he's up in arms about it?"

"Sometimes a person just gets fed up."

I didn't get to hear what her sister had to say to that because a radio went off in the break room. There was, it said, a 103 on Wescott Drive. I didn't have the first idea what a 103 was, but apparently the Wonder Twins considered it important, because they abandoned their Cokes and tore out of the break room as if the place were on fire. So much for that diversion.

Fortunately when life closes a door, it opens a cliché. When I turned my attention back to the waiting room, after watching the twins' exit, I saw a burly guy with a greying moustache standing beside my chair.

"'Scuse me if I'm wrong, but you look like the guy that writes those books."

"I am a guy who writes some books," I allowed and patted the seat beside me. "Are you a fan?"

He took the chair next to mine and laughed. "I guess. My sister keeps giving me those Seven Leagues books for Christmas, and I read 'em in case she asks me things. But I don't mind too much."

He said it amiably enough that I laughed along with him. He probably didn't mind the books too much, or he wouldn't have taken the chair. A guy who was planning to lay into me would have stayed on his feet.

"I'm working on a North American one right now," I told him. "Might be a series. It's a big topic."

"Bigger than Australia," he agreed. "You're writing about the Dominion?"

"That's the plan."

He looked around the waiting room. I did the same, mostly to make sure Karsten was still breathing. It was hard to tell with him bent so far over his reading material, but he seemed to be all right.

"You're really getting the nitty gritty," my new friend said.

"What, this place? I'm waiting for a friend. He's in private security, and he had to run somethi—one… in."

He nodded. His hands were folded neatly and lying in his lap. It was a very delicate gesture for such a thickly moustached man.

"I ran a violet," he said. I looked at his face to see if he was making a joke. His brown eyes showed no trace of humour.

"Like a traffic light?" I asked.

"Kind of," he said. "Sometimes when there's low-flying traffic, they turn on violet lights, and you have to clear the area until the flying traffic's gone. Dragons or whatever, you know? I didn't see traffic, and I figured I could make it through, so I hit the gas and damned if there wasn't a fucking cop right there. I bet there never was any air traffic. Son of a bitch was just sitting there writing tickets, filling his quota."

"Sounds that way," I agreed. "I'd have thought cops in this town would have better things to do."

"People would be let down," he said. "I mean, if we didn't have so many murders. You know? Everyone around here looks forward to seeing the Bell Toll. It's gotta go up every year, right, like… like if you're running a lottery. You always need a bigger prize."

I kept my voice low as I responded. "You're saying people in the Dominion are proud of their crime rate?"

"It's one thing that's not bigger in Texas," he told me.

I had an urge, hearing this callous talk from a man who didn't seem monstrous, to test a theory.

"You hear about that cop who died?" I asked. "That Detective Harper?"

"Yeah," my new friend said, suddenly subdued. "Hell of a thing. That guy. I was at a bar about ten years ago, and I got in a fight. He broke it up. Good about it, though, you know? Nice guy."

I was trying to think what to say next when a cop leaned around the corner and waved to him.

"Okay, Mr. Waldtz. You're free to go."

He leaned closer to me until his shoulder touched mine. "They took my car in because they thought I had undeclared nonspace in it. Guess they didn't find anything."

"Was there something to find?" I asked.

He gave me a shy smile. "I take the fifth, Mr. Stuart."

Excerpt from *Seven Leagues Over the Dominion*

"You can't expect me to have known he was a zombie. He never once said 'brains.'"
—*Testimony from a Dominion City court transcript*

THERE'S A familiar joke about Canada that it could have had American efficiency, British culture, and French cuisine but instead wound up with American culture, British cuisine, and French efficiency.

When the Dominion decided to customize its legal system in light of its unique blend of citizenry, the city's leaders had both Canadian and American law to choose from. Initially the approach was simple: crimes were tried according to the side of the former border on which they had occurred. In those rare cases where this was impossible, enough common ground was found between the two systems that the Dominion was, by and large, able to stand on it.

Procedure was determined by the courtroom in which the case was heard for trial cases, and by the judge otherwise. Change of venue petitions had been known to have longer arguments than the case itself.

For the first two decades of the Dominion's existence, it was led by politicians with traditional backgrounds and long memories of the way things had always been. The fire that destroyed the Dominion's city hall in 1976 came mere months before an equally dramatic change in civic leadership. In the Dominion this was as important a change as a governmental coup might be in any other town. After all the Dominion was well accustomed by this point to being an essentially independent state.

The next government—headed by Bernie Krejci, who is today still mayor of the town—felt that the American and Canadian systems were not adequate to handle the kinds of issues brought up by a city full of magicians, psychics, and shapeshifters.

The civic leaders argued that existing laws assumed people consistently looked more or less the same, and that seeing was generally believing. In the Dominion that wasn't the case.

There were always laws in the Dominion, as there are today. Every predator carries a Rights and Responsibilities card outlining what they may eat and under what circumstances. Werewolves, for example, are not permitted to attack people when the moon isn't full.

Similarly, all manner of self-defence against werewolves, including proactive self-defence, is permitted during a full moon. Shooting a werewolf in bed two weeks later, however, is murder and is punishable by law.

Many lesser offences, particularly non-violent ones, are not crimes in the Dominion. Fraud for example. You can sue someone for fraud if you can prove it, but the Dominion won't prosecute it. The rationale for this is simple: it's too hard. It's too difficult to keep track of what whammies have been laid where. It's expensive and time-consuming, and frankly if you're in the Dominion, you're supposed to be able to handle your affairs better than that. In fact residents have been heavily fined for failing to take reasonable steps to protect their bodies, identities, and passports against nefarious use. Caveat everyone.

Much of this was always understood by the residents of the Dominion, but at first little of it was written down. The assumption was that the Dominion's residents could and would take care of themselves. The legal system worked to whatever extent it did because most people wanted nothing to do with it. The Dominion investigated and prosecuted those crimes about which it gave a damn, such as murder. The rest was arbitrary. Call a cop and see what happens.

When Dominion City University opened the magically inclined Rubedo College in the early 1970s, it soon became apparent that the existing system—with its assumption of "if you're in the kitchen, you must be able to stand the heat"— wasn't adequate for new chefs. Three hundred freshman Rubedo students arrived in the college's first year, and only seventy-three went on to graduate. A little over one hundred either flunked or dropped out. You're free to guess what happened to the rest. Be imaginative, because the stories are pretty wild.

This, along with increasing tourist traffic and the revenue it generated, helped to create a climate in which the reform-minded Krejci and his crew could be elected to power.

Though the will to change came to City Hall in the late '70s, and most residents agreed that tourists and students did require a higher level of security (or at least recompense), the Dominion's leaders were at first only able to put new laws (such as the law against unregistered virgin sacrifice) on the books. It wasn't until the vampire influx of the early 1980s that the city council was able to win a referendum for a wholesale change to a new legal system—one that was a hybrid of civil and common law.

Vampires, you may recall, could be tricky to deal with. Apart from their taste for blood, they had a number of unsettling knacks. "Forget what you've seen," they would tell you at the scene of a murder, and you would. "Shoot that man for me," they might say, and you might do it. You might even think it had been your idea.

I'm certainly not claiming that mind control and the power of illusion weren't rampant in the Dominion before the vampires arrived en masse, but the addition of so many mentalists to the city's population tipped some kind of balance and pushed the existing legal system from ad hoc and insufficient to downright laughable.

Witness testimony was useless. Even testimony recorded on camera or captured by psych-screened clairvoyants was useless, because you never knew who you were seeing or who might be pulling their strings. Of course this had always been true to some extent, but the twin demands of a broader set of laws and a more mentally dominating populace resulted in entire weeks in which no case came up that could be effectively tried.

What's more, a system with such firmly drawn lines between prosecution and defence often resulted in battles more magical than legal. "I now show the court that the man before them is actually a giant spider in disguise, and as such he was the one who poisoned the victim! Shazam!" And then the defence would, with equal and opposite shazam, prevent the arachnid's unmasking and say the prosecution had the wrong guy.

The Dominion's leaders considered the Napoleonic Code, the basis of legal structures still used in many countries worldwide. Its focus on a specific set of laws, rather than an evolving common law system in which cases helped to define law, wasn't suitable for a place where the unexpected was something that came with your bagel each morning. However, the city's leaders were intrigued by the idea of dropping the requirement that cases be proved beyond a reasonable doubt.

In the Dominion, doubt is always reasonable. The person you're talking to might not be who they look like or who you think they are. They might be a ghost. Or they might be an astral projection and not really there at all. Prosecuting anything to the standard of "beyond a reasonable doubt" was impossible. When juries were interviewed after a conviction, they admitted to either ignoring that requirement or focusing on other issues. In the famous case of Harold Weissmuller, the dragon convicted of starting the 1976 city hall fire, one juror told a reporter, "I don't know if he did it or not. I just hated that guy. He was smug."

Cause for a retrial? Not in the Dominion. The jury had been psych scanned and accepted by both sides before the trial began, so that was the end of it.

A word about psych scanning: This procedure, performed by city-approved psychics, is supposed to verify the intention of honesty, the lack of criminal motives, and the lack of undue prejudice in trial witnesses. It's also used on city employees working in the justice system—from judges, lawyers, and cops to pathologists and even receptionists.

Does it work? It seems to, though critics say an inaccurate psych scan can easily go undetected until the underlying lie is discovered. Certainly suspects can and do lie on the stand. Once a previously scanned suspect has been caught in a lie, the suspect is assumed to be immune to scanning. This makes psych scanning a good profession for those who want to never be wrong.

Psych scans are also optional among employees who are not actively involved in trials. It's understood, however, that turning down a psych scan is never a good career move.

Between the possibility of scan immunity in witnesses and the misgivings some residents have about the efficacy of scanning in the first place, doubt is alive and well in Dominion courtrooms.

In most civil law systems, as in civil cases in the United States, proof is determined not by a lack of reasonable doubt but by a "preponderance of evidence." In other words, who brought the biggest and best pile of evidence to the show? In light of the city's unique circumstances, the Dominion's leaders decided to adopt the civil standard for all cases, a change that was enacted in 1982.

Another change brought about in 1982 was the addition of a city investigator to all cases. These investigators, sworn to (and presumably scanned for) neutrality, work independently of lawyers and the police to study the facts of the case, provided any can be determined. The investigators attend trials and speak up when they have something to contribute—including the refutation of any evidence they can more or less prove to be untrue.

The investigators help keep the circus atmosphere of the Dominion's courts to a minimum. In practical terms, that means the typical Dominion trial is a one- or two-ring circus, instead of a full three-ring affair with clown cars and elephants.

Oddly, though the Dominion has very few laws compared to most places, it has a staggering number of bylaws. Chips, papers, and scans are needed for nearly everything, and even a barista might ask to see your species identification before serving you, explaining with a shrug that she can't sell coffee to plant-based hominids. You can protest that you clearly aren't a plant, but this is the Dominion and you never know. So papers, please.

Chapter Six

Karsten Roth

LIFETIMES SEEMED to pass before Jake reappeared. My stomach was roiling from the smell of the station, which was of blood and sulfur and the disinfectant someone had used trying vainly to clean the place. I was certain Innis would be in a fight at any moment, and I didn't know if I, as his employee, would be honour-bound to fight alongside him.

A man was dragged screaming through our waiting room by three police officers. Two wrestled him into a side room. The third stayed behind to speak with the startled and alarmed officers who had come to the waiting room in answer to the screaming.

"Stupid fucker was in Roserood with a couple of his buddies," she told them. "They got drunk, figured they'd cross the Heart. Three of 'em went in, but we caught this one. Now he figures we should go back for his pals."

"Jesus." A burly cop standing near the door shook his head. "What does 'no one comes out of the Heart alive' mean to these people? Do they think we're kidding with the warning signs?"

I could not have been more relieved to see Jake come into the waiting room. "I hope you got what you needed," he said, "because we're going."

Innis and I stood. A scaly man with leather wings stood as well. Jake stared at him until the man sat down again, wings shaking. Something in the way Jake looked made me want to do the same. I almost wished for wings to quiver.

"Yes, sir," Innis said, with a salute.

Jake didn't respond. We had to move quickly to stay with him. I half thought if he arrived at the Land Rover before we did, he would leave us behind.

A young couple was leaning against the side of the vehicle. I admit I would not have thought them a couple had they not been drunkenly showing the world their love. She was tall and long-legged, as antelopes were. She was much as antelopes were from the waist down as well: four legs ending in hooves and covered in light brown hair. She was wearing a dress of sorts. It fit her human top and was wide across her back. Her hands were human and busy with her companion's belt buckle.

"Break it up," Jake said. He walked toward them as if he would go through them, and they separated. They saw where Jake was going and so also stepped away from the car.

The woman's companion was a dwarf. Not to say that was a human born with one of the conditions of this kind, but to say that he was wide and knobbly and powerful in the way the dwarves of fairy tales had been. Since the Turn, such dwarves were seen from time to time.

"Sorry," the antelope woman said. The dwarf said nothing. He was probably thinking, could he get his teeth into Jake's leg? They were said to be biters. Some said there was poison in their mouths. I believed there was not. Just bile.

Once we were inside the car, Innis laughed. "Anyone else trying to picture how those two get it on?"

"For the right money," Jake said, "she'd probably let you watch."

Innis seemed intrigued. "She's a sex worker?"

Jake shrugged. I heard something crack in his shoulders. "Could be. It's good business here. A lot of people come to the Dominion to get drunk and work out some kinks."

"Where the beer and the antelope play," Innis said.

I glared at him, and he dropped his self-impressed smile.

"Imagine if they were a serious couple, though," he added. "Maybe they are. How do you…? I guess kids are out of the question. Heh. Kids. That's what you call the babies, isn't it? Not fawns."

"Calves," Jake said.

I was surprised he would know something of the kind.

"Either way," Innis said.

"Don't be so sure," Jake told him. "Anything's possible."

He glanced over his shoulder at me. I kept still, hoping to be boring enough that he would look back to the road. "This must seem pretty weird to someone who's used to Europe."

"I think it is weird to someone who's used to physics," I said.

Jake then turned to face forward. "You people have everything all divided up. Trolls over here. Orcs over there."

"Come on," Innis said. "That's not fair. Just because they have some designated areas—"

"And designated magic-free zones," Jake said.

Innis shut his eyes. "Okay, whatever. You're obviously in the mood to harp on this."

It seemed odd, suddenly, that Innis had gotten into the back seat with me, instead of taking the passenger seat beside his friend as he usually did. What was I to make of that? And the fact that I was glad of it?

Jake was less in the mood to harp than Innis thought, because he did not say anything further on the topic of Europe. He said instead, "There are a lot of cross-fertility experts in the Dominion. It's one of our local specialties."

I knew this, in a way. "Serenity Kirk came here when she wanted to have a child," I said. "This is what the tabloids told us. But you cannot make too much of what the German tabloids say."

Innis looked surprised. "I saw that French movie she was in. She was having trouble with fertility?"

"She was not, but her husband is long dead. He walks around, yes, but his… swimmers, do you say?"

"Sure," Innis said. He was smirking. "The swimmers weren't swimming?"

"It seems not. She did have twins, though. The tabloids say."

"A lot of people say it's some kind of supreme judgment of fate or whatever," Jake said. "Like those couples weren't ever supposed to be together anyhow. But they can solve pretty much anything around here in terms of reproducing. Unless you want to get nasty with a werecat. That's never gonna work out right."

"Why is this?" I asked. Jake looked at me again. Again with the unpleasant smile.

"Barbed penis," he said. "I found a whole string of hookers one year with their own kitty cats all clawed up. New one every week. Never caught the guy either. Guess he must've left town."

I could hear him laughing a little, thinking of this. I glanced at Innis. Innis appeared ill. He saw that I was looking at him and touched my shirtsleeve lightly with two fingers. A gesture of solidarity, I thought, or apology about his friend. I gave him what I could manage of a smile to show that I did not hold him responsible for the horrible things Jake said.

No one spoke the rest of the way to the hotel.

As we pulled up, Innis said, "I've got that appointment with the mayor tomorrow."

Jake grunted. "That's what you think. Getting an appointment with the mayor is a lot easier than getting the mayor to keep one."

Innis laughed, as well he might. I had no doubt that Innis would say something, anything really, and his appointment would be kept. Was it merely wavy brown hair and dark eyes of the film star sort, and of course his charm? Or were people right to say that Innis Stuart was persuasive beyond what one might expect, even of a man with his natural graces? I stared out the window so Innis would not see me contemplating him.

"Just pick us up at nine," Innis said. "And we'll see how it goes."

Morning, June 16
Innis Stuart

KARSTEN AND I had raided the snack machines on the way to our rooms the night before since we didn't want to get up a second earlier than we had to. At five minutes to nine, I appeared in the lobby to find Karsten at the front desk, complaining to a young, white-haired clerk about a painting in his room.

"Sir," the clerk was saying, "the Pickman prides itself on going beyond the generic non-art provided in most hotel rooms. Yes, the subject matter may be challenging or disturbing at times, but…."

"The subject matter is not the concern," Karsten said. "Do you think a murdered woman in a mirror is the most disturbing thing I have seen since my arrival?"

"Well...." She shifted from one foot to the other. Her brow wrinkled, and the formal manner dropped away. "So what's the problem?"

"The mirror has been fogging up as if someone is breathing on it."

"Oh!" She was bouncing on her toes, happy to have a grasp on the problem at last. "Is your picture haunted? We have a lot of those. We got them from an auction in New England."

"You can send mine back there," Karsten said.

I smiled behind my hand. The clerk frowned.

"We can't do that, sir. But I'll see about having the painting covered or moved."

"Thank you."

I fell into step beside him as he walked away from the desk. "Chicken."

He glanced at me. "I beg your pardon?"

"Scared of a widdle haunted painting?"

"Yes," he said. "I am. Perhaps we could switch rooms."

"If you want," I said. "Chicken."

Jake came through the front doors and stood inside them, expressionless. I went to him.

"Ready?"

Jake nodded, turned and walked out.

"Charming man," Karsten said.

I put a hand on his shoulder. He gave me a faintly surprised look in response. Not upset, only surprised. Maybe intrigued.

"He's a little cranky these days," I said, "but at least he's not a chicken."

Karsten nodded thoughtfully before elbowing me in the ribs and preceding me to the vehicle.

"I hope you two don't have anything to do for the next year or so," Jake said as we slid into the back seat of the Land Rover, "if you're really intent on seeing the mayor."

"I told you last night," I said. "I have an appointment."

"Yeah," Jake said. "And I told you, appointments are cheap and plentiful."

I glanced at Karsten, who shrugged. He probably didn't care. His portfolio showed little in the way of portrait photography, so I assumed it wasn't an interest of his. During an interview with the mayor, there'd be little for him to do but take pictures of the man. Or woman. Or neither or both or something else. There wasn't much agreement among those who'd met Mayor Krejci.

"So," I asked Jake, "are you saying actual visits with the mayor are expensive? I do have a discretionary fund."

Jake laughed as he pulled into traffic. His laugh was loud, but more than that, it was unexpected. Karsten wasn't the only one in the back seat who jumped a little on hearing it.

"You think you can just bribe your way around town, Innis? I thought you knew a few things about this place."

"Very few," I said. My teeth didn't want to separate. I shut my eyes and forced myself to unclench my jaw. "That's why I'm here. And why I have a guide."

I felt something on my leg and opened my eyes to find Karsten giving me a reassuring pat. It was a nice thing for him to do, and he was welcome to leave his hand there all day if he liked. It was not lost on me, however, that I was being soothed by a sourpuss. There could be no clearer sign that I had to get my temper under control.

"Bribery is strictly forbidden around here," Jake said, seemingly either unaware or unconcerned that he had pissed me off. "Strictly. You'd be better off getting caught shoving five hundred and eight dead pigs into a police car than offering or accepting a bribe."

Karsten's neutral expression hadn't changed, yet somehow he looked amused.

"This thing with the pigs," he said, "may I assume this has happened?"

Jake didn't honour that with a response.

"Bribery's forbidden in most places," I said. "What makes it any different here?"

Jake shrugged. "Don't know. Don't care. The other cops told me how it was when I moved here, and I said, when in Rome."

"Snobbery," Karsten said.

I looked at him. "What?"

"It is most likely snobbery," he said. "Bribing officials, that is something you do in Africa or Columbia or Russia. Your country cannot pay you half so well as I can. Have my spare change."

I snorted. Karsten's face told me he didn't like that, probably as much because it was uncouth as because I was laughing at him.

"Kar, look... I prefer not to bribe people, and I rarely do it."

"Has my whole name become a burden to you?" Karsten asked politely.

I laughed outright. "I guess I must be getting comfortable with you."

He raised his eyebrows in mock surprise. "Is that how one can tell?"

"If you really hate it—"

He shook his head. "It is the most common diminutive for my name. You may assume I have heard it before. You were telling me you do not bribe people."

"Right," I said, "A person can get a long way with a smile and some pleasant conversation. But I'm also a realist. How do you think things get built in rich countries? How do you think politicians make money for campaigns? How do you think people get cushy jobs?"

He shrugged. "Those things happen in many ways. Yes, of course money and favours are exchanged. But the style of bribery where you give small amounts of money to everyone... this is considered backwater. And the Dominion is already not taken so seriously as it would like to be."

"The kid may have a point," Jake said.

"He's not a kid," I said.

Karsten gave me a puzzled glance, and I understood that. It wasn't really my place to take umbrage. For all I knew, he liked being mistaken for a university student. Something about the way Jake said "kid," though, bothered me, and I wanted him to stop.

"I'm two hundred and seventy-five," Karsten said. It came out of left field for me, but it seemed to mean something to Jake, who swerved to the side of the road, cutting off a moving van, and hit the brakes.

"You think that's funny?" he spat, turning our way and leaning as far into the back as his seat belt would allow.

Karsten tilted his head like a curious bird. "No," he said calmly. He was studying Jake's face, looking for something there.

"He was a good cop!" Jake said, and then I almost laughed. Not because I got it, suddenly, that the cop who had been cut up and left around town had been two hundred and seventy-five. Not because of Karsten's little joke, if joke it had been. But because Jake's line sounded like something from a terrible movie, worse even than the one Donna had been in when she'd declared herself to be on the trail of "something big."

"What do you think happened to him?" Karsten asked in that calm, mild tone.

Jake's eyes widened. "Everyone knows what happened to him."

Karsten inclined his head, another birdlike gesture. "True. I meant instead, do you have a suspect?"

"I don't know," Jake growled. "Where were you six months ago?"

"Berlin," Karsten said.

Simply telling it like it was. That kind of tone was pretty well guaranteed to make an angry person angrier, and it appeared to be working on Jake. I put a hand on Jake's arm. The skin was hot.

"Jake, come on. The number stuck in his head because of that story in the *Phoenix*."

"It is not a goddamned joke," Jake said.

"No one's saying it is," I told him. "It's obviously a sore point in this city."

Jake moved away from me a little, toward the front of the Rover. "What do you mean by that?"

Outside our vehicle, traffic was missing us by inches. Drivers were honking. More than one car flickered and vanished, most likely teleporting away to avoid a collision. Jake hadn't done the best parking job of his career. I was tempted to suggest that we continue the conversation elsewhere, after my meeting with the mayor, but I got the sense that Jake might not be open to discussing Aloysius Harper again.

"The crime rate's sky high in this place," I said. "Add in the things that would be considered crimes anywhere else on Earth, and it's halfway to the moon. Jake, man, you used to be a cop. You must see that the police and the reporters are used to moving on to the next thing. It's not usual for one murder to keep attracting interest this long after the fact."

"So we should just drop it?" Jake asked. "That what you think?"

He sounded funny when he said it. Far away. I took my hand off his arm.

"You know that's not how I work," I said. "I'm not here to judge the town or the people living here. I'm here to say, 'that's interesting' and ask questions until I think I understand it. Kar's here to take pictures. Though I've spent a little time with him now, and I suspect he's judging everything in sight."

I wasn't sure which came first, Karsten hitting my arm or Jake laughing. I would have to apologize to Karsten later, but it was worth it to break the tension.

"Look," Jake said. "Both of you. Al was a cop in the Dominion before it was the Dominion. He was walking a beat before the place had cement sidewalks. Since the war, the Wall got torn up and City Hall burned down. Even the goddamned rivers aren't where they used to be. So, what, it's crazy that people miss Al?"

"Do you miss Al?"

Karsten's voice came from close beside me. He'd somehow moved forward without making a sound. Jake gave him a dark look, but the clouds cleared as he stared at Karsten's face.

"Sure," Jake said. He had that distant sound to his voice again. I had to strain to hear him over the noise outside. "I never worked with him much, but sure. You'd see him around, you know. You get used to seeing a guy around."

"I'm sorry," Karsten said simply.

Sorry for Jake's loss or for the… well, the joke, or whatever it was. I wasn't sure which he meant. Maybe both. Jake nodded.

"Do you have any leads?" I asked. Jake looked exhausted. At nine thirty in the morning.

"If we did," he said, "do you think this case would still be open?"

"You can't be serious," I said. "The DCPD has the best retrocognitives anywhere. Can't they do a reconstruction?"

"The Dominion has the best of everything," Jake told me. "Even the worst."

He glanced at his watch. It was thick, a brown-leather and brushed-nickel contraption that would have looked ridiculously heavy on any other arm.

"We'd better get rolling. Don't want to be late."

"I thought," Karsten said, "there was no point being on time for an appointment here."

"Being late," he said, "would be worse."

Karsten Roth

I HAD, for myself, little desire to see this mayor. I was curious, yes, about who might agree to be considered responsible for such a place. However, I was not curious enough to want to queue in an office building when I could be seeing more of the city instead. I didn't know what Innis thought he would learn in such a place.

He didn't visit mayors anywhere else that he traveled, unless he was bribing them to let him work undisturbed.

I was starting to believe we might learn more about the Dominion, and about our own dubious level of safety, if we spent more time with Jake. Perhaps if Jake told us why his former brethren had been so unhappy to see him the night before, even as he brought them a criminal ready for booking. If I had known Innis better, or if Innis had known Jake less well, I might have taken Innis aside and told him about the workings of my mind. As it was I suspected he would only call me paranoid. And then he might say it was a quality of my Germanic people.

In fairness I did not believe Innis had anything more against Germany than against any other place on Earth.

I was thinking these things as Jake circled and circled the stack of grey and pitted concrete blocks that was the Dominion City Hall. I thought immediately, of course, he is searching for a place to park. Then I thought, but he does not do that. He places a placard in the window and parks where he likes.

I was about to ask about this when we slowed for a turn and I saw a piece of paper appear on the windshield of a city car that was half on the street, half on the sidewalk. I nudged Innis.

"Did you see that?"

He glanced at me. He seemed amused.

"Karsten. If you want to stay in this line of work, you are going to have to learn to be more specific. If there aren't ten things worth looking at in any given location, I shouldn't be there."

"A ticket appeared on the window of that car," I told him, pointing for added specificity. Innis craned over his shoulder as we made the turn and pulled away.

"Huh," he said. "Well. They do that in Rome too. They don't do it in Germany?"

"I've never seen it in Rome," I told him. "What do they do, exactly? It can't be that they have clairvoyants watching the parking spaces and teleporters giving out tickets. That would be an extraordinary waste of ability."

Jake laughed and slapped the steering wheel. "Waste of ability."

"He has a point," Innis said. "I never really thought about it, but the amount you'd have to pay psychics just to ticket people… it's not gonna be worth it."

"Except in Rome?" I asked.

Innis smiled at me. "Lots of people park like assholes in Rome."

This was true. I thought it might be revenge for the city's decision to abandon a nearly finished parking garage that could have held eight hundred vehicles. The construction of a ramp leading to the garage had turned up haunted ground. Ancient ghosts. Violent ghosts and strong. Ghosts, whatever they truly were, were sometimes addled, and these Roman ghosts would not see reason. The city said they were history and not to be removed. And so the people of Rome parked where they could from desperation or spite. Perhaps both.

"I am surprised anyone cares about something so inconsequential," I said, "in a place of such chaos."

"That's the point, ki—Karsten," Jake said. "You gotta tell your—shit."

That was all the warning we received before Jake claimed a spot by accelerating and braking, seemingly at once.

"Too small!" Innis yelled. I was at least as startled by that as by the motion of the vehicle, and I cursed. I did this in German, as always when was I alarmed. Jake waved a hand, irritated. I heard us for a moment as I imagined he did, buzzing around his ears. It was an effort to make anything of what we said. And then I did not know why I had thought such a thing, apart from the insect-swatting way Jake had moved his hand.

I felt fuzzy, as if it were late and I had been drinking. Innis was pressing his temples with long fingers. I knew people who did this to ward off headaches, though it had never worked for me.

"You'll feel better when you get out of the car," Jake told us. As I began to open the door, I saw it flicker.

"Shut your eyes," Jake said. I did so and left the Land Rover that way, forgetting for the moment that traffic here filled every available bit of pavement and that I could be run over as I stepped outside.

Once I was outside, my head cleared. I looked for Innis, expecting to see him across the top of the vehicle, and saw him instead across the hood of a yellow sports car of some kind. Yet I could extend my hand and touch the door I had just closed.

"Jesus," Innis said. He sounded as uncertain as I felt. Jake walked around the vehicle and put a broad hand on Innis's shoulder.

"Nonspace," Jake said. He gave Innis a shove. "Get moving. Don't want to be late."

I stepped around the front of the Land Rover, as Jake had, to join Innis as he started to walk toward the front doors of City Hall.

"Jesus," Innis said again, but softly, for me alone.

Jake was already a few metres ahead of us, and Innis seemed content that he be there.

"I did not know they used nonspace in this way," I said. "I thought it was just in buildings, in added rooms."

"Me too," Innis said. "Haven't even met the mayor yet, and already we've learned something."

He was attempting, I thought, to sound chipper. It was not a successful attempt.

"It is practical, I suppose," I said.

Innis smiled. "And naturally you would be a fan of that."

"I can't see why anyone would not be," I said.

He laughed and put a hand on my back as we followed Jake around the corner of the building. This touch was unaffected and reassuring, and so I let his hand remain there. Innis had been touching me often, and I had been finding that it was not unpleasant, though I did not often like to be touched by people I did not know well. Innis had a manner about him that made one feel comfortable with him. It might have been his mysterious charm, but I thought instead that it was merely his way. He seemed genuinely to like people. It was a novelty for me, and even agreeable, to be in the presence of such simple good will.

Every city hall I have seen in my travels has borne some crest or flag or item of distinction atop its entryway. This one did not. As we approached the front doors, I saw polished dark granite around them, distinct from the rough concrete of the building's walls, and the doors themselves were glass. Aside from this, there was nothing to indicate that the building was in any way special, a celebration of its community. The words "City Hall" did not even appear.

"All business, hey?" Innis commented. I nodded. He gave me a foolish grin and said, "Practical."

"Yes, fuck yourself," I said.

He was laughing loudly as we passed through the doors, and everyone turned to look.

Perhaps not everyone. Perhaps I exaggerate. But a hundred of them at least, the residents of the Dominion, standing on line after endless line. They stared at Innis with curiosity and annoyance and some other thing. It was, I soon decided, pity. Because this was a place where one lost one's sense of humour, and they expected Innis to lose his as well.

My first instinct was to take photographs, as that is what I do when… well, it is what I do, full stop. But it is also what I most want to do when I come across something I could never properly describe. I wasn't certain, however, that a photographer would be welcome here.

"Photos?" I asked softly.

Innis frowned. "Yes, but wait until they've stopped staring."

"Obviously," I told him. I was not an amateur.

In order to do something other than simply stand there, I looked for Jake. He was at the back of one of the shorter lines, which meant there were only a dozen or so people in front of him.

The city hall resembled a huge and inefficient train station. We were in a single large room. There were stairs and elevators at the far end, and above us I could see halls ringing the open space that led, eventually, to a dingy yellow ceiling. At each level of the building, the halls extended farther into the space, toward the center. I guessed that each hall was surrounded by offices and that the offices on the top floor would be the largest.

In this room I could see no offices. The room was ringed by wickets and, near where Innis and I stood, a single washroom. No accommodations for size or shape here.

Each wicket was manned by one person. In its employees, at least, the city hall did show variety in size and shape. I saw fur and metal and one woman, tall and thin, who was not substantial. The bulletin board behind her could be seen, faintly, through her.

The residents of the city, also a wide assortment of types, were waiting with the snappish disgust of those who hate where they are but are not going anywhere. In this respect the room was unlike a train station. A train station offers hope that you might get away.

"Shit," Innis said.

I barely heard him, even in this strangely quiet room. I followed his gaze and saw a uniformed police officer standing beside Jake, her face angry. She was speaking and pointing toward the door. Jake, also angry, was shaking his head. Before I could respond, Innis began to walk toward Jake. He was moving quickly, taking full advantage of his long-legged build. I had to nearly run to stay beside him.

"Nobody wants to see you," the officer was saying as we drew close enough to hear. She was nearly as tall as Jake, if not so wide, and her skin was the same light grey as the walls of the building. "That little stunt last night—"

"I didn't know bringing in a killer was a stunt," Jake said. "I have a PI , in case you forgot. I'm responsible for—"

"Fucking tell me about it," the officer hissed. I say hissed because this is what she did. I thought for a moment I might have seen the end of an oddly shaped tongue. "Why don't you tell me what you're responsible for?"

"Fuck you, Zahia," Jake said.

She—Zahia—laughed. It was not with humour.

"Don't change the subject," she said.

"Okay, people," Innis said. He stepped nearly between them, and each of them stepped back. "I don't know what this is about, but maybe this isn't the place. Huh?"

"There isn't a place," Jake growled, but Zahia eyed Innis thoughtfully. Her narrow face was pleasant when she was not enraged.

"Yeah," she said. "Fine. Jake?"

Jake rolled his eyes but, to my astonishment, followed Zahia as she walked quickly toward and through the front doors.

Innis bumped his arm against mine. "We got his place in line."

I regarded him. He was tall, such that when we stood so close, I had to strain my neck to see his face.

"What do you suppose that was about?" I asked.

Innis stared at the doors as if he thought they might overhear. "That was his partner. Like, cop partner. He mentioned her to me sometimes… before he quit."

"I thought you said he was a detective," I said. "Do the detectives here wear uniforms?"

Innis looked at me now. His eyebrows were raised. "No. That's strange, isn't it?"

I wanted to say that Jake was strange and that many people seemed angry with him. I said, carefully, "He does not seem to have left the police force on good terms."

"Yeah," Innis said.

He was watching the doors again. I waited. He said nothing more.

"What I said about my age," I said after a moment. "I wanted him to talk about Aloysius Harper."

Innis laughed. It was a huff of air. "Mission accomplished. Were you trying to royally piss him off while you were at it?"

"No," I said. "I'm sorry about that. I should take photographs now."

He nodded. "Go for it. I can hold down this fort until Jake comes back."

Innis Stuart

KARSTEN SEEMED eminently relieved to be able to run around with a camera and not speak to anyone for a while. It amazed me that he spoke English so well, considering the effort it must have taken to learn and how little interest he generally had in speaking to anyone.

I watched him for a few minutes, and would have been content to keep doing it for an hour, but then he went outside the building for exterior shots, and I had to find a new hobby. I turned to the dark-haired man in front of me, who was both four-eyed and bespectacled. That had probably earned him a hell of a ride through elementary school.

"You waiting to see the mayor?" I asked.

He snorted. "You nuts? Who has that kinda time?"

"Not you?" I ventured.

"Damn right," he said.

He would probably have left it at that, but I was still bored.

"So, what are you in for?" I asked.

"In for," he said. "Good one. Fuckin' ten to twenny."

"The lines do seem pretty slow," I said.

He squinted at me. The effect was more than doubled by the extra eyes. "Must be newta town."

"Just visiting," I told him.

"Lucky," he observed. "I'm tryina leave. You wanna buy a house?"

"Got one," I said. "In the Yukon."

"Crazy," he said. "Bears are crazy up there."

"Can be," I said. I hadn't come to the Dominion to talk about bears, no matter how crazy they were. "You here about the land title or something? On your house?"

He looked at me like I was as crazy as a bear.

"Not gonna sell it without sales permits," he said.

"You need a permit to put your house up for sale?" I asked. "That's unusual."

"Never un-fuckin'-usual to need a permit," he said and turned his back to me.

The room had some kind of noise dampener on it, but I managed to pick out enough of what was happening at the front of the line to determine there was no theme going on. It wasn't the "seeing the mayor" line or the "pissed off at the Dominion" line. It was a mixed bag of people and problems. To the credit of my bear-hating buddy, most of them did seem to need a permit of some kind. Generally the lady in the wicket told folks their permit wasn't available. More than a few were told to go stand in another line.

No sign of Jake, but I wasn't worried about it. The appointment was in my name, and thanks to Jake's insistence on good time management, I still had about twenty minutes to make it to the front of the line. I'd see the mayor by myself if I had to. Considering how many people Jake seemed to be rubbing wrong lately, maybe it would be better that way.

Karsten sure as hell couldn't stand Jake, but then again, Karsten hadn't been practising "if you want a friend, be a friend" with the guy, so it was hard to tell who, if anyone, was to blame for their little personality conflict. As long as it didn't come to fisticuffs, I didn't care if they wanted to snipe at each other. I did, however, see Karsten's point. The cops had not been glad to see Jake. Even Manya—though, granted, a criminal overlord—had been strange with him compared to the way she'd treated Karsten and me. And in truth I was finding him a little off-putting myself. Something was bothering my old pal.

Karsten Roth

I PRETENDED very hard that I had gone outside merely to take photographs of the building, but I needn't have bothered. Jake was already gone by the time I arrived on the sidewalk. His former partner was still there, as I had hoped she would be. I slung my camera strap over my shoulder and approached her.

"I'm sorry," I said, "that we interrupted you earlier."

Zahia smiled and shrugged. In natural light, I could see a faint repeating pattern on her skin.

"It wasn't a conversation worth having," she said.

"I'm Karsten Roth," I told her, offering a hand. "I'm a photographer. I'm here working with Innis Stuart."

I paused there to see if she knew of Innis. Some people did.

She shook my hand. Her hand was smooth and dry. "So that was the infamous Innis Stuart. I thought so. Jake acted like he didn't know the guy, but I've seen pictures."

"Pictures?" I asked.

"Yeah. Jake had a picture on his desk of the two of them fishing somewhere. Total cliché, right? And he read Stuart's books, so I saw the author photo one time. He's cute."

She spoke as if she were younger than me, and I could tell nothing from her skin, but I thought that she must be older than she seemed to have been a detective. I wondered if she spoke that way to disarm people, to make them think her inconsequential.

"You were Jake's partner," I said.

She rolled her eyes as Jake had done when she'd asked him to step outside.

"Two wonderful years," she said. "And look where it got me."

"Where did it get you?" I asked. I tried to keep my voice neutral.

"Nowhere," she said, and her expression hardened, and then she did look older than me. "How do you like working with the great Innis Stuart?"

"Is he the great Innis Stuart?" I asked. "His books are quite popular, I suppose."

"He's pretty popular with Jake," she said. "I used to hear all about him."

That was the sort of thing I had been hoping to hear.

"I have no desire to go back to a queue," I told her. "Could I buy you coffee instead?"

She smiled. It was a careful smile that did not show much of her teeth. "Not my drink. But there's a park two blocks down if you want to sit for a few."

I agreed and followed her to a small and hideous inner-city park. It had a few patches of lawn and paths between the patches, though the entire park took up less than a block. There was a bench along each path and a statue next to each bench. She chose a bench beside a statue of turtles, a stack of them, taller than she stood.

We sat, and I set my camera down between us. She glanced at it.

"Just a digital?" she asked. "Normal pictures?"

My camera was not "just" anything, in my view. And I liked to think my pictures were not so ordinary as to be called normal. But that was probably not what she had intended by her question.

"It sees what the eye sees," I told her, "more or less."

"Less of the ghosts?" she asked, smiling. "And more of the things you've been bewitched into not seeing?"

"As you say," I said. "It is a lens and a machine. A small computer."

"Very old-fashioned," she said. She ran her fingertips over the leather case that held the body of the camera. I could not tell if she meant it as a seductive act or if she was simply fond of photography.

"Not really," I said. "I am a photographer, not a psychic investigator or some other thing. So I own cameras and not some other device."

"Fair enough," she said. "So you never answered me about working with Innis Stuart. Is it that bad?"

"Why would you think it would be bad?" I asked. "I thought your former partner spoke well of him."

Zahia laughed. A bulge in her throat, wider than an Adam's apple, moved up and down.

"That right there makes me wonder," she said.

I tried to look friendly, the way Innis did. It was not natural to me. "To be honest,I am finding Jake difficult. He is our guide to the city, and he seems... temperamental."

"Oh, he's temperamental all right," she said. "He's also not your best choice of a guide if you—"

I could see nothing that had distracted her.

"If I what?" I asked.

She shook her head. "He just doesn't get along with people all that well. You know? You don't want to be associated with him if he's going around town pissing people off."

"Such as yourself," I said.

She laughed. "Jake can't piss me off much more than he already has. But he should stay away from the police station. That's a word of advice. Keep your guide away from the station."

I cocked my head in curiosity, and she laughed. I frowned, puzzled. She covered her mouth and pointed at the back of the bench. A pigeon sat there, beside my shoulder, cocking its head as well.

"Copycat," I told it.

It looked at me and straightened its head, as if it had understood.

"Wow," she said. "That's amazing."

"Birds are imitative," I said, but in truth I had never seen a bird do such a thing before.

"No, not just the head-tilt thing," she said. "The pigeon. We don't have them here. I didn't think we did."

I smiled. "Pigeons are everywhere. What do they call them in New York? Winged rats?"

"Yeah, sure," she said, "but they all left the Dominion in the mid-eighties. No one knows why. The theory is that someone in town who fucking hated them made them disappear."

"Except for this one," I pointed out. "Why should Jake stay away from the police station, if I may ask?"

Zahia looked at the pigeon and not at me as she said, "It's not something I'd like to talk about."

"We're meant to be speaking about Innis," I said, and at this she faced me again.

"Exactly. You keep evading my question. What's he like?"

I opened my mouth before realizing that I did not know what to say.

"I… suppose he is all right," I said.

She laughed. "Oh, that's convincing."

"No," I said. "I mean that he is fine to work for. So far. This is my first trip with him. I have worked for worse people. But I find him odd."

"Seriously?" she said. "What is it you do, again?"

"I am a photographer," I told her.

She nodded. "Yeah, but you're not in the Dominion because the light's really good here. Like, you shoot weird stuff, right, and that's why you came here?"

It was my turn now to watch the pigeon. It looked back at me. It seemed as if it were trying to understand me. In this, I wished it luck.

"I like to think I'm just a photographer," I said. "But it seems that I do take many pictures of… weird stuff."

"Well," she said, "to be fair, there's a lot of it."

I gave her another smile. It was becoming more natural. "That is true. And so you wonder, why would I find Innis so odd?"

"That's what I'm wondering," she agreed. "Jake talked him up as a meat-and-potatoes guy. You know, an adventurer type. Fearless, bold, daring, all that crap."

"Yes, that crap," I said, still smiling. "I don't know that he is fearless. I think if he were, he would not have lived this long. But did Jake ever say there was something different about him? Some… quirk?"

She curled toward me on the seat, bringing her legs up and tucking her feet beneath her. This was, I thought, not good for the uniform. It did not look to be serge, but even polyester would pick up dirt.

"Jake never said anything about Innis having a quirk," she said. "What are we talking about here?"

I shook my head. Obviously she had nothing to tell me. "Perhaps nothing. It only seemed strange to me that Innis has never been arrested. Not that I could discover. In some of the places he has traveled, it is nearly impossible not to be arrested at some point, if only until money has changed hands."

"No kidding," she said. "Jake used to tell stories about when he was traveling, you know, with the military. He's been in jail about a billion times. Hey, do you want me to check on Innis's record? Not that he probably has one in a lot of those places, especially if there was a bribe involved, but maybe I can get a little more information than you did."

"That would be very kind," I said.

"You figure he's some kind of creepy-ass mind controller?" she asked. "That wouldn't fit in too well with his boy's own adventure image, would it? How I Daringly Mind-Fucked My Way Across Africa."

I shrugged. I did think Innis had done something of the kind, and yet I did not want to see him, as they say, tarred and feathered. Perhaps this was his subtle influence at work upon me. Or perhaps it was simply that he showed none of the casual disregard I had seen in other mentalists. Of those I had met, he would be the first who had offered me the best seat at a pub table and the last of a basket of french fries.

He was, in fine, not what I had expected. He thought of me and of others. He showed, more than kindness, a taste for unique qualities in people. Even in this bad-humoured photographer who had perhaps not been fair to him at first.

As well, I sometimes sensed that he was courting me. I mean precisely this old word. He held doors and chairs and put a hand at my back. He did nothing crude. He did nothing untoward. He merely treated me as if I were worthy of great care. It would be a lie to say that this did not charm me.

I would say these things to myself, but not to Zahia. To her I said, "No, but I feel something is amiss. But there is one other thing I wanted to ask you."

"Sure," she said. "Shoot."

"Do you know of anyone else who might know Innis? I am thinking he and Jake may have friends in common."

She frowned. The lines of her forehead went very deep. "Yeah… actually, yeah. Um…. Donna… something or other. She's a crime reporter for the *Phoenix*. She goes way back with both of those guys. She mentioned it once when she was interviewing Jake about some case we were on."

"And she is still there?" I asked. "At the *Phoenix*?"

"Oh yeah," Zahia said. "She's one of those old soldiers, you know? She'll be there forever."

"I can find her, then," I said. "Thank you."

"Hey," she said. "No need to thank me. I figure if I find something on his buddy, maybe it'll fuck up Jake's Christmas."

"His Christmas?" I asked, puzzled. December was months away. She laughed.

"Figure of speech. All I'm saying is, I want to make his life hard. So I'll see what I can do."

As she walked away, I could see the marks her shoe heels had left on the seat of her pants. The pigeon made a sound as if twitting her for this.

"You should probably leave," I told him. "She said something here does not like your kind."

He said nothing further, so I bid him farewell and went on my way.

Chapter Seven

Innis Stuart

WHEN THE bear-hater reached the head of the line, putting me in second place, I looked around for my guide and my photographer and found they were both still AWOL. Not that I needed either at the moment, but I liked to know where they were. More than that, I liked to know that they were not in the process of beating each other senseless.

Okay, that Jake was not in the process of beating Karsten senseless. I had no idea whether Karsten could handle himself, but considering that Jake had military training and was nearly twice Karsten's size, I didn't think it would matter.

The bear-hater was eliding his way through a diatribe about the sheer number of permits and other pieces of paper he needed in order to sell his privately owned home to another private citizen, assuming he could find a private citizen who would want to buy it. Privately I sympathized. The whole thing sounded unreasonable. Bear-hater didn't sound that reasonable either, and probably never did, but that didn't mean he had invalid complaints.

The woman at our wicket seemed unconcerned. She had narrow features, small deep-set eyes, and greying hair pulled into a bun. I wondered if it were possible to purchase employees like that, maybe from a place called Bitter Civil Servants and Bank-Tellers, Incorporated. They all seemed to come from the same production line. Of course this was the Dominion, so maybe that wasn't a joke. The place could actually have production lines for civil servants. For all I knew, they were golems.

She was explaining the facts of life to Bear-hater in a bored and scratchy voice when Karsten finally showed up.

"Your house was grandfathered in when the unmechanized flight height restrictions went into place," she was telling him as Karsten spotted me and mouthed something that looked like an apology. "The new owner will have to acquire a permit signed by all registered non-mechanized flying residents within a twenty-block radius, or he will have to lower the roof accordingly. You are required to note this in your terms and conditions of sale, unless you obtain the permit yourself."

"Jesus Christ, lady," Bear-hater said. "I dunno who flies. Whaddami, supposed to ask?"

Karsten hurried across the room. I let him hurry, though there was no rush, because the bastard had made me wonder where the hell he was. I didn't care for that.

"You can obtain a list of registered non-mechanized flying residents in your section of your zone at Wicket A."

I would have laid money that Bear-hater didn't know what his section of his zone was and that this was going to be a problem when he got to the front of the line at Wicket A, but he didn't inquire further. Instead he shrugged and slapped money onto the counter. Because paperwork isn't enough fun if you don't have to pay to do it.

The civil servant was printing out multiple copies of copies of multiple receipts when Karsten arrived at my side.

"I'm sorry," he said. "I was photographing."

"This building?" I asked. "Outside? It's not much to look at."

He gave me a flat expression. I wouldn't have wanted to play poker with him. After a long pause, he said, "I spoke with Zahia."

That was about the last thing I would have expected. I raised my eyebrows at him. "Really? Why?"

He shrugged. "She saw me taking photos and asked about you. She has seen your books."

"Well, sure," I said. "She used to work with Jake. He talked about her sometimes. Why didn't she come talk to me?"

"She was tired of hearing Jake talk about the Great Innis Stuart. I think she wanted me to say you were an ogre."

I grinned. It was childish, but I liked hearing that Jake had been talking me up. Especially considering that he'd run hot and cold since I got to town.

"Not literally, I assume," I said.

Karsten smiled. "I don't know. I told her I had taken photographs for worse people."

"High praise," I said. Karsten was scanning the room, searching for his next shot. He was nearly always doing that whether he realized it or not.

"I once took pictures," he said, "at gunpoint. A solider wanted photos of his family."

"You would probably have done it without the inducement," I observed.

He kept scanning the room. "And the photos would have been less blurry as my hands would not have been shaking."

"You see Jake out there?" I asked. Karsten shook his head. He was watching a tentacled man at the front of a nearby line who was going through his many pockets searching for something. Probably a form he didn't have.

Bear-hater stepped away from the wicket and stomped past us to what I presumed to be Wicket A.

"I'm up," I said to Karsten, who finally looked at me.

"Congratulations," he said.

I rubbed my hands together and faced the civil servant. "Good morning. I have an appointment with the mayor."

She did not check a computer screen or a notebook or a clock. "Their Worship is running a little behind."

"I'm sure they are," I said, "but I've come a long way to talk with them, and I made the appointment pretty far in advance. Is there any way I could get in for just a few minutes?"

I capped it off with a smile. I didn't know when she'd last seen a smile in this place, and I thought it might dazzle or confuse her.

She blinked, and for the first time, her expression was not completely hostile.

"A few minutes would probably be all right," she said. "Take the stairs at the back to the top floor and turn left. I'll let them know to expect you."

Beside me, Karsten took a deep breath. Relieved, apparently.

"Thank you," I told the woman and put a hand on Karsten's arm. "Stairs," I told him.

"I heard," he said and pulled his arm away.

The stairs were covered in a seventies vintage linoleum that some designer, probably through a haze of reality-bending smoke, had thought resembled rusty orange stone. I was confident that it never had, even less so now that it was worn from all the thwarted elevator-takers trudging up the stairs, putting their feet down in the middle of each broad step. Everyone in Canada, even this putative Canada, aimed hard for the middle.

Kar was definitely put out about something, to more than his usual extent. I could tell not only because he was snubbing me, out of the blue, but because he didn't look left or right as we climbed the stairs. There were a few points at which even I could see a good shot waiting to be taken, but he either didn't notice or didn't care. I considered asking to borrow his camera, which would probably shake him out of whatever this was, but I thought it would be better to meet with the mayor without blood streaming from where my testicles had recently been.

At Karsten's angry pace, we made it to the top of the stairs in remarkably good time. I took a moment to look around the top floor. It was fancier by far than the dull, utile grey of the ground floor, but it was still nothing like the showpiece I would have expected. Not that the Dominion was necessarily wealthy—though it might have been. No one seemed to know. But when you have enough magic around, it's not hard to doll the place up.

There were some potted plants, and the hallways were wide and covered in recently vacuumed Moroccan-patterned carpet. It was a sign of how few people came upstairs that a carpet could stand up to the traffic. The skylight had not been cleaned recently, but its light did warm the cold fluorescents that provided the rest of the illumination.

I turned left, and as promised there was a door with a plaque indicating that this was the mayor's office. Karsten had stopped outside it, waiting for me. I passed him and opened the door, expecting to find a desk and a receptionist guarding the inner sanctum. Instead I stepped into a spacious corner office with a single large desk along the back wall and a single obscurity behind that desk.

It would be more descriptive to say a person or three people or an orc, but I wasn't up to the task, and I'm still not. In my defence, I don't know of anyone who is.

"Kar," I said under my breath. He was close beside me, as I'd figured he would be. Whatever had crawled up him and died, he still knew enough to stay close when walking into a strange room. "You may want to take pictures after all."

Karsten said something so quietly that I didn't think he'd intended for me to hear it. It was German, and I was pretty sure it was a curse. I saw his hand move, quickly but subtly, to drop the lens cap from his camera.

"Your Honour," I said, stepping forward and offering a hand. "I'm Innis Stuart, and this is Karsten Roth."

The mayor stood and offered a blur in return.

"A pleasure," the mayor said.

Karsten Roth

I THOUGHT moment after moment that I knew what I was seeing. The mayor was an older man with greying hair cut close to his balding head. A woman, fifty at most, with bottled auburn hair and thick-framed tortoiseshell glasses. A younger man, perhaps forty-five, with a hairless and translucent blue scalp showing the bone beneath. A lion, for a single heartbeat. A stack of plasticine, forming and reforming itself as it reached for our hands, closed a folder, sat back in its chair. A mouth forming because now it was to speak. And then an old man again. And now a blur.

I wondered if Innis were seeing this as I was, or if he might be seeing different things, but it was not a good time to ask. What had the mayor's hand felt like to him? I could feel nothing but pressure, no texture or warmth.

"Bernie Krejci. Call me Bernie."

This what the mayor had said in response to our names. It was no help at all. Even the voice was everything and nothing at once.

What would my camera capture? The flash was off, and this office had enough light that I thought I could get an acceptable image. I moved my arm so that the mayor was in sight of the lens and pressed the button several times. I was careful not to look at the camera, to draw attention to it in any way. Once I was certain I had something I could use, I would ask if I might take some photographs.

We were invited to sit in dark brown leather chairs facing the mayor's cherrywood desk. Unlike the rest of the building, there was nothing of the 1970s in this room. It was all from a decade or two before the Turn.

"Thank you for agreeing to see us," Innis said. "I know you're very busy."

"Well, you had an appointment," the mayor said, as if this were explanation enough for our presence. How could it be that I could hear cheerfulness in the voice but not whether it was pitched high or low? "And I am, I must admit, a great fan of your books."

"Always good to meet a fan," Innis said brightly. "Your Honour—Bernie—I wanted to meet you because I'm introducing readers to the Dominion, and there are people who say you *are* the Dominion."

Bernie laughed. A hand reached for a tissue and blurred into something else, perhaps a hook. I studied the tissue box. Bernie was giving me vertigo.

"I don't know who told you that. Whatever the Dominion is, I'm not it."

I was not so sure. Innis sat up straight, and it was an excuse to look at him instead of Bernie. I did so.

"You've been mayor a long time," Innis said. "Decades. And you were living here before that. Some people say you were living in Dominion City during the Turn."

"Well, I have been here awhile," Bernie said.

Innis smiled. "During the Turn?"

"Innis—can I call you Innis?"

"Of course."

"Innis, past a certain point, asking where someone was and when they were there is like asking that person's age. And we all know that's not polite."

"I don't think I'm known for being polite," Innis pointed out, but he settled back into his chair. "Anyway, however long you've been here, people associate you with this place."

"The Dominion does as it does," Bernie said. "It's on a kind of level, you see. It's up there."

A hand, or something, waved toward the ceiling. The skylight did not extend into this office, and so I tilted my head to see the winter-white moulded ceiling. It had a repeating pattern that was familiar, somehow, but I could not place it. My neck hurt, and I looked forward again.

"What do you mean, up there?" Innis asked.

"It's high level. What I see to here is what you might call the nuts and bolts. Services. Policing."

"Parking tickets?" Innis asked, smiling. The mayor did not smile, though how I knew this was beyond me. I could not see a mouth of any kind. The mayor was mainly a blur now, to the relief of my tired eyes.

"Yes, of course. We approach a one hundred percent enforcement rate in the five blocks surrounding City Hall. Beyond that point, it's a bit too expensive to police parking as thoroughly as we'd like. But we do try."

"Okay," Innis said. "Let's talk about that. One of the things the Dominion is known for, beside its mayor—"

Bernie nodded and I somehow saw amusement in it.

"—is its crime rate."

Now Bernie was not amused.

"We do what we can."

"I'm not unsympathetic," Innis said. "I'm sure it must be hard coming up with the resources to manage crime in this town. But you're putting all of this effort into parking enforcement, and I can't help thinking that's misdirected. Not to mention the red tape jungle we fought our way through downstairs. From what I've heard, people here are licenced and ticketed half to death."

"What did I just tell you?" Bernie asked with impatience.

"That you do what you can," Innis said. "But my point is, if you would redirect your energies—"

"You misunderstand me," Bernie said. "I said we do what we can. Parking tickets, we can do. Handing out R&R cards, we can also do. Controlling the crime rate in the Dominion, well, we've already done the one thing that would change that, and it changed it for the worse. On paper."

I was lost. Innis was leaning forward again. "Do you mean when you changed the laws? In the eighties?"

"We can redefine crime," Bernie said. "We made more things crimes, and the crime rate went up. If we made fewer things crimes, it would go down. But in a real way, we can't hope to change it."

"Why bother redefining it, then?" Innis said irritably. "It's a make-work project for philosophers if you're not making the city safer. Isn't it?"

"I should not have said these laws have had no effect," Bernie said. "It is safer for students and visitors. But this is a dangerous place by its nature. There are powers that run through it. I shouldn't say this to a travel writer, but it is never going to be safe."

"Well, we agree there," Innis said. "I look at your tourist fatality rates and I think, anywhere else in the world, there wouldn't be tourists the next year. The industry would collapse."

"We don't promote this city to tourists," Bernie said. "It promotes itself somehow. It could be we offer something people don't find elsewhere. That's true enough. But I think it draws people too. See, it does its own thing. It's at that higher level."

"And you're a functionary?" Innis asked. "Your Worship? I'm not trying to be rude, believe it or not. I just want to be sure about what I think I'm hearing. Are you saying you work for the city, not in the sense of being on the civic payroll, but in the sense of being its butler or something?"

Bernie laughed. "A butler would have far more influence. I simply do what I can to make the city make a bit more sense."

"I didn't see sense downstairs," Innis said. "No offence, but have you been down there? No one has the forms they need. People stand in lines for hours. It's like that all over the city, anytime you bump up against an actual rule or law. Appointments and reservations go missing. There are support groups for people who've gone through Customs here. Your own elevators, in this very building, don't work."

"Well," Bernie said, rocking now without a rocking chair. I tried not to think about how. "She does fight back. She does."

Innis narrowed his eyes. It was not an angry look. He was intense. He was trying to understand. "She?"

"The city," Bernie said. It was a placid sound, like crickets at night. "She fights back. But we keep up our end."

"I'm sorry," Innis said. "I am not understanding you."

"We do what we can," Bernie said. "We hand out tickets when people are parking in the wrong spot. When people are in two places at once, or two times at once, that's the city. That's the Dominion at its higher level. It is chaotic, young man. It is near-complete chaos. But do you know why it is only near-complete chaos? Parking tickets."

"Parking tickets?" Innis echoed. He sounded like an echo, bouncing without control in a large and lonely place.

"Parking tickets and forms and licensure," Bernie said. "Order, my friend. We generate order. The Dominion generates chaos. It fights our little forms and erases reservations, but we can always make more. We made more laws, as you seem to know. That helped. Helped us get our courts in order too. We're not going to win, but we don't need to. All we've got to do is keep enough order in the mix that you can get up and tie your shoes in the morning without having to reach into an alternate dimension for your left foot. Unless you want to do that and you built your house that way. But you'd have to have—"

Innis said it with him: "A licence for that."

Innis Stuart

BERNIE WAS nodding at me, pleased that I was finally catching on. I didn't know how to explain that understanding what he was—or they were—trying to tell me was different from catching on, because that last one implied that I saw the sense in what they were saying. I'd seen a lot of strangeness worldwide, and I wasn't prepared to declare anything impossible, but the notion that parking tickets were the fragile threads holding consensual reality together along the northwest coast… that was pushing it.

I glanced at Karsten to see if he was buying it. He was looking anywhere but at the mayor, which I could understand. The blur was creepy. What was worse was that I kept thinking I could see them clearly for a moment when I turned my head. Only out of the corner of my eye.

"Yes?" Karsten said, having noticed that I was staring at him. His odd fit of anger with me seemed to have passed.

"You're a big fan of order," I said. "Do you have anything you'd like to ask Bernie? You could swap train scheduling techniques."

Karsten took a moment to glare at me before looking at Bernie—or nearly anyway. From where I sat, I could tell that he was focusing over Bernie's shoulder. Where a shoulder would be.

"I apologize for the behaviour of my colleague," Karsten said, "because it is unlikely that he will apologize for himself. He believes himself to be amusing."

"No, no," Bernie said, "don't apologize. We've been working hard to increase the reliability of our light-rail transit. People talk about the trains running on time as a stand-in for the most ruthless of efficiency, as if it's something you would only do if you meant to herd people into those trains and take them to concentration camps. My apologies, young man, if this is an upsetting topic for you."

"It's all right," Karsten said, though it wasn't, and Bernie wasn't sorry.

"The thing to understand," Bernie said, "is this: The bylaws we've enacted, these R&R cards we assign, the comprehensive and precise title papers we generate… these are conveniences. Even the parking tickets are conveniences because without them people would park all day and never think to clear a space for the convenience of someone else. Rules are not evil, though it is fashionable for young people to believe they are. There is not an inherent evil in making trains run on time."

I wondered what the people lined up downstairs would say if I told them the mayor had their convenience in mind. I was tempted to go down there and ask them. Or maybe I could stroll down to the cop shop and ask *them* if it was convenient for them to see funds diverted from law enforcement to the administration of permits.

My inclination toward some kind of display must have shown on my face, because Karsten put a hand on my arm and pressed down hard enough to send the message that I should keep my ass in the chair. Despite this there was no strain in his voice as he spoke to Bernie again.

"Would it be all right for me to take a photograph of you? It would be for use in Innis's book."

Bernie smiled, or did something that gave the impression of a smile. I couldn't tell how the mayor's face worked. In fact, I couldn't have sworn there even was a face. And yet I somehow felt as if I were seeing one, with the regular complement of expressions.

"Well, now, you would need a permit for that."

Karsten tilted his head. "Really, Your Worship? It is your likeness. It would be, I think, your decision."

"Oh no. No. This is a public building, and photography in public buildings requires a permit. There's a separate permit for each building. You don't mean to tell me you haven't been getting your proper permits since you arrived here, do you?"

"Our guide made the arrangements," I said quickly. Photogs, in my experience, didn't take kindly to being told where they could or could not shoot, and I didn't want Karsten getting into an argument about it. As far as I was concerned, he could shoot whatever the hell he liked, once we were out of this office, and I'd put it in the book. I doubted there'd be any noteworthy consequences.

"But you don't have a permit for this building?" Bernie asked.

I shook my head. "Sadly, we are missing that one."

"You could get one downstairs," Bernie suggested. "There are some forms to be filled out, I believe, but they can tell you that at any wicket."

"We'll look into it," I said. "Thanks."

"And then you can make another appointment," Bernie said. "For the photograph."

I didn't bother to point out that my last appointment had been made months in advance and that I'd had to wheedle to have it honoured. Either they wouldn't believe that, or they'd say it was the city fighting back. I'd seen Kar drop the lens cap, so I was pretty sure there were already photos on the memory card. It was mainly from curiosity that I said, "I don't suppose you could make an exception for us? Just let Karsten take a few shots. You're the mayor, aren't you? Shouldn't you be able to make exceptions once in a while?"

Bernie laughed and shook their head. "That would be chaos, wouldn't it? I'd be playing for the wrong team."

"No special treatment?" I asked. "Even for the mayor?"

"The laws of the Dominion apply equally to everyone," Bernie assured me. "The laws of nature, on the other hand... there I can make no promises."

"What about the Scree?" I asked. "I've heard the law doesn't apply at all there."

The mayor frowned. "The law applies. It's just difficult to enforce. I know how it has to look to outsiders, but this is not an easy place to administrate. We have made choices, decisions. And to some extent, every city has a Scree."

I wanted to say that the mayor probably didn't live in the Scree, else maybe they would have made different choices and decisions. But I also wanted to continue exploring the Dominion, and I had a feeling that topic would, if pressed, result in a one-way ticket out of town.

"I've been to a lot of Screes," I said instead. I didn't mention where. "My guide tells me there are people trying to gentrify the northeast corner, near Roserood Park."

"That's true," the mayor said. "We've issued a fair number of permits, and I understand it's acceptable to the community. So it will probably go ahead to some extent. But the poor are always with you, aren't they? So there'd best be someplace for them to live."

"Does it have to be such a dangerous place?" Karsten asked. His voice startled me. The guy was damned quiet, even for a photog. He didn't talk a lot. He didn't move around much. He even breathed quietly.

Bernie hesitated before answering him. "That's up to the residents to some extent. And there are other factors and influences, yes, but I don't think anyone wants... I don't think the violence is something the community leaders have an investment in. I think it's being driven at the street level, and it may change. It may yet change."

"We're told," I said, "that people from outside the Scree go there on full moons to hunt. So you can't pin it all on the residents."

Bernie smiled. "People do hunt there, yes, and that's regrettable. But here in the Dominion, we believe that sort of behaviour will sort itself out. One way or another."

"A law of nature?" I asked.

Bernie laughed. "Oh no. Lord no. Far more predictable than that. That's why we don't bother to legislate it."

The phone on the desk rang and Bernie sighed. "I believe that's my cue to move on."

"From the Dominion?" I asked with a smile.

Bernie laughed again. "Not today. Fate willing, not anytime soon. But we will see. Anyway, gentlemen, I will have to end this here."

I nodded and stood. Bernie did not offer a hand again, which was fine by me. I hadn't enjoyed it the first time.

"Thanks again for squeezing us in," I said. "We'll let you get back to your war on chaos."

"Unwinnable," the mayor said, demonstrating a keen grasp of the laws of nature that supposedly didn't work here. "A stalemate will do."

Karsten Roth

INNIS WALKED shoulder to shoulder, or arm to shoulder, with me as we went down the stairs. I no longer had the urge to move away from his touch as I had when he had finessed the clerk to keep his appointment.

He whispered to me, "Did you get anything?"

I shrugged. It was all the response required, as he would surely feel it.

"Don't count your money while sitting at the table," he said. He sounded approving.

I looked at him. "It is best not to."

Innis put a hand on my back, resting on my shoulder blade. I had a bad moment, then, thinking perhaps this was not, ah, courtship, but instead his way of using the power he had. Had he touched the clerk before, or the auditor at the hotel? Or the customs agent, the first night? Was it what he did when he convinced people to take his view?

I thought back. No. He had not touched many people, in fact, since we had arrived. Mainly he had put his hand on me in his unobtrusive way. It was not, I thought, intended to manipulate. To intrigue me, perhaps, or to say that he had an interest in me beyond photography, but not to change my mind. More even than this, I felt it was his way of inviting me to be with him there, in that moment, and not so much inside myself. In short, a kindness.

I was not always at ease with kindness, but Innis continued to extend it, tolerant of my ways. Kindness seemed natural to him.

"Do you know anyone who doesn't know that song?" he was saying. "I mean, anyone who speaks English at all? I said something about knowing when to hold 'em and when to fold 'em the last time I was in Bhutan, and some guy at the next table sang the rest of the chorus. Bhutan didn't even have TV until ten minutes ago."

"There have been tourists," I said, "since the seventies at least."

"Yeah," Innis said. "That's true. Searching for the thunder dragon. I don't think there actually is one. You see any dragons in Nepal?"

He was taking the stairs slowly, and I slowed my pace accordingly. Perhaps he felt the sight of someone moving quickly would be an aggravation to the queued people on the ground floor.

"Did I say I was there?" I asked. I could hear his smile when he answered me.

"You have a portfolio, Mystery Man. Seven Shamans, Seven Summits, remember? To take pictures at Everest's southeast base camp, you pretty much have to be in Nepal."

I could not help shivering. Innis had his hand on my back still, and I could feel his eyes on me.

"I saw no dragons," I said.

Innis, to my surprise, let the subject fall as his hand fell from my back.

"Maybe I should show Jake your portfolio," he said. "Then he'd stop calling you 'kid.'"

"*Es macht nicht*," I said. "I know I look young."

"That you do," Innis said. He was smiling again. "Probably doesn't hurt in some situations, if people don't take you too seriously."

"It has been helpful at times," I admitted.

As we left the bottom step, I saw something and blinked twice. I thought it impossible that I was seeing Jake there, near the front doors.

"Son of a bitch," Innis said. "I thought he'd fucked right off."

So it was a shared hallucination.

"Perhaps he was just waiting," I said, "until he was certain his partner was gone."

"Ex-partner," Innis said. I sensed that I had only the barest shred of his attention. He raised a hand at Jake, and Jake nodded in response. Innis was walking quickly now. Never mind the frustrated people in their endless queues. I hurried to catch up.

"I'm sorry," Jake said, proving his vocabulary broader than I had thought. "I figured you'd be in line for another hour at least."

"I had an appointment," Innis explained, as if to a child.

Was it my imagination, or did Jake seem curious for a moment?

"Guess you were safe enough up there," he said. "How's Bernie?"

"Blurry," Innis replied. "Do you know them?"

"Not really," Jake said. "Bernie and I shook hands one time at a press conference."

This was likely when Zahia had met Innis and Jake's reporter friend, the big case Jake had cracked.

"A press conference?" I asked. Jake moved his shoulders uncomfortably, as if he had left the coat hanger in when he'd pulled on his jacket.

"We had a serial murderer. The old-fashioned kind—no magic. I caught the case, and I put it down. They gave me a—" He stopped. "Come on."

We fell in on the sides of him as he went toward the half space where we'd left the car.

"They gave me an award," he said, "for catching the guy, getting him locked up. They sent him to Kingston."

"Why would they send him to Jamaica?" I asked. Innis laughed and Jake, after a moment, gave a gruff chuckle.

"Sorry," Innis said. "You're not from around here. Kingston, Ontario. It's a Canadian prison town. Well. Prison and university town."

"Same thing," Jake said.

"So this man was sent to a Canadian prison?" I asked. "I thought the Dominion had its own system."

"Yeah," Jake said, "but he wasn't a supernatural type, and he'd broken some pretty straightforward laws. The Dominion doesn't have its own prisons, anyway, so we've got to send them somewhere if the courts give them time."

Innis was wide-eyed. "I didn't know that. I never thought about it. How the hell does that work?"

"We have access to the Canadian and American prison systems," Jake said. "Sometimes, if we've got something really special on our hands, we'll make a deal to incarcerate elsewhere. But we don't give out a lot of prison time around here. It's mostly punishment fits the crime. Sentencing circles. Whatever. Case by case."

"Except in this case, it was Kingston," Innis said. "Kingston Pen proper?"

Jake nodded. "Fucker's still there. See, here's the thing—if I'd just let him keep on, he'd be dead now. I guarantee it. You think humans are the most dangerous game, guess again. All I did when I brought him in was extend his life."

"And win an award," Innis said with sympathy.

"Right," Jake said. We had arrived at the car, the front part of it that we could see. He stared at us across the roof. "Getting around to lunchtime. I figured I'd show you Chaplin House."

Innis grinned. "The travel agencies say no trip to the Dominion is complete without it."

"The travel agencies can get fucked," Jake said. "But the steaks are good."

Innis Stuart

I WASN'T falling out of my pants about trying to locate and use the rear door to the Land Rover, and I could tell from Karsten's face that he felt the same way. I asked

Jake to please pull out to let us in. He glared at me as if I'd asked someone to hold my hand crossing the street. He did it, though, so he could glare at me all he liked.

Karsten began gazing out his window the second he got into his seat. I didn't take it personally. I knew it was part of his job. But I did sometimes want to light a sparkler or something to get him to face me as we talked. It was irritating.

"You heard of Chaplin House?" I asked him.

He looked out the window. "No."

"It's haunted," I told him.

He looked out the window. "And what is not, around here?"

"I hear the steaks are good," I said.

He looked out the window. "I hear this."

For a change, he took out his camera and began to flip through the shots. I was impatient to see his pictures of the mayor, but he had gone back to the beginning of the day's work and was reviewing each photo with care.

"They say the unicorn steaks are excellent," I said.

"Oh?" Karsten murmured. "Are they wild-caught or farmed?"

As he probably knew, there was no such thing as a unicorn farm. I smiled, picturing the specialized staff that would be needed to run that kind of enterprise.

"They're from Our Mother of Pent-Up Urges Unicorn Farm and Nunnery," I said. Kar smiled at his camera, but I think he meant it for me.

"You guys ever stop talking?" Jake asked. He met my eyes in the rearview mirror, and I grinned at him.

"You know me better than that." I did actually stop talking for a few blocks. Then I said, "Weird about the mayor. That blurriness thing."

"Weird," Jake agreed.

"You did a press conference with the mayor," I said. "How does Bernie look in photos?"

"Blurry," Jake said.

Karsten began to move rapidly through his shots. He sighed and held the viewer up for me. A desk and a pen stand and a blotter and a blur. The blur faded out around its edges, making it tough to even tell exactly how large the mayor was.

"It's a good shot actually," I told him. "It gets the experience across. My readers like that sort of thing."

He frowned. "Badly framed."

I patted his shoulder. "It was illicit. It's fine."

"I don't want to hear this," Jake said. "You want to talk about taking shots in City Hall without a permit, do it when I'm not around."

"Apparently you need a permit everywhere in the Dominion," I said. "Which is ridiculous."

"Only on public property," Jake said. "Private landowners can give you permission themselves. But no one enforces the law except City Hall."

"And you can't fight City Hall?" I asked. Jake turned around, which I wished he would stop doing while he was driving.

"Shut up, Innis. I'm not kidding around. I don't give a shit what you do, but I need to not know about it."

"Oh. Kay," I said. "Did either of you notice, when you look at the mayor kind of sideways, you can see them better?"

"Never tried it," Jake said.

I glanced at Karsten, who shrugged. "I tried not to see them."

"I was thinking," I said, "it's kind of like prosopagnosia."

"What is that?" Karsten asked. I liked that he was confident enough to admit it when he had no clue what I was talking about.

"Face blindness. I read an article about it a few months ago. Apparently people process visual information about faces separately from all other visual information. There are people who have a brain disorder where they can see just fine, except for faces. Faces are a blur."

That finally compelled Karsten to glance at me. "But if they took a photograph…."

"It'd be normal," I said. "Yeah. I'm not saying the mayor causes prosopagnosia. I'm saying looking at Bernie must be a similar kind of experience. Actually this is kind of funny—I think face-blind people do better when they're not seeing faces straight-on. I wonder if Bernie's little knack is related to that somehow."

"Can they see expression?" Karsten asked. "These… prosopagnosiacs?" He was interested enough to have put his camera down.

"The person who wrote the article had it, and she said she could determine expressions. I don't know how that works."

"It worked with Bernie," Karsten said.

"You saw that too?" I said. "Like, you knew they were smiling, but fucked if you could tell how you knew that?"

"Yes."

"Everyone sees that," Jake said. He wasn't interested enough to turn around, which was good "Everyone sees Bernie the same way. First you see ten different things, and then you're not sure what the hell you're seeing, and then it's a blur that smiles at you. We're over it around here."

"Hang on a sec," I said. "You see through people's illusions. You must see what the mayor actually looks like."

"That *is*," Jake said firmly, "what Bernie actually looks like. Jesus. Can we drop this?"

"I'm sorry to be boring you," I said, "but Karsten and I are new to town. We find these little things interesting. We may even talk more about it later."

"Try to wait until I've dropped you at the hotel," Jake said.

"You're not a very good guide," I told him. "In some respects."

"You're not dead yet," Jake said. "In any respects. So shut the hell up."

Karsten seemed amused.

I nudged his arm. "Stop smirking. I pay you to take my side."

"No," he said placidly. "Only to take photographs."

"Is there enough money in the world for the other thing?" I asked him. He looked me right in the eye and gave me a brilliant smile. I wouldn't have thought he had a smile like that in him.

He said, simply, "No."

I had, for a moment, a crazy urge to tell Jake to skip lunch. Drop us at the hotel. I wanted to see if I could convince Karsten to take my side, or to at least try for that smile again. But we were on the clock, more or less, and I wasn't at all sure that Karsten would care for the idea. I bit my tongue and stared out my window instead.

Q1, or the Old Quarter, as they called this part of town, was a hell of a lot nicer than the Scree, and it had much of the character of East Hills, with the same old houses. These old houses, however, were behind tall metal fences and had expensive cars out front, which was a world away from the slightly run-down East Hills mansions that bulged with students and mailboxes.

"What do the people in this part of town do for a living?" I asked.

Jake glanced at me. "What?"

"There's more money here than I've seen anywhere else in the Dominion. I'm wondering where it comes from."

Jake shrugged. "Where does it usually come from? We've got lawyers here, doctors, some big-time magical consultants. A lot of that, actually. Lot of importers, families that got rich before the Turn. And some asshole celebrities. They seem to think there's caché or some shit to having a house here. Most of them only come up for Halloween and the solstices."

"Must get a lot of burglaries," I said, "if people know those homes are sitting empty most of the year."

Jake smiled. I could see it in the rearview mirror. "We get a lot of attempted burglaries. Most of the burglars don't survive."

"This is a nice town," I said. "Real good-natured place. Have I mentioned how nice this town is?"

Jake shook his head. "It's not a tough fate to avoid. Don't break into houses."

"I'm impressed by your sensitivity," I said.

Jake's hands tightened on the steering wheel. "You don't know a fucking thing about it, Innis. You've never dealt with an actual crime problem. You've never stayed in one place for more than half an hour. If I want your opinion on anything, it'll be how to pack light and get moving before anyone figures out I'm a greasy ball sack."

I raised my hands in surrender. "Hey, come on. I was just saying, the death penalty seems a little harsh for breaking into an empty house. And I know you well enough to know you prefer the people in the Scree to the celebrity assholes."

"People in the Scree mostly rob each other," Jake said. "You'd think they'd figure out they're passing the same twenty-dollar bill around, but that's how it is. You want to know who breaks into these houses? College kids, looking for souvenirs. And they're welcome to whatever nasty souvenir they get as far as I'm concerned. They're no loss."

"Jake… they're kids," I reminded him.

Jake scowled. "Fuck 'em."

He took a hard enough left that I had to grab the door handle to stay on my side. Then the Rover lurched upward for a few seconds, followed by an equally hard right before Jake slammed on the brakes in what I hoped was a parking spot.

"Okay," Jake said. "We're here."

Chapter Eight

CHAPLIN HOUSE was a mansion on a hill, dark and turreted. It looked to have been a private home in its past. It was now surrounded by a parking lot, but I could see the remains of outbuildings beyond the newer asphalt. A garage, perhaps, or even a carriage house. People here probably considered it old.

There were many cars and other vehicles in the lot. Most were more expensive than Jake's, or at least newer. All of them had been washed more recently.

"Are we dressed for this restaurant?" I asked. Jake laughed, tension broken, and got out of the Rover. Innis and I followed.

"You're out west," he said once we were all in the lot and walking toward the mansion. "Most places west of Ontario, if you're wearing pants, you're fine."

"Oh come on," Innis said. "There are places with dress codes. There are even places up north with dress codes. Not that I'm a fan of dress codes, but that's not accurate." After a moment, he added, "Most of the signs say No Shirt, No Shoes, No Service anyway. In theory, you could show up in a T-shirt and sneakers and ask for a table."

I wondered if Innis had ever tried such a thing and decided not to ask. Happily we did have shirts and shoes and pants. We were not even in jeans, in honour of our meeting with the mayor.

"This was gravel the last time I was here," Jake said. He kicked the ground in a friendly way, as if he were congratulating it for being solid and smooth. "It's always a risk, laying asphalt in this place."

"Why's that?" Innis asked. He had his hands in his jacket pockets and was interesting himself in the vehicles.

"Land might not like it," Jake said. "You get a lot of cracking and buckling. Some people've sworn their new driveways disappeared overnight."

As we drew closer to the house, I could see penny-farthing bicycles decorating either side of an enclosed upstairs veranda. It was eccentric.

"Does the land have opinions about buildings too?" I asked.

"Not so far," Jake said, "but I figure you never know when it's going to raise an objection. You wouldn't see me starting construction in the Dominion limits."

"You don't have a lot of housing starts?" Innis said as we arrived at the restaurant's front doors. Jake held the doors open for us.

"Not a lot of open land," he said as we passed.

"Like Berlin," I said. "Before the wall came down."

There was a hostess behind a slim grey stand. She was not what I had come to expect in Canada, the young women in skirts both too short and too tight. She was elegant instead, in a sleek business suit and with straight hair carefully curled at the ends.

"Reservation's in your name," Jake said, and he gave Innis a gentle shove toward the hostess. Innis seemed confused as to why the reservation was not in Jake's name.

"Innis Stuart," he told the woman at the podium. "For three."

She frowned and checked at the leather book on the stand in front of her.

"I'm afraid," she said, "that I have nothing under that name."

I stole a glance at Jake. He was hanging back a bit, watching. He seemed expectant.

In that moment I understood something as clearly as if Jake had said it to me. More clearly, in fact, because I trusted few of the things Jake said.

I understood that Jake expected Innis to be able to talk his way into the restaurant. That despite what he had said to us, he had expected Innis to be able to see the mayor. He believed as firmly as I did that Innis was unusual in this respect, and this was why Jake was watching him closely now.

Having now seen Innis do this trick a few times, I could have told Jake it would not be much of a show.

"Sounds like some wires must have gotten crossed," Innis said. He did not ever seem frustrated when this sort of thing occurred. Or angry. He seemed to expect that all would be well. As it would, that being his experience. "These things happen. Look, there are only three of us, and two of us are from out of town. We don't need your best table, you know, just whatever you might have. Is there some way you could manage to squeeze us in?"

I watched Innis as he spoke. There was nothing unusual in his face or his eyes. He looked into her eyes, but not in a fixed way. His tone, too, was normal. It was simply his voice, the way he spoke all of the time. More polite, perhaps, but anyone would be polite asking a stranger for a favour.

She hesitated, then smiled at him. It was a real smile, not simply a professional one. "Well, since you're a visitor, we should be able to manage something. I'll go see what we can do."

"Thanks so much," Innis said. Once she had gone, he faced Jake and me. "You know, people have a reputation for being kind of unreasonable here, but they've generally been pretty good."

"Huh," Jake said.

I felt a chill. I could not have said exactly what it was, but there was something in Jake's tone that said he was beyond my point of mere speculation. He knew more about this matter than I did. Possibly more than Innis did. When he watched Innis so closely, was it to see how Innis worked this magic of his? Or was it to see whether Innis knew he was working magic at all?

Or another reason, perhaps, so strange as to be unguessable?

My best chance at an answer was to ask Jake, whose words I did not trust and whose demeanour gave me concern. And to do this when Innis would not be able to overhear.

I did not believe I would have much appetite for lunch.

Innis Stuart

THE HOSTESS returned quickly to guide us to a small table not far from the kitchen doors. I looked for her nametag so I could use her name when I thanked her, but she didn't have one.

The place had a subtle 1920s theme. There were no life-size stand-ups of Al Capone or murals of flappers, but everything—from the furniture to the linen to the framed painting on the walls—was true to the period. Not that I figured the owner had somehow found so many matching antique chairs and tables and bought them, but obviously some decent replicas had been chosen. The fitted business suit adorning our hostess was more forties than twenties, but however far off the mark, it still seemed to be an attempt to fit in.

The patrons showed no interest in the theme. They were colourful and trendy, mostly, those Q1 celebrities and other well-off professionals enjoying a long lunch atop Chaplin Hill—the highest point in the Dominion proper, though the Sasquatch lands to the north went far into the mountains. Many of the people we passed on the way to our table wore more subtle and elegant variations on the animal modifications we'd seen in East Hills. Others sported animal-print dresses, scarves, and ties.

People were laughing and talking, loud but not obnoxious. As we walked to our table, the sound of broken dishes came from somewhere at the back of the room. Diners clapped for that, as they will when the wine has been flowing for a while. I looked around for Mr. Butterfingers but couldn't spot him.

After we'd taken our seats, the hostess set menus on the table and leaned down toward us. Her cleavage was tastefully contained, light and shadow. She was wearing Clinique's Happy perfume, which I recognized because my editor also wore it and I had, the year before, given her a gift pack of the stuff for Christmas. Perfume, body wash, shampoo, lotion... my editor's a lovely women, but I'm always surprised that I can't smell her a block away.

That perfume thing right there told me the restaurant wasn't as fancy as it liked to pretend, because a hostess in a truly fancy restaurant would have been wearing a mere touch of something fashionably and outrageously overpriced or no perfume at all.

"You won't know it for a little while," she said, her voice low, "but this is one of our better tables. People ask to be moved from here because it's near the kitchen, but they don't realize… well, you'll see. Just trust me." She stood. "Your waiter will be Tim," she said in a normal voice. "Enjoy yourselves, gentlemen."

Jake appeared amused behind his menu, which was delicate and seemed in danger of being torn to pieces simply by being in his large hands.

"I miss something?" I asked.

Jake looked at me. "Nope. Like she said, you'll see."

"The floor show," I said.

Jake smiled. "Your guide books tell you about that?"

"No details," I said. "They just called it 'not to be missed.'"

Jake nodded. "You won't miss it. Next show's in—" He checked his watch against a pendulum wall clock near the door, then reset his watch. "—forty-three minutes."

Karsten frowned at me. "Your guide book didn't tell you what this floor show was?"

I had to laugh. Of course a guy from Berlin would want to know what kind of floor show he was walking in on. The possibilities were, to his mind, limitless.

"They were sworn to secrecy," I told him. "I heard they swear everyone to secrecy on the way out, to keep the surprise. Whatever that is."

Karsten raised his eyebrows at Jake, then at me.

"What is the point in being here, then, if you will not be able to write about it?"

I glanced at Jake. "Cover your ears. Hum something."

Jake scowled at me. "Aw hell, I'm gonna find a washroom."

Once he'd retreated to the foyer, where I assumed the restrooms could be found, I smiled at Karsten.

"I don't care what I swear to while I'm here. I'll print whatever I want."

He stared at me, unimpressed. "Are you mad? You are making oaths. You do not know to what or to whom."

"That's what makes it fun."

He didn't smile. I put a hand on his forearm.

"Kar. I do this all the time. If I kept every secrecy oath I swore, my books would be pamphlets. I have never had a problem."

He cocked his head. "Yes? And you have done this in the Dominion?"

I laughed. "You've started to believe this town's press releases, my friend. Come on. This place is different in some ways, sure, but magic's the same game wherever it's played. An oath here is like an oath anywhere. The spirits or the gods or whatever will have to come after me to punish me, and nobody cares enough. It's too much like work. So," I added, patting his arm with each word, "stop worrying."

He pulled his arm away. "You're an ass, Innis Stuart. Not the 'greasy ball sack' your friend says you are, but certainly an ass."

I picked up my water glass and tapped it against his. It rang nicely. "Never claimed otherwise."

I took a sip, set the glass down, and picked up my menu. It wasn't long, a single sheet of parchment in a leather holder, but it made up for the lack of selection by being what my mother would have called "strange as all get-out."

They didn't offer unicorn, to my disappointment, but did offer cobra, tiger, and lion. The cobra came in a stir-fry, the others as steaks. I wondered if they were always available or if the menu was following the exotic animal trend that was so hot throughout the city.

John the Conqueror root was available as the seasoning in a chicken sandwich, and there was a fried mushroom dish I wasn't brave enough to even consider.

The menu was careful to list the herbs and other additives in each dish. I didn't know enough about magic to know what half of them were supposed to do, but I assumed they weren't around to do nothing but taste good.

Karsten nudged my arm and pointed out an asterisk next to Baked Oik with Yogurt. "Permit required," the small print at the bottom said.

"Oik?" he asked.

I shrugged. "Whatever it is, we don't have the paperwork for it."

Jake returned and glanced at his menu before dropping it to his plate again.

"Paperwork?" he asked.

"For the oik," I said. "Whatever it is."

"Werewolf," Jake said.

I stared at him. "I beg your what?"

"Keep your voice down," Jake said pleasantly, though no one seemed to have noticed my outburst.

"But—but that is a person," Karsten pointed out.

I pointed at Karsten. "What he said."

"Meat's different when you shoot the wolf," Jake said. "Wouldn't catch me eating it, though."

"Because," I said, "you are not a cannibal. Right?"

Jake shook his head. "What cannibal? I'm no werewolf."

"But it's a person," I said.

Jake shrugged. "Meat's different," he repeated. "And they're always getting shot around here anyway."

"Good lord," Karsten said. "Is that a reason to eat something? Are people not always getting shot around here as well?"

"It's more getting mauled or sucked dry," Jake said. "Not so much shot. But there are places in town you can order up the long pig. Strictly off the menu. You gotta ask for it, but it's there."

"Never a good idea," I said. "Cannibalism. If nothing else, it's bad for your health."

"Never said people were the ones ordering long pig," Jake said. Which was true. I wasn't sure it made anything better, but it was true. "Anyway, I'd be a lot happier if people stayed away from the oik. That shit's like PCP for some people. Not everyone's susceptible to it, but those who are… watch out. They don't need a full moon to go apeshit. They'll do it before dessert."

"Always learning new things on this job," I said. I hoped I sounded more enthusiastic than I felt. "Is that what the permits are about?"

"Yeah," Jake said. "Someone got the idea you could test for sensitivity with bloodwork. The test only works about half the time, but City Hall fell out of their pants for it because it meant a whole pile of paperwork—testing permits, bloodwork request, lab results—and that's before you even get around to making a permit request. So they voted in a permit law. You know, instead of banning the shit outright, which would be a lot safer for everyone and no big loss to the food pyramid."

"Paperwork for the sake of paperwork," I said. "People joke about that in a lot of places, but Bernie told me it's your actual deal around here."

Jake downed half his water and wiped his mouth with the back of his hand. Good thing it was only a faux-fancy restaurant.

"Yeah, city council's got a theory that they're the flip side of the coin. They sweat the small stuff so we can afford to let the big stuff go. I figure if balance was so damned important, the world wouldn't be the way it is. You don't have to have this much order and this much chaos, like you're balancing a ball on your nose and it's gonna hit the ground if you don't do it right. But Bernie and friends have a lot of people buying into their line of garbage, so they'll likely be running things for a while."

"You think Bernie believes their line of garbage?" I asked.

Jake flicked his finger at his water glass. His glass didn't ring. "Probably. But who cares? They've got the voters buying it, so we have to live with it either way."

Our waiter, the aforementioned Tim, appeared beside our table as Jake expressed that opinion. I'm not saying Tim came out of nowhere, but I didn't notice him arrive. Mind you, with the best waiters you usually don't.

"Good afternoon," Tim said. "I'm Tim, your waiter. Sorry about the delay. We had a small time shift. Can I bring you something to drink?"

Tim looked like a kid working his way through school. He had spiky hair, freckles, and the Lennon glasses that had, about a decade ago, given way in college-kid popularity to Buddy Holly glasses. The thin-framed circle style was only now starting to make a recovery.

"Two of us are from out of town," I said, "so we may need a little help."

Tim smiled. It was either sincere or a nice imitation. "I can handle that. What are you wondering about?"

"Well," I told him, "I'd like to start with a beer. Do you have a local microbrew?"

Tim pursed his lips and nodded. It was as if I'd asked him the square root of some huge number.

"Yes… the Dominion has two microbreweries, and we carry beers from both. My recommendation would depend on what kind of experience you're after."

I leaned back in my chair. "Are you asking whether I prefer lager or ale, Tim?" I already knew the answer.

"Uh, no," Tim said. "Actually all of the microbrews we carry are ales. I mean residual effects. And not in the sense of alcohol by volume."

"He means magical shit," Jake tossed in. Tim glanced at him before turning back to me. His expression didn't change from pleasant neutrality.

"There are additives in some of our local beers," he said. "Many visitors to the Dominion are looking for singular experiences."

I nodded. "That's what I figured. I'm looking to have a plain old beer."

Jake raised his bushy eyebrows at me. "You sure about that? Aren't you supposed to be trying everything the Dominion has to offer?"

"I'm supposed to be coherent enough to write about what the Dominion has to offer," I told him. "But you're welcome to partake so I can write about your experience."

Tim's eyes widened a little. "Are you a reviewer?"

"No, just a travel writer," I admitted, though I did toy for a second with the idea of lying. It would have guaranteed exceptional service.

Tim rocked back on his heels and surveyed our table thoughtfully.

"In that case, do you want me to bring out sampler trays? On the house?"

"I seriously do have to be able to write about my experiences," I said. "It's a nice offer, but I'm concerned about the consequences."

"He writes adventure travel guides," Jake said.

Tim didn't give Jake so much as a glance that time.

"You wouldn't want to miss the floor show," he informed me. I was starting to wonder if people around here got that tattooed inside their eyelids, lest they forget. "We've got a nice wheat ale with no side effects, aside from the usual. It's from Pegasus Rock."

I ordered one, and Karsten made it two. Jake asked for something called Raven Dark. Tim nodded and slipped away from the table.

"What did he mean, small time shift?" I asked Jake.

Jake shrugged. "Thin walls around here. Some haunted places have ghosts, other places bump up against another time. He probably stepped in the wrong place and wound up in 1924 or whenever."

"Could that happen to us?" Karsten asked.

Jake broke out his shrug again. "Sure, but it's no big deal. Stay where you are and you'll get back eventually."

"After decades' worth of eventually?" I asked. "You stand there from 1924 onward?"

"Nah, it's just a few minutes." Jake considered for a moment, then added, "Except one guy used the washroom back in '86. He was in there for about half an hour before somebody went to get him, and by that time, he was gone. No one ever saw him again. So that guy could be taking the long way home."

"He would be here by now," Karsten pointed out.

I frowned at him. "He'd be dead by now. Depending on how far back he went."

"So his problems are over," Jake observed.

He sounded as if he considered the washroom guy a lucky bastard. Maybe that was why he'd taken so long to return from his own trip to the washroom. I pictured Jake standing in front of a line of sinks, staring at himself in the mirror and wishing 1924 would appear behind him.

"He's never going to have another beer, either," I said. "Since when have you had a death wish?"

Jake laughed, a sound so ugly that a few nearby diners stared at him over their shoulders. I couldn't tell if they were annoyed, fascinated, or frightened.

"This is the magic city, Innis," he said. "Wishes come true here. If I really wanted to be dead, trust me—I would be."

That was Tim's cue to place mugs and bottles of beer in front of us. Karsten poured his beer in his mug, but Jake and I pushed our mugs aside. We'd never be as sophisticated as Europeans.

"Might as well take those," Jake told Tim. "Make more room for the food."

"Have you decided?" Tim asked. "Or do you want to talk about the menu?"

"We'll need to talk," I said. "I notice you've got John the Conqueror root in a sandwich. What does that do?"

"If you've got the stomach for it," Tim said, "it'll make you… ah… a very attractive person. And lucky in other ways as well. But a lot of people don't have the stomach for it."

"And if you don't?" I said.

Tim smiled, showing teeth that had been bleached to an opalescent sheen and specked with glitter. Vain, these kids. Or at least trying to keep up with the vanity of others.

"You'll spend time in many of the Dominion's lovely washrooms."

"Okay," I said. "Good to know. Since I'm already handsome and lucky, I'll give that a miss."

"The albatross is good today," Tim said. "Our albatross supplier grain-feeds them so you don't get the fishy taste."

"Are they bad luck?" Karsten asked. "I always thought they were."

Tim gave Karsten a speculative look. Probably trying to place the accent, which really was far more British than German most of the time.

"Some people say they're bad luck to anyone who kills them. Eating them is supposed to be okay. Anyway, I think that was just a rumour people spread back when they were endangered, before the Royal Theurgic Preservation Society was started. You know, a story to keep people from eating them."

"But," I said, "if you're creating demand by eating farmed albatross, aren't you supporting those farms and thereby indirectly killing the birds?"

Tim slipped his hands into the pockets of his 1920s suit. "Curses aren't usually that sophisticated," he said.

"I thought you were not concerned about curses anyway," Karsten said to me.

"I don't care for seabird," I said. "Even if it is grain-fed. The cobra curry sounds good."

"I'll have the albatross," Jake said.

He probably would have ordered it even before the RTPS un-endangered the world's animals, if only to be a hard case.

Tim turned to Karsten. Before Karsten could say anything, the room filled with the sound of people, mostly women, shrieking. I looked around, panicked, for the threat. What I saw instead was my fellow diners smiling and raising their glasses in salute to the sound, which seemed to come from everywhere at once. After a few seconds, the shrieking stopped and the soft swing music I'd barely noticed before began to play again.

"This joint used to be hoppin'," Tim said, with neither a wink nor a smile. He stared at Karsten. "I'm sorry... you were saying?"

"I see taimen here," he said.

"Yes, in pirog with coriander and cumin," he said. "We source the taimen locally as well. It's a good opportunity to try taimen that hasn't been dried for export."

Karsten evidently agreed with that, since he opted for the dish. I wondered if their local source knew Manya, she of the taimen table. Hell, maybe their local source was Manya.

My wheat ale had gone down so smoothly that I'd barely noticed it, so I got another round of beer for the table. Tim nodded and set a plate of sliced Scotch eggs in the middle of the table.

"Phoenix eggs," he said. "Compliments of the house."

After Tim had gone, Karsten poked at one of the eggs with his salad fork. "Why would a phoenix have eggs? Don't they rise from ashes?"

"Some say their eggs are ashes coated in myrrh," I said.

Jake grunted and took a swig of his beer. "Some say chicken eggs are phoenix eggs. Not to cast fuckin' aspersions."

That marked the first time I'd seen Karsten smile in response to something Jake said.

I stabbed a slice of egg and popped it in my mouth. Definitely not ashes or myrrh. Maybe it was a chicken's egg and maybe it wasn't, but there wasn't anything unusual about it. I considered clutching my throat and pretending to die, but Karsten got offended enough when I talked with food in my mouth. A stunt like that would probably mean he'd never be seen with me again.

"Could be chicken," I told Karsten and Jake. "Could be anything. Maybe even phoenix. I guess, if it gives me heartburn, we'll—"

Karsten Roth

BEFORE HIS sentence was complete, Innis disappeared. It was instantaneous, to my eyes. Not a fade or a flicker. I looked at Jake.

"Is this, what, a time slip?"

"Shift," he said. "Yeah, probably."

He seemed too relaxed for a man who was uncertain as to the whereabouts of his good friend.

"Probably? What else might it be? Shouldn't we be trying to get him back?"

Jake drank the last of his beer and put the bottle down on the table, hard.

"If he shows up again in a few minutes, no problem. If he doesn't, we can worry about it then."

"If you are wondering how this city got its reputation for being callous," I began.

Jake snorted. "We're fucking cavalier. Get it right. Look, kid, no matter what happened, there's no benefit to getting wound up about it."

Innis had not been gone one minute and already I was "kid" again.

"He may need help," I said. Jake raised a hand for our waiter, whom I could not see. This did not, I supposed, mean he was not around.

"What kind of help are you and I going to give him? Huh? Settle down, have another beer, and we'll know in a few minutes whether we've got a problem or not."

I had barely started my second beer and was not in dire need of another. I did not say this to Jake, who would probably call me something worse than "kid."

As Jake ordered another round of beer from our waiter, who had approached the table from behind me, I decided that Jake was not being altogether unreasonable. There was nothing I could do at the moment, and there was reason to hope all would be well.

It would be more intelligent if instead of fretting, I used this time to speak with Jake. In public. Not in a dark alley or my hotel room. Somewhere safe, with Innis expected back at any moment. It was the best opportunity I was likely to find.

"Tell me something," I said. "Why did you put this reservation in Innis's name?"

Jake picked up his empty beer bottle and began turning it, this way and that. "He's good at talking his way into places. Reservations are a bitch around here."

"And then you watched him," I said, "as if you hoped to learn something."

Jake kept his eyes on the bottle. It caught the light from the front windows and made patterns on his face.

"He's a smooth talker. Didn't you say that to me?"

"He's more than a smooth talker," I said. "And you know this."

Now he looked at me. "What the hell's that supposed to mean?"

But he knew. I could see this in his eyes and around his mouth. Jake was not a good liar.

"Did he do this as a boy?" I asked. "When you were growing up?"

Jake put his bottle back on the table. "Why don't you ask Innis? He'll tell you he doesn't do anything."

"I do think he would say that," I said as Tim set new beer on our table. "But does he believe it?"

Once Tim had gone, Jake leaned far forward. "I don't know whether someone sent you," he said, low and deep, "or whether you just have a bee in your bonnet, but this is none of your fucking business. I am none of your business. Al Harper is none of your business. Take photos and keep your mouth shut, and maybe I'll forget we had this talk."

I was saved from having to answer that by Innis reappearing in his seat.

"Wow," he said. He picked up his beer and shook his head. "Wow."

"That," I said, "is why readers hang upon your every word."

"There's a house party going on," he said as he raised a meaningful finger to me. "No one seems too concerned about Prohibition. Could be gangsters. I couldn't tell for sure."

"Time will tell," Jake said. Innis showed him a particular finger as well.

"They're having a lot more fun than we are, I'll tell you that."

"I'm relieved to see you," I admitted. "I thought you'd met the fate of the washroom man."

Innis checked his watch. "I was gone for about five minutes?"

I nodded.

"It's the same timeline," Jake said. "Same universe. It's not gonna pass any differently."

"You don't know that," Innis said. "What if you jump to another universe when you think you're going back in time? What if all of that is going on right now somewhere else, and that's what we're picking up?"

Jake seemed annoyed. Really, he had not stopped seeming annoyed since I had annoyed him.

"It's the same event, over and over. And it made the papers back in the day."

"What made the papers?" Innis asked.

"The floor show," Jake said.

"Did they see you?" I asked. "When you went back in time?"

Innis frowned. "I don't think so. They didn't pay any attention to me anyway. So either they couldn't see me, or they just didn't notice me."

"Or people go back there so often they don't care anymore," Jake said.

He stabbed a few slices of Scotch egg with his fork and stuck them in his mouth. Innis shrugged and offered the plate to me. At the shake of my head, he finished the egg off himself.

"Enjoy the heartburn," I said.

Innis smiled. "It sounds like the least unpleasant side effect a person could expect in this place."

"When did you get so goddamned squeamish?" Jake asked. "I've seen you eat fried spiders."

"And took a photo of me with spider goo on my chin. Thanks very much for posting that."

They spoke of such things for what seemed a lifetime while I watched others eating and tried to hear as little as possible. I was much relieved when Tim delivered our meals and ended that conversation.

The fish pie was excellent, and I found the taimen much better fresh than dried. Innis seemed pleased with his curry and placed a bit of the meat on the edge of my plate before taking a sample of my taimen. Neither of us reached across to Jake's albatross, which might have been both fresh and grain-fed but still had an unpleasant odour and an aura of misfortune.

We ate in silence for a few minutes, and then Tim placed a small tumbler in front of Innis. It had a clear liquid inside and, at the bottom, a yellowish-green object with ribbons of slime trailing it.

"Comes with your meal," Tim said. "Just toss it back. Don't sip. Don't chew it."

"Ah," Innis said. "That the gallbladder?"

I looked at him. He did not seem to be kidding.

"Yeah," Tim said. "It's good magic."

"So I hear," Innis said. He held the glass up to the light. "And this is vodka? To help me forget that I've swallowed a gallbladder?"

"Makes it go down easier," Tim said. He seemed uncomfortable with this part of his job.

He did not, I imagined, order this dish as his staff meal.

Innis shrugged and did as he was instructed.

"Whoa," he said as he put the glass down. "That is bitter."

"That is bile," I said.

Innis did not respond. His mouth was moving as if trying to push the taste away.

"Bleh," he said. Then he faced me. "Bile. Well, you'd know, surly-pants."

I ate the snake meat from the side of my plate. It wasn't bad. It had the feel of tender fish meat, and the only taste was of curry.

"Kind of a letdown," Innis said. "I thought cobra might be different from rattlesnake."

"For all you know," Jake said, "that is rattlesnake."

"And that," Innis said, waving a fork at Jake's plate, "could be Canada goose from the park. I heard there was a place in Edmonton that got caught with coyotes in the freezer."

"You never know what you're getting in a restaurant," Jake declared, seeming unsurprised by this information. "You pays your money. You takes your chances."

As if to emphasize this point, at that moment the floor show began.

Chapter Nine

Innis Stuart

I THOUGHT for a moment that I'd time-shifted again. The room no longer resembled a restaurant dining area, carefully done up in 1920s style. It seemed, instead, to be an actual 1920s living room—the same one, in fact, that I'd visited shortly before my meal.

What was different this time was that Karsten and Jake were with me, and we were sitting at our table. All of the tables were in place, with diners around them. What had seemed to this point a random scattering of small round tables could now be seen as a careful arrangement that did not interfere with the furniture or people in the room overlying our own.

The diners were looking around with happy, expectant faces. The 1920s crowd seemed oblivious to our presence. I nudged Jake, who was watching the entrance to the room.

"They don't see us, do they?"

"Nope," Jake said. He continued to watch the entrance and, on the theory that he knew what he was doing, I did the same.

My theory was proven correct seconds later when a group of men in black suits rushed through the entrance and began to fire Tommy guns at the living room gang.

That meant they were firing in our direction, and I had to fight my instinct to hit the ground. From the corner of my eye, I saw Karsten make it halfway to the floor before he stopped himself and returned sheepishly to his seat.

Jake laughed and threw a napkin at him. "Here. You might want to hide your eyes."

Karsten dropped the napkin to the floor and glared at Jake. I put a hand on Kar's shoulder.

"Nothing wrong with your instincts," I told him, then promptly showed him there was nothing wrong with mine either. A gun went off behind me and to my left, and I ducked. I could hear Jake laughing as I turned to see a desperate flapper in a beaded red dress, crouched in the corner with a Derringer .22. She was firing at someone on the other side of our table, behind Jake. As I watched, she was hit. She fell backward, and the gun fell from her hand.

"Her gun was a single shot," Jake said. "She never had a chance."

I could say it was like watching a movie in the sense that we could hear and see everything going on around us but were untouched by it. We couldn't get splashed by blood or anything else and, mercifully, couldn't smell the death.

It wasn't like a movie, though. A movie is designed to look a certain way, usually an appealing or attractive way even when the scene is violent. Even when a movie is horrifying or disgusting, it's horrifying or disgusting in an artful way.

This wasn't art. This was people dying any which way and not giving a damn how they came across while doing it.

Sure, it was a hit with the crowd. They were cheering, pointing things out to each other, checking out the part they missed the last time they ate at Chaplin House. But contrary to popular belief, the presence of an audience doesn't automatically make everything into something new. Some things stay just as ugly, no matter who's watching.

Karsten was taking photos in the efficient, mechanical way that photographers have when they can't stand to think about what they're photographing. I wasn't sure taking photos in here was allowed, or that he'd necessarily get the whole picture in his pictures, but there was no reason for him not to try. And he was probably relieved to have something to do besides sit there and watch the slaughter.

"Lighten up," Jake said and punched my arm. "They're long dead. And no one in this room was what you'd call a wide-eyed innocent."

I thought of the flapper and her pathetic little pistol. She'd probably carried it in her purse for years, thinking it would save her from one big bad wolf or another.

I considered telling Jake that the lady, though probably not exactly a lady, hadn't been Al Capone either. I was worried that he'd say she'd gotten what she had coming for bringing a .22 to a Tommy gun fight, and then I'd have to throw my beer bottle at his head. It was better to keep quiet.

The floor show, by my watch, didn't last long. Five minutes, maybe, and then the other room faded as the diners applauded. Karsten photographed them as they beamed and clapped, and I might have been imagining it, but I thought I saw a grim judgment in that.

Once he'd gotten a few shots, Karsten quickly slipped his camera under the table. I tapped my beer bottle against his glass.

"Instincts," I said. He gave me a less than half-hearted smile.

"Not instinct. Experience. I had enough cameras taken away that I did eventually learn."

"This is why I don't carry a recorder anymore," I said.

"Can I get you anything else? A dessert menu?"

I was jumpy enough that it startled me when Tim spoke. I put my hand over my heart and turned my head to face him.

"Do you have a defibrillator?" I said. "Healing potion?"

Tim laughed. "First time's always a little surprising. It's pretty loud."

It had been, but loud didn't bother me. I had a feeling Tim didn't want to hear about what was bothering me.

"I think we're good here," I said.

"Just the bill," Jake said, and in spite of everything, I had a moment of feeling at home. Americans asked for the cheque for some reason. I'd never understood it.

Hell, what did I understand?

Karsten Roth

MY MEAL, though it had been quite good, did not sit well in the wake of the floor show. Innis seemed no more comfortable than I was. When the bill arrived, he put it on his card without hesitation, and I thought that was a sign of how eager he was to leave. Yes, he could write it off, but I still thought he would have waited a moment to see if Jake might offer. Instead he did what would get us out of the restaurant with the most alacrity.

Jake seemed disappointed that we had not properly appreciated the entertainment and said something to this effect as we crossed the parking lot to the Land Rover.

"Oh, I appreciated it," Innis said. "Don't get me wrong. I'm here to get the flavour of the Dominion, and I am by-God getting it."

"Those people are long dead," Jake said as he had in the restaurant.

Innis said nothing. He was angry. Not at Jake, precisely, for bringing us there. Jake had been right to do so. It had been, as Innis had said, a flavour of the Dominion. Callous and laughing was the flavour, and we did not care for it. Innis and myself, I mean to say. Jake had been laughing with the crowd. I felt as if Innis and I were aliens here, and of course we were strangers to this place. But I had been many places far from my home, and I had never felt so alien before.

Innis was being the bad traveler, perhaps, in being angry. He was passing judgement on the crowd and on Jake. I did not blame him, because I was doing the same.

In this we were not only different from the people of the Dominion but from other travelers who crossed the world the same way, as if all they saw had happened a hundred years before and now served only to amuse them.

As devil-may-care as Innis might like to appear, he felt for the suffering of those people in their lives and for the loss of dignity in their afterlives. Beneath this image of his, the insouciant adventurer, I had come to believe there was a man of substance.

And I had not failed to notice that as the shooting began and terrified us both, his first impulse was to be solicitous of me.

We were silent getting into the car and as we drove down the hill toward the tree-lined avenue. When we turned north instead of back toward downtown, Innis said, "Jake?"

"You want some hippie-dippy shit?" Jake said. "That more your speed?"

"I think," Innis said, "there's a pretty long road between being a hippie and thinking that floor show was a little morbid."

"Hey," Jake said, "I'm just gonna give you some more flavour of the town. Like you want."

I had once climbed into a taxi in Berlin to find that the driver had been driving for forty-eight hours straight and was half mad on amphetamine. He'd had a few good tips and thought he was on a roll. He had driven with one tire on the sidewalk most of the way and had laughed when I'd demanded to be let out of the car. We were in this together, he'd told me. I would have my full ride.

I thought of that trip with nostalgia now. How safe and pleasant it had been compared to this.

"What the hell is up your ass?" Innis inquired.

"When'd you get a fucking yardstick up yours?" Jake responded.

"What?" Innis seemed both offended and hurt.

"You didn't have a fucking moral compass in your hand when you were two-fisting it with those mercenaries in the Stans."

Innis hit the seat between us, hard enough that the dent stayed long after he pulled his hand away.

"Hey, I may have gotten shit-faced with some questionable motherfuckers in my time, but that doesn't mean I liked what they were up to. I was getting the fucking story, Jake."

"Oh, right," Jake said. "You're a fucking journalist now. I keep forgetting."

"I'm a fucking author," Innis said. "Fuck you."

Was this always the way they spoke to each other? Did they curse and accuse and then forget about it until the cursing began again? Had they done this when they were six years old and could only guess what "fuck you" meant? I could not tell by looking at Innis whether he was accustomed to this. He simply seemed angry.

We drove for many blocks. The houses became less impressive as we went farther from downtown. We passed strip malls. I had seen no shopping malls here, to my surprise. I had thought it was a law in North America that every city had to have a certain number of malls.

As we passed a row of identical houses done in what someone had likely thought a Bavarian style, Jake spoke again.

"There's a commune just inside the city line," he said. His voice was gruff but calm. "They don't believe in magic."

"I have news for them," Innis said. He sounded calm as well, and even amused. "Magic doesn't care."

"Nah, not like that," Jake said. "They know magic exists. They just don't like to use it."

"Oh, fuck me," Innis said. "C'mon, Jake, man, not these assholes. They're all over the place. I don't need to meet a bunch of SciCos here."

It was not a nice way to speak of the Science Core Coalition. They were extreme, yes, and obnoxious, but they also had a point. They said magic had come from nowhere, and we did not understand it. Perhaps the thing to do was leave it alone and continue on with science, which had been with us for longer and would not, for example, suddenly go back to where it had come from someday.

"These guys aren't real into science either," Jake said. "They're Quaker-ass bastards."

"Even better," Innis said. "Actual Quakers? Or just Luddites? You know what? Don't answer that. It doesn't matter. Turn the car around."

"Why would a magic-free community be here," I asked, "if the land itself is so charged?"

"Aha," Jake said. He raised his index finger. "See? That's the question. What are they doing here?"

Innis frowned and stared out the window. He did not seem happy, but he was no longer demanding that Jake turn the car around.

"Fine," he said after a few moments. "We'll meet the Luddites."

I wasn't much more excited about this than Innis seemed to be. I was not even certain I would be allowed to take photographs if these people were against science and complicated machines. But it was as Jake had said—whatever we saw at this commune, it was unlikely to be so cheerfully callous as what we had witnessed over lunch. And so in that respect, I welcomed it.

Innis Stuart

KARSTEN'S CAMERA was on the floor of the Land Rover. He wasn't flipping through his photos to see what he'd captured in the restaurant, and he wasn't holding the camera on his lap in case he got a rare chance to take a decent shot out the window. It was impossible to know what he was thinking, at least without the help of a telepath, but I got the sense he was trying to keep his taimen down.

Apparently he was a goddamned hippie, just like me.

Jake was right in a way. I'd changed some since our paths had crossed in war zones. I'd gotten softer talking to civilians instead of soldiers and hunting for places that were dangerous because of magic or geography instead of violence. Maybe I'd rubbed off a few edges, and maybe some of those edges had been the ones that had kept me alive so far. I could see his point—to a point.

Jake had changed too, though. Since moving to the Dominion, he'd gotten harder. Angrier. It probably served him, being that way. The sense of humour, though, that was a problem. He still had one, but it was limited and mostly bad-natured. It wasn't enough to do what a sense of humour was supposed to do in stressful situations, which was keep a person from losing it.

Normally Jake's emotional life wouldn't have been my business, exactly. We'd known each other a long time, sure, but he'd always been a private guy. Thing was, though, he was driving me around town and picking places he thought I should visit. If he was liable to drive us off a cliff or into a bottomless portal, that was my business.

As little as I liked the idea, I was going to have to have a private talk with Jake. I'd send Karsten off somewhere and have dinner with Jake, maybe. We'd talk about old times. I'd bring up his piss-poor mood. He'd call me an asshole and possibly throw something at me. A good time had by none.

We were getting into the foothills along the north edge of the city when Jake slowed and turned right onto a gravel road. A lot of ups and downs and a bit of washboarding, but overall the ride wasn't bad.

"So is it part of the Dominion?" I asked. "This commune?"

"Said it was inside the city limits," Jake said.

You couldn't have proved it by me. I saw pine trees. Ravens. Fireweed and brush. And I sensed something that wasn't there. I couldn't tell what it was, but I had a definite sense of something missing.

"Doesn't feel like city," I said.

"Used to be a private estate," Jake said. "The owner died, kids inherited, didn't want a damned thing to do with the Dominion and sold off the land. This was in the sixties, so the hippies have been out there for a while."

"And they're not much into lawn maintenance," I observed. "Good for them. I hate lawns."

Karsten shot me an amused glance. "I thought they would evict you from this continent if you did not keep a proper lawn."

"Not in Dawson," I told him. "You should come up and visit sometime."

He looked thoughtful. "Ghosts," he said finally.

I nodded. "Yeah, ghosts, and the bears are acting weird. Not sure what that's about. But it's pretty quiet overall."

"A virtue," Karsten said, and I believed he meant it. If Karsten had been in charge of naming the seven virtues, "quiet" would definitely have been on the list. Chewing with one's mouth open would have topped the seven sins.

Jake followed the road around a tight curve to the north. It widened after that and stopped at a gate that seemed like iron and probably was. Nothing like cold iron for keeping the supernatural away.

Jake pulled in next to the gate.

"Stay put," he ordered, then got out and started patting his pockets.

From the inside of his jacket, he retrieved a small vial with a spray nozzle on top. A lock de-icer, maybe? Seemed a strange thing to pull out on a warm day in June. I leaned forward to watch through the gap between the front seats and bumped shoulders with Karsten, who was doing the same thing.

Jake sprayed the gate's lock, and I saw a flash of orange light before the mechanism moved of its own accord. Jake gave the gate a shove, and it opened easily, baring the roadway to us. Jake stuck an arm out in that direction before returning to the car and getting back inside.

"Hope you don't mind getting wet," he said, holding up his arm.

"The fuck?" I said intelligently.

The cloth of Jake's jacket where he'd held his arm through the gateway was dotted with moisture—clear drops of something like rain.

"They have weather control?" Karsten asked. "Did you not say this commune disliked magic?"

"It's not the commune that has weather control," Jake said. "It's the Dominion. People were bitching last week about all the rain we'd had this spring, so the city council took out the civic pocketbook and hired up a few nice days. Lucky for the two of you, arriving when you did."

"Weather control," I repeated.

I'd heard of places that did it, mostly in Europe where the population density—and so the tax base—made it affordable. It was rarer in Canada, unless it was an effort to stop a forest fire or save crops.

"Apparently it's raining," Jake said.

He sounded happy about it. Maybe he preferred that the weather be itself, good or bad.

It was like driving into an automatic car wash the way the rain inched onto the car as we moved slowly up the road. I almost expected big blue brushes to stick out from the trees and scrub the sides of the Land Rover.

Jake stopped the car again a little past the gate, got out, and locked the gate behind us. It was a surprisingly considerate thing to do, given his overall fuck-it attitude.

Karsten cracked a window after a quick glance to make sure Jake wouldn't see him. I didn't think Jake would care in this place, but I'd have been the same way if Jake had bitten my head off on the topic of open windows the way he'd bitten off Kar's.

Once he was convinced he'd gotten away with his small act of mutiny, Kar tilted his head back, shut his eyes, and took a deep breath. Rain splashed onto his forehead, and he smiled as he felt it. Apparently there was a hedonist in there somewhere. Never would've guessed.

The scent of clean rain, earth, and pine spread throughout the car, and Jake must have known a window was open, but he said nothing. Either it was safe here, or Jake himself was enjoying the rain enough to consider it worth the risk.

It was a short drive from the gate to a small bridge over a stream and to a tidy white house with rounded corners and a pointed roof that sat in a modest cleared lot on the other side. The house had no number or mailbox. It didn't even have a wooden sign with The Cutesy Fuckertons burned into it. If you arrived at this house, it seemed, you were supposed to know who was inside.

Jake stopped in the wide dirt driveway that faced the house and turned off the Rover.

"You might as well get out," he told us. "We'll see how this goes."

Karsten Roth

UNLIKE THE overdone "Bavarian-style" houses we'd passed on the way to the commune, this plain house with smooth walls and a low-hanging roof truly reminded me of Bavaria. It was a pity that I had little affection for that state.

Innis and I stayed a few steps behind Jake as he went up the stone walk to the front door. Innis glanced at me a few times as if he expected me to have some comment on this latest adventure. I disappointed him with silence.

The front door opened as Jake raised his hand to knock. Innis and I stopped upon seeing this and stood perfectly still, the rain soaking us. I believe that deep inside we hoped we would blend in with the rain barrels at our sides and thus go unnoticed.

A man with thick, curly grey hair stepped outside and pulled the door of the house shut behind him.

"Ex-detective Adler," he said and offered a hand. Despite this, the man did not seem pleased to see Jake.

"I'm still a private cop," Jake said, shaking the man's hand. "How are you, Syd?"

"Wondering why you're here, Jake," Syd said. "And who your friends are."

So the rain barrel disguise had not worked. Innis stepped forward and shook Syd's hand.

"Innis Stuart. I'm writing a travelogue piece about the Dominion. This is my photographer, Karsten Roth."

I shook Syd's hand as well. It was rough from work.

"Sydney Madur," he said. And to Innis: "You say you're a writer."

"Yeah, I write travel books," Innis said. "Why?"

"That's what you're doing here? Working on a travel book?"

Now Syd faced Jake, who breathed deeply through his nose. In and out again. He did this twice before he said, "Yes, Syd. He is working on a travel book. I wanted to show him another side of the Dominion."

"I don't have to talk to a private cop," Syd said. "I know my rights."

"I know you do," Jake said. "Would you be willing to talk to these guys about your setup here? The whole magic-free thing?"

Syd looked at Innis and then at me and then at Jake. Jake shook his head and turned to face us.

"There was a murder here two years ago. That road we came up on leads through the grounds, and people own plots facing it. The guy who was killed was found lying in the middle of the road, about halfway up through the, ah, community."

"Marvelous, Jake," Syd said. "Thank you for sharing this with your writer friend."

Jake glared at Syd. "I'm just explaining why you're acting so goddamned squirrelly. Innis doesn't give a crap about your murder. I'm not being paid to care anymore, so I don't give a crap either."

I was not so certain that Innis did not give a crap about the murder, as he seemed quite interested and was generally curious about such things. However, I could sense that it was not wise to say so.

Syd was plucking at a loose thread in his bulky grey sweater. He did this for long moments as the three of us became increasingly damp. Then he turned to Innis.

"You want to know what we're doing out here."

"Seems like an odd place to have a magic-free community," Innis said.

Syd raised his eyebrows. "Some might say that, but I say it's the best place in the world. Wipe your shoes when you come inside."

He opened the door and went back into his house. We followed, Jake going first, and wiped our shoes on a thick braided mat as we stepped through the doorway. I closed the door behind me. When I turned from the door, Syd was beside me with a towel. Innis and Jake were already drying their hair.

I dried my hair quickly and studied the room, which was softly lit and gently curved. Everything about this small house was soothing and rustic. The colours were muted browns and greys, with unpainted pine in the furniture. In many places there were no chairs or shelves. Instead there would be a seat curving out from below a window, or a set of books placed in a wall's cubbyhole. Everything was of a piece, covered in the same greyish-white plaster.

Most everything in the house could be seen from this room, though rounded walls swept up to partially conceal the kitchen and dining room. The bedroom was a loft, and a single door at the back of the house led to what I assumed must be the washroom.

Windows provided most of the light, though a few candles were lit on the thick-legged coffee table.

Syd took the towel from my hands. "Have a seat. I'll throw these in the hamper and get us some tea."

We sat, Jake taking a wicker chair across from the plain cotton futon where I sat next to Innis. Jake leaned forward.

"Guy got an axe in the back," he said.

"Syd?" I said, confused.

Jake scowled at me. "No, the murder victim. Axe to the back. Mailman found the poor bastard face down in the road. I got out here, started looking at people's axes, and guess what—everyone had a brand-new axe. Whole damn commune bought new axes and told me they didn't know who'd owned the murder weapon."

"You arrest anyone?" Innis asked.

Jake shook his head. "Impossible. No one saw anything. No one knew the dead guy. Near as I can tell, he was some unlucky son of a bitch who wandered out here one dark night and startled one of Syd's happy campers."

"Startled them?" I asked. "It is not a reflex to follow someone and put an axe in their back."

Jake smiled nastily. "Maybe the guy saw something they didn't want him to see. Why don't you ask Syd about that?"

"I think I'll pass," I said.

Jake sat back in his chair, and we said nothing further, merely looked around the comfortable room until Syd returned with a tray and set it on the table.

"Red ginseng," he announced. "I grow it out back. It'll keep you from getting a cold after standing out in that rain."

"I was told ginseng was difficult to grow," I said, taking a mug of tea.

"Time and patience," Syd told me. "These days, people like to wave wands over their gardens, but I prefer the natural way."

"You're saying magic isn't natural?" Innis said. He had taken a mug and was holding it in his hands, letting the steam rise over his face. "You think there's a machine somewhere churning the stuff out?"

The way Innis said this was friendly and curious, and so Syd did not seem to mind.

"Maybe," he said. "No one knows. Where's it coming from? What does it want? Does it have plans for us? No one wants to ask these questions, do they? Because—"

He was stopped by the sound of someone knocking on his front door.

"Ah, excuse me."

I thought I could hear angry voices outside and became certain when Syd opened his front door. A man of about Syd's age, maybe sixty, and a woman who was not yet forty were standing there, speaking loudly and over one another. It was still raining quite hard, but neither seemed to care.

"...not interested in what you think," the woman was saying. "I wasn't talking to you."

The man turned to Syd. "She was talking to my wives."

Syd put his fingertips to his temples. "Not this again."

"I can talk to whoever I want," the woman said.

"She can talk to whomever she wants," Syd agreed. He looked at the woman, who had long dark hair in spiraling curls. "Yes, you can, but you know this winds him up, so why do you keep doing it?"

She narrowed her eyes. "This has nothing to do with him."

"That is my family, and I am head of that household," the man said.

"If your wives don't want to talk to me," the woman told him, "they don't have to."

"You are to speak to me, not to them," the man said.

"Buddy," the woman said, "I am not a member of your household. Don't tell me what to do."

"Women are to be silent in the temple," the man insisted. Syd started to rub his own temples as if that had reminded him of why his fingers were there.

"Oh," the woman said, "I forgot—I have something for you." She reached into the front pocket of her capri jeans and slowly pulled her hand out again, revealing an extended middle finger, which she proudly presented to him. "There it is!"

"All right, children," Syd said. "Grow up. Be adults. Settle this yourselves."

"It wasn't my idea to come here," the woman said. I did not know this woman, but I believed her. She seemed no happier about this argument than Syd was.

"Just go back to your own lots," Syd said. "Both of you. Marie, stay off Isaac's land. Isaac, people can talk to your wives if they want to. You have a problem with that, go get yourself some land up north where you won't see anyone else."

Marie was already walking away. Isaac glared at Syd for a few moments longer, then hurried after Marie. He was probably concerned that she would speak to his wives again on her way home.

Syd closed the door and sat down with us again. "The joys of communal living," he said.

Jake snorted. "You get every kind of wacko out here, Sydney."

Syd sipped his tea, unconcerned by this. "People have their reasons for rejecting magic. Some believe magic is a danger to man and the Earth. Others think magic is the devil's work. We all find a way to live together, and mostly we live in peace. Squabbling is not important next to our shared goal."

"Shared goal?" Innis said. "What goal is that?"

"To live free from magic," Syd said.

Innis leaned back and looked at Syd as if trying to take his measure.

"That's interesting," Innis said. "You must know that there are places on Earth where there's very little magical energy. There are also countries where magic is strictly regulated or flat-out illegal."

Syd smiled. "And yet I am in the Dominion."

One of the candles began to gutter. Syd licked his fingers and put it out. "We want to show that it's possible to live this way everywhere. If you're in Iceland or India or Australia, there's still no reason to put up with this magic bullshit. It can be controlled, and it can be vanquished."

"How?" I said.

Innis glanced at me, and I thought he might tell me to keep quiet as I was the photographer and not the interviewer. But he smiled.

"That's a good question," he said to Syd. "Most warders use magic."

"The Earth produces its own protection against magic," Syd said. "We grow rowan and wolfsbane. You may have noticed our front gate, which is cold iron. We've also amassed a good supply of silver."

Jake was regarding his tea. I did not think he was trying to read his future in it. I thought instead that there was something in his face he did not want seen.

"I beg your pardon," Innis said, "but that's pretty mild, isn't it? I'm having a hard time believing that rowan and wolfsbane are going to keep back something like weather control. Especially around here."

Syd eyed him coolly. "But you can see that it does work."

"But I can see that it doesn't," Innis protested. "Look at Jake, for example."

"What does that mean?"

"Well…." Innis set his mug down on the tray. "Jake has a… quirk that lets him see through illusions. Not that he's ever had it checked out, but it seems safe to assume this is a little bit of magic he does. So in theory, shouldn't Jake have been stopped at the gate?"

Syd set his mug down as well. I thought, madly, that the mugs might start to fight, acting out the hostility in the room. "Our defences exclude purely supernatural beings," he said, "but they don't exclude people who have some kind of magical quality to them. We do ask that people don't employ these qualities while they're in this community, as residents or visitors."

"Wow," Innis said. He was not even trying to sound sincere. "Who knew you could get that specific with wolfsbane?"

"Obviously," Syd said, "we do not give away all of our secrets. There are many who are hostile to our goal."

I was fascinated watching them talk. Innis was not charming this man. This was clear. But I was not certain it was due to a collection of herbs or to another ward of some kind. Innis was not, I believed, interested in charming this man. He was not joking or smiling. He was on the edge of anger.

And Jake was not watching any of it. He looked at his tea and his shoes and the wall and the candles. Especially the candles. They had an attraction for him.

"So your ultimate goal," Innis said, "just to be straight on this—your ultimate goal would be what? The elimination of magic from the world?"

Syd smiled. It was a tight and painful smile, worse because he seemed to intend it as friendly and calm.

"That's a lofty ambition. I simply want to live the way I want to live, and I want others to understand that they can do this too."

"What about people who don't want to live this way?" Innis said. "What about people who like magic? Or those 'purely supernatural' beings you mentioned, whatever you classify that way—and I don't know how you even make that classification—but what do you want for them? Live and let live?"

Syd licked his fingertips again, not to put out another candle but to clear away the soot.

"Now, Innis. We all have people we think the world would be better off without. Don't we? Don't you? But you don't murder these people, do you? You just go your own way."

Innis looked at Jake as if hoping Jake would say something, perhaps back him up. Jake was now staring out the window at the rain. He did not notice Innis, and so Innis turned to me.

"I rarely murder anyone," I told him.

Innis smiled.

This and the other time he had smiled at me—these were the only times he had smiled since we had arrived at the commune. It was pleasing, even flattering, that this gregarious and likable man seemed to like me so well. In the bar the night before, surrounded by people much friendlier and more pleasant than I, then too he had behaved as if he would rather speak with me than with any of them. For some reason, this made me like both Innis and myself somewhat better.

"But do you think about it a lot?" he asked. "Murdering people?"

"I don't know what you would consider a lot," I said, and he smiled a third time.

Syd stood and took the tray from the table. "Best not to live in a world," he said, "where wishing makes things so."

Chapter Ten

Innis Stuart

I'D HAD more than enough of Jake's murder suspect. And no matter what Jake said, I was under no illusions about his motives in bringing us to the commune. He might genuinely have thought it would be helpful for my writing about the Dominion. Actually I agreed. But that didn't change the fact that Jake, cop or not, was not happy about having an open case.

What he thought he'd accomplish by sitting me and Karsten down in front of Syd, though… that was a greater mystery than the unsolved murder.

"Rain's let up," Jake said.

We all looked where Jake was looking, out a narrow window beside his chair. The sun hadn't reappeared, but the only water still falling was dripping from the needles of the pine trees.

"The beauty of weather is that you can't truly predict it," Sydney said.

Jake shook his head. "You can keep your natural weather. Dominion Week hasn't been rained out in thirty years."

"Dominion Week?" I said.

Jake set his mug down. "First week of July. Canada Day through Independence Day. It's a hell of a party."

"I'm sure it is," I said, though I did summer solstice in Dawson most years and had a hard time believing parties got much better than that.

Jake put his hands on his knees and stood. "Syd, you mind if we take a walk through the community?"

Syd stood as well. A guy like that would be damned if he'd sit while anyone else in the room was standing. Someone might get the impression he wasn't in charge.

"Feel free. But I'd advise you to stick to the main road unless you've been invited onto someone's property. People like their privacy out here."

Jake snorted a laugh. Syd didn't smile. I stood, and Karsten stood beside me.

"Thanks for your time," I said, offering a hand to Syd.

He shook my hand, even though I probably had magic cooties all over me. He shook Karsten's hand too. Jake didn't offer a hand, and Syd didn't seem to mind.

"May I take photographs?" Karsten asked.

I almost laughed. He was willing to take secret shots of the mayor, but here he asked. I couldn't blame him, though. Who wanted an axe in the back?

"It's a free country," Syd told him. "But not everyone likes having their picture taken, so you might want to ask first. Feel free to take all the shots you want of my house and this lot."

Karsten took a few pictures of Sydney and his house, inside and outside
the building, walking him around and asking questions about the house as they
went. Syd seemed happy to sing the praises of his home and was willing to do
whatever Karsten asked as long as he could keep talking about the place. Straw-
bale construction apparently. Warm in winter. Cool in summer. It was humid as
hell in the rain and probably would have been a smarter idea out on the prairies
somewhere, but Syd didn't say anything about that.

Jake wandered the house in a way that he probably thought seemed casual,
though it was pretty obvious—to me at least—that he was hunting a lost clue
to sew up the axe murder mystery. A receipt for a dozen new axes, maybe. Or a
framed photo of Sydney standing over the body and wiping his prints off the axe.

Once Karsten had something he was happy with, Syd walked the three of us
to the main road and pointed down its length.

"Stay on this road and you'll be fine," he said.

"As far as I'm concerned," Jake said, as soon as Syd had returned to his
house, "they're all fucking guilty. Not that black-haired chick at the door. She's
new. But the rest of the fuckers."

"And you're going to nail them for it," I said.

Jake put his hands in his jacket pockets and lowered his head to watch the
ground as he walked. "Not at this point."

"But you wanted to get another look at the place," I said. "You brought us
out here for a reason."

Karsten gazed at me and then at Jake with open curiosity.

"I'm your guide," Jake said. "I thought this would be educational." At my
disbelieving stare, he added, "We had every psychic in the department out here. We
had the best gear. I'm not expecting to accomplish a damned thing today outside of
doing what you hired me to do."

"Do you want photos of anything?" Karsten asked Jake.

It was a generous offer, considering the terms he and Jake were on. I was
surprised to hear him make it.

Jake shook his head. "I have plenty of photos of this place. All kinds of
cameras. You seen those new retrocog cameras?"

"Yes," Karsten said. He didn't sound impressed. "I don't use such."

"Next thing you know," Jake said, "Syd'll have you signed up for a lot."

"Hah," Karsten scoffed. "I have no problems with magic. But I am a
photographer, not a magician."

"No problems with magic," Jake repeated.

Karsten gave him the same flat, poker-player expression he had given me
earlier at City Hall. "That's right."

I considered asking what the hell that had been about, but I doubted either
of them would tell me.

We were passing the road to the first lot. It was a longer driveway than the one in front of Syd's house, so I could only catch glimpses of the property down the lane and through the trees. I saw women in long cotton dresses working over steel tubs that had been lined up along wooden tables.

"Isaac's lot," Jake said, unnecessarily.

"Wanna go talk to them?" I asked Karsten. He didn't bother to reply. Instead he squinted through the trees.

"What are they doing?" he asked, sounding somewhat disgusted. I peered over the top of his head and saw one woman lifting a handful of squirming red worms from a tub.

"Vermicomposting," I said. "I thought you Europeans were into composting."

"I live in an apartment in Berlin," Karsten pointed out. "And as much as I like nature, I prefer that it stay outdoors where it belongs."

We moved on, stepping on a few earthworms as we went. Whether they were escapees from the composting program or local residents flushed by the rain, I couldn't have said.

The next few lots were quiet, whoever lived there either away at work or inside tidy off-white houses that resembled Syd's.

It should have been a nice walk. The woods smelled fresh, and it wasn't too buggy along the road. It was just warm enough, not hot, and the clouds gave everything a soft, even light that Karsten probably appreciated.

Something was bothering me, though. It wasn't the thought of the murder. That was long over, and this was one place where I had no expectation of running into the victim's ghost. It was something else. Something in the air or the ground. Or maybe it would have been better to say that it was something missing from the air and the ground.

I had been born after the Turn. We all had, the three of us walking this road. I had traveled, of course, to places where the magical energy was low. Even in the places where it was high, like the ones Syd had mentioned—India, Australia, Iceland—it ebbed and surged. I wasn't accustomed to a steady stream of magic flowing through me, and I wasn't someone who relied on it to live.

But I was accustomed to some magic being present wherever I went. It wasn't something I felt exactly, not in a way I could identify. But I could feel it better now in its absence. The closest thing I'd experienced was a change in pressure from a deep dive or a high climb. It was an inequality between the inside and outside of my skin, and it made me feel as if my will alone were dragging my flesh and bones. Step by wearying step.

Jake looked uncomfortable as well, slogging along with his head down, though Karsten seemed as agile as ever. He was taking pictures with care, avoiding the lots, shooting down the gravel road or through tree branches into the sky. Jake silently pointed at a patch of road, and Karsten nodded, took shots. That was where the man had been found. That was where they'd put him, after they'd all decided to buy new axes… and to lie.

We said nothing about it and moved on.

The last lot, on our right-hand side made all three of us burst out laughing. It featured a log cabin, an old pickup, and a yard chock full of pot.

"That fucking well takes me back," Jake said. "Remember?"

I did. An aging hippie in our hometown had grown the stuff in the basement of his used bookstore. Jake and I had thought it was old-fashioned and funny, even then, that someone still bothered with a ride that tame.

Karsten got up the nerve to take a few shots of that yard, then slung his camera over his shoulder. "I suppose, what are you to do when you live here and get tired of reality?"

Jake grinned. "Drive into town. And don't think they don't. This place is a ghost town on Thursday nights."

Karsten looked at him, puzzled. "Thursday nights? Not Fridays?"

Jake nodded. "Late-night shopping. Thursday's the only night it's allowed."

Karsten Roth

ON OUR return to downtown, I went through my photographs as Innis and Jake discussed their boyhood in Manitoba. I tried to seem uninterested in the hopes that they would forget I was there and let something slip about Innis's quirk, or even Jake's.

They did not mention this. Instead there was much talk of lakes and prairies. Girls they had dated. Pranks they had played. Innis's parents, who had been "cool," and Jake's parents, who had not. All of their parents, it seemed, had passed away by now.

"This has got to be boring you at least halfway to death," Innis said to me.

I pretended to be startled. "What?"

"Yeah," he said, clapping my shoulder. "This old home week stuff can't be too interesting if you weren't there. When we get back to the hotel, why don't you take the rest of the day off? Jake and I can catch up, have dinner, and you can do whatever strikes your fancy."

"If you go down Aleister Drive in the Scree," Jake advised, "you can find someone to strike your fancy for twenty bucks."

"I have no doubt of it," I told him, "but I believe I can find other ways to occupy my time."

"To each his own," Jake said.

I returned to my camera and they returned to their conversation, which was now about Sydney and his commune. Innis bitched mightily about it and said that Sydney was a danger to all of us. I thought that Sydney was an old man paddling upstream and, as such, far too busy to be a danger to anyone. I said nothing, however, because I had no desire to argue with Innis about it.

"Syd can talk about magic all he wants," Jake said. "You know how he keeps the magic out? It's not fucking rowan, I can tell you that."

"Of course it's not fucking rowan," Innis said. "That place is warded to hell and back."

"Fuckin' right it is," Jake said. "And you know who did it? Sydney Madur himself. The man, the legend. He started warding in the '50s. By the time he and his buddies bought up that estate in '65, he was the best in town. Word is, you can still get him to set up a ward for you, if the price is right. Not that any of the idealist fuckholes living in that place have any idea. They think it's all rowan and flowers and goddamned rainbows."

"You think he did the murder?" Innis asked. "You think maybe that guy was going to tell people about Syd's wards, and that's how he got an axe to the back?"

Jake shrugged. He turned off the heater, which he had used to clear the car windows. With the clouds cut off behind us, the Dominion's sun was making the car unpleasantly warm.

"I don't care who did it. I told you. As far as I'm concerned, they're all guilty. They conspired to cover it up. The law says they're accessories after the fact—even in the Dominion. And they do fall under Dominion law whether they think so or not."

"You couldn't get anything from psychics?" Innis asked. "Seriously? Did you try dragging everyone into the police station to get them away from the wards?"

"No," Jake said. "We're idiots. Never occurred to us. Innis, you may be a clever shit, but that doesn't mean the rest of the world is stupid."

As much as Jake both irritated and frightened me, I was starting to see the value of his role in Innis's life. He said things Innis desperately needed to hear.

"I wasn't saying you were stupid," Innis protested. "I was just saying that I thought the warding would stop once you got to the edge of their property."

"Apparently Syd warded the residents too," Jake said. "They move around in their own little magic-repelling bubbles."

"Gonna be a bitch if they need serious medical attention," Innis mused.

Jake smiled. "I sincerely hope so. But I have a feeling they can turn those bubbles off and on."

They dropped that subject, and all subjects, for the rest of the drive. At the hotel, I was seen off with a wave and a "see you in the morning" as Innis switched from the back seat to the front. Innis and I were to meet for breakfast in Hounfor.

I hurried to my room, where the painting had still not been removed, and looked in the phone book for the number of the *Dominion City Phoenix*.

Asking for Donna in Crime put me through to the extension of a Donna Hartley. Her strong and direct voice told me that she was away from her desk or on another line and that she would return my call as soon as she could.

This was a problem because I didn't know her relationship with Innis or Jake. Did she think well of them and speak to them often? If I were to leave a message saying why I wished to speak with her, would she immediately call Innis and tell him about my call? But if I merely left my name, would she bother to call me back? I had been hoping to reach her in person so that I could guide myself by the tone of her voice as we spoke.

I thought quickly as the voicemail beeped in my ear and finally said, "Ms. Hartley, I would like to speak with you about Brandon, Manitoba, where I understand you grew up. You may reach me by calling room 1208 at the Pickman Hotel."

I then went to the washroom to brush my hair, which was still in disarray from the toweling. As I set the brush down, my phone rang.

"Yes, hello?" I answered.

"Honey," that strong voice replied, "no one ever wants to talk about Brandon, Manitoba. Who are you, and what do you really want?"

There was nothing for it but to forge ahead.

"My name is Karsten Roth. I'm a photographer working on a travelogue with Innis Stuart. I would like to discuss Innis," I said, "and also Jake Adler. Is there a place where I might buy you coffee and ask you questions?"

"You want to ask me about Innis?" she said. She sounded amused by this.

"Yes," I said.

"And Jake."

"Yes," I said again.

"For reals," she said.

"Yes," I told her. "As you say, for reals."

"Well," she said. "Goddamn."

I said nothing. After a few beats, she said, "There's a Tim's two blocks north of the Pickman. Can you be there in half an hour?"

I did not know the place she spoke of, but half an hour was more than enough time to find it.

"Yes," I said. "And thank you. I'll see you then."

"Oh, honey," she said, "don't thank me yet." And the line went dead.

Innis Stuart

MY FIRST thought as we pulled away from the Pickman was that it was odd to leave Karsten behind. I felt as if I'd forgotten a travel mug with my favourite coffee or my most comfortable jacket—something apt and agreeable that would improve things wherever I went. It was a weird way to feel about anyone I'd known only two days, let alone a guy who routinely implied I was an idiot.

"Your photog going to be okay?" Jake asked, as if he could read my thoughts.

"Aw, yeah," I said. "I know he looks young, but he's been in the shit. Do you know he was at Tunguska when it bounced back? Only photographer to get anywhere near it. *National Geographic* gave him a cover."

"Stop bragging," Jake said. "It's not like you did it."

I laughed. "Hey, he's my photographer. There's got to be some kind of reflected glory."

"And you like staring at him."

I shrugged, which was not a denial, and I knew Jake would know that. I was also pretty sure Jake wouldn't want to talk about it. Not beyond letting me know he had my number. He'd never been interested in my social pursuits.

To be honest, I didn't really want to discuss Karsten with Jake, either.

"Where'd you meet the guy?" Jake asked, apparently not done with Karsten after all.

I was starting to wonder what he was after. Maybe just digging for something to criticize.

"He contacted my publisher and said he wanted to do something for a Seven Leagues book," I said. "We arranged this trip, but I didn't actually meet him until he got on the plane in Frankfurt."

"He asks a lot of questions," Jake said. He was taking us over the bridge to East Hills, which surprised me, considering his distaste for the whole college scene. "He seems to think he's a journalist."

"He is, kind of," I said. "He goes places and tells the story. Only with pictures. There are probably times when he has to ask questions to figure out what the story is. That's how he knows what to shoot."

"Maybe so," Jake said noncommittally. Once we were past the bridge, Jake turned north and stayed close to the river. "They've got kayak rentals up here if you're interested. Little bit of whitewater, but no reason to roll, so you won't need a wetsuit."

"I'm up for that," I said. I'd spent too much time on planes and in hotel rooms over the past few weeks. "You've got a good setup here. Two rivers, ocean, mountains."

"Weather control," Jake added. "It's all right. I miss Manitoba sometimes."

Jake had always liked the space and the lakes of our home province more than I had. Not that I had anything against all of that, but I was the one who'd been eager to see the world, while Jake would happily have stayed home if the armed forces had let him. It hadn't been Jake's idea to get shipped all over the planet.

"Join the army," I said.

"See the navy," Jake finished. "Yeah, I know. I was stupid to think they weren't gonna ship me out. But I liked the work."

"Better than what you do now?" I asked.

"Some ways," Jake said. We stopped in a small gravel circle next to a red-and-white boathouse. Jake pulled out some bills and told the teenage girl inside to free up a pair of kayaks and a couple of life jackets. She nodded, and I saw gill slits open and close where her neck and shoulder met.

As Jake filled out the paperwork, I watched a construction crew working across the street. They seemed to be renovating an old office building. A woman with a hard hat was giving everyone directions. After listening to her for a minute or so, I realized she was scanning the building. X-ray vision, or something like it. Nice to have, as long as you could control it. Otherwise it could drive you crazy.

Once Jake had cut through the stack of paper, we got ourselves settled and into the river. It was clean and cold, with the slight turquoise tint often found in mountain water. Something about the riverbed and the reflection.

Jake indicated that we should go north, upstream. It meant the second half of our trip, when we were tired, would be downstream. I nodded and followed him.

"You have to get out of the city," he said once I'd pulled up alongside him, "to get the sense that you're out of the city. You're always going to see buildings off this river. But at least you get a little space around you."

"I never understood why you moved here," I said.

Jake gazed up the river, and I wondered if he'd heard me. Then he said, "I never really understood it, either. I was planning to head back to Manitoba after I left the army, but I had an urge to move here. Figured I'd give it a try."

A duck swerved to avoid us and gave us a dirty look. I kept still until we'd floated past it.

"You've been here a long time," I said, "for someone who's just giving it a try."

"Yeah," Jake said. "I know. I got interested in the job. Now... I don't know what I'm still doing here. Maybe I should go home."

"Maybe," I said. "What's stopping you?"

"Dunno."

We didn't talk much after that. Jake seemed lost in thought, and I decided to let him think. He might well be thinking about whatever was bothering him, and maybe that would help him to talk about it.

We passed buildings that took advantage of their river view with windows, balconies, and patios. But we also passed a lot of brick buildings that showed the river their broad backs and had few or no windows aimed at it. I was puzzled until I remembered that the rivers had shifted after the Turn, destroying many of those old brick buildings but somehow leaving others standing. Those windowless backs had once faced alleys and the backs of other buildings. Of course they hadn't been built for a view.

"You still like your job?" Jake asked me.

I was a little startled to hear his voice.

"Love it," I said. "I set my own hours, decide where to go, travel all over the planet... and when I get tired of it, I go back to Dawson and write. I can't imagine anything better."

Jack shook his head.

"Spending half your life in hotels and another quarter of it in airports," he said. "No thanks."

"I was thinking I'd spent too much time in hotels lately," I admitted. "Might be time to head to Dawson for a while. You could come up if you want. Take a vacation."

"I have business here," Jake said. "I can't pick up and leave."

"Since when?" I asked. "You used to live out of a pack."

"Now I live out of a house," Jake told me. "And I have clients. Hey—check it out."

He pointed at the sky ahead of us, and I saw the glint of sunlight against prismatic scales. I leaned back and squinted at it.

"Dragon?" I asked. "It's too small, isn't it?"

"Yeah," Jake said. "We have some other flying reptiles around here. No one's caught one yet, so it's anyone's guess what exactly they are. I think they fish the river."

"You can fish this river?" I asked.

Jake laughed. "You can if you want, but I wouldn't. You can catch some pretty surprising shit in these rivers. People aren't always prepared to deal with what they pull out."

Jake seemed, like most Dominion residents I'd met, perversely proud of the trouble and danger the city generated. Maybe that was really what kept him from leaving. He'd always liked risk. It was why he'd joined the army. Well, that and grades that weren't quite good enough for university. Jake wasn't a dumb guy, not in the least, but school hadn't offered enough risk to hold his interest.

I considered that while we paddled north. Most cops had post-secondary education these days. Especially cops that worked in homicide or major crimes. Jake had a lot of army training, and that had likely helped him, but it might still have been a struggle to get something better than security-guard work. Maybe the notorious Dominion was the only place desperate enough for cops to overlook Jake's lack of a degree.

I stopped thinking about that because we'd entered the "little bit of whitewater" Jake had mentioned earlier. It wasn't anything serious, to be fair, but I hadn't been in a kayak in a while, and I had to concentrate to keep from regretting my lack of a wetsuit.

I was pretty sure I heard Jake laughing at me a few times, but I decided not to worry about it. Hell, if it was making Jake happy to laugh at me, I was a good enough friend to let him. Right?

Jake must have eventually decided he was a good enough friend to stop laughing at me and get on with his day, because he turned around and started taking us back downstream. I checked my watch as we moved into smoother waters again and realized we'd been on the water for nearly two hours. I'd barely noticed the time, which was the real beauty of being in a kayak on a river. I felt better than I had for days, and far better than I'd felt walking around Syd's commune.

I hoped Jake was feeling better too.

Karsten Roth

A TIM'S, apparently, was one of a well-loved chain of coffee and doughnut shops. A soulless place, most likely, with wipeable seats and paper napkins, yet the Pickman's clerk had looked at me with astonishment and some disapproval when I told her I needed to find this Tim's and did not know what it was.

"Wow," she had said. "You haven't been in Canada too long, hey?"

"A few days," I'd told her. "I was here this morning, for example, when I told you I wanted the painting in my room covered or removed."

"Right," she'd said, snapping her fingers and pointing at me. "Right. I'm sorry, sir. I'll get someone to see to that. Uh, Tim's… that's a Tim Hortons. They're everywhere. She said north of the hotel?"

I had confirmed this, and she had smiled.

"That's my Timmy's," she'd said. Meaning, most likely, that she went there often and not that she owned it and worked as a hotel clerk for enjoyment. "Go out the front doors, turn left, turn left again at the first corner and go up two blocks. Red writing, yellow sign. You'll see it."

When I had asked her what sort of place it was and she had told me, she had behaved as if I had asked someone in Agra what a Taj Mahal was.

Now I was following her directions, around the corner and up the busy street, and saw a sign that was the right colours, though I could not yet make out the words.

The sidewalks were crowded here, and I was used to this from Berlin, but the people were somewhat ruder. They pushed and jostled and gave dirty looks to anyone who did not move quickly enough. Despite what I had told the clerk, I had been to Canada several times before, though never for more than a week at once. I might not have known every doughnut shop in the country, but I had formed an opinion about the pushiness of its residents. They were not pushy.

But this was not Canada, and it felt typical of the Dominion, this being jostled by giants and horned creatures and people who had grown leathery skin for armour. I began to fear the stroll would leave bruises.

On my left I passed a tattoo parlour, now out of business, that had catered to vampires. It had likely done a brisk trade for a time, as vampires had to have their tattoos redone each night. A tattoo was a scar, after all, no different from all the other scars and wounds they healed as they slept. Now, of course, most vampires were far beyond caring about such vanities.

In the loft above this place, a sign offered psychic self-defence courses. Was it recommended to have such knowledge to walk safely in this neighbourhood? I quickened my step.

Donna had not said how I was to recognize her, nor had I given her a way to recognize me. This did not strike me until I was outside the Tim's and confirming that it was everything I had suspected—moulded plastic everywhere and arborite tables on steel poles. The one surprise was a badly patched hole in one wall, the size and shape of an average man. Except that average men did not tend to walk through walls.

It was crowded, and I had to stop beside the door to check the room. A woman with thick, medium-length dark hair and broad shoulders waved at me from a table for two in the far corner. I went to the table and saw a mug of coffee waiting in front of the empty chair.

"I'm sorry," I said. "You must be waiting for someone else."

"I don't think so," she said, and it was the voice from the telephone. "I'm Donna. You must be Karsten."

I sat. Donna was holding her own mug of coffee and seeming pleased with herself. I was willing to concede this right to her as I had no idea how she had picked me out.

"How did you know?" I asked.

Donna's shoulders moved forward and back and I realized this was how she shrugged. Not up and down as most people did.

"You came in here and looked confused," she said. "No one does that. They walk in, get in line, crane past people to see what's on the racks, maybe read the menu. You walked in here and goggled like you didn't know what planet you'd landed on."

"Perhaps I don't," I said.

She nodded and raised her mug to me. "Welcome to the Dominion. I got you a coffee but I didn't know what else you'd want. I usually grab a maple."

"I'm fine," I told her. "Thank you."

"Well then, Karsten Roth," she said. "Why don't you tell me what it is you want to know about Innis and Jake and Brandon, Manitoba?"

"You knew them there?" I asked. "As children?"

"What do you consider a child?" she asked in return. "I did my final year of high school in Brandon. My dad set up new offices for a construction company, and he was doing it in Brandon that year."

"You moved a great deal?" I asked.

"You got that right," she said. She waved a hand at the mug in front of me. The pottery was old-fashioned, crème and brown. "Drink up."

I wanted to say that I had no need of coffee, but I had the sense that it would be like refusing a communion wafer. I took a sip, and it was unusual. Not unpleasant, and not bad or weak, but different from what a roastery would have served.

"Yeah," Donna said, once I had partaken of the drink. "First eighteen years of my life, I moved all over the place. I was pretty worried about senior year because it's hard to make friends at that point, but I was living down the street from a punk freshman kid and wound up making friends with him and his gang. Not gang like this is my turf, yo, just the other punkasses he hung around with."

"And this was Innis?" I asked. "Or Jake?"

"Innis was the one who lived near me," she said. "But Jake was usually over there too. Jake's folks weren't parents of the year, I don't think. I'm not saying it was ideal, senior year spending time with a bunch of kids. But better than not having any friends at all. Shit, when you're in high school, anything's better than that. But here's my question for you, Mr. Roth—why do you want to know about this?"

I had thought about ways to approach this question, which I knew she would surely ask. None of the ways seemed good, and so I did what came naturally to me and simply said it.

"I know that Jake has a magical talent," I said. "He is able to see through masks and other illusions. I believe Innis may have a talent as well, of a different sort, yet he does not speak of it, and Jake denies it is so."

Donna tapped her finger against the rim of her mug. "That is real interesting. What exactly are we talking about, here?"

"Influence," I said. "I'm not saying that he knows, himself, but I believe he convinces people to... what does the bumper sticker say? Save Time: See It My Way. I have seen this many times in the short while we have worked together and have heard of it from others in my line of work."

"Oh, that is interesting," Donna said. She was nearly vibrating with energy, staring into my eyes. "I've been wondering because that guy is such a loudmouth, but everywhere he goes, doors open for him. And do you know he has never been in jail?"

"I do," I told her.

She grinned and tilted her head. "Nuts. No way is that possible unless he's got a dash of pepper. Man. I never thought of this before, but it explains a lot."

I drank more coffee. I wasn't certain but thought I might be starting to like it.

"This is nice for you," I said, "but not helpful for me, as I was hoping you would know something about what Innis does."

"Sorry," she said. "I got nothing. I can tell you, when they were boys, I never saw anything unusual in either of them. Innis got in Dutch plenty of times. He wasn't talking his way out of anything back then."

"You only knew them for one year?" I asked.

She nodded. "Not even a year, really, if you want the truth. I made some friends my own age during second semester. I didn't see a lot of the boys after that. They were mostly grounded anyway, the second half of that year."

"Grounded?" I asked. "Punished, do you mean? Told to stay at home?"

"That's the proud tradition of grounding," Donna confirmed. "To hear them tell it, they never even did anything. But some kid in their grade vanished, and a lot of the parents put their kids in lockdown. They were probably scared some guy with a van and candy would get their kids next."

"There are many things for parents to worry about, these days," I said.

Donna snorted. I was surprised to hear it from a woman.

"Oh, right. It was better back when you had to worry about your kids being eaten by a marsupial lion. Parents always have worries."

"I suppose so," I said. "Do you have children?"

"Two," she said. "Away at university. Which reminds me—I should get back to work. I have books and Kraft Dinner to pay for."

"Can I pay you for the coffee?" I asked.

She laughed. It was loud, the way Innis laughed, and people around us turned to stare. I pictured them, the two of them, standing in a bright gold wheat field and laughing together, their voices reaching to the horizon.

"I'm not that hard up, honey. Thanks anyway." She paused. "Wait—one thing. Is Innis really in town to write another one of his travel books?"

I nearly dropped the mug in my hands, so surprised was I by that question.

"What else would he be doing?"

"I don't know," she said. "I heard he was asking questions about Aloysius Harper. I thought maybe he planned to write about that. You know who Al Harper was?"

And here was the dead police officer again. Innis had been right when he said something about this man's death had worked its way into the soul of the Dominion.

"I read about him in your paper," I said. "It may have been your byline."

"It better have been," she said. "That's my beat." She looked around the restaurant, and I did the same, following her eyes. At the same moment, we both saw police officers at a nearby table. I smiled and she laughed, quietly this time.

"All the cops in the doughnut shops," she said. "Ever listen to a police scanner?"

I shook my head.

"Mostly boring," she told me. "But whenever Timmy's comes out with a new doughnut of the month or whatever, they make a general announcement. I always get a kick out of that."

I would not have had the patience to sit next to a police scanner for hours, hoping to hear a lead worth chasing.

"Your job sounds unending," I said.

"Yeah, well, there's always the hope that you can write a book, maybe get into the true-crime racket. Better pay. Better hours."

Her eyes told me that this was her concern about Innis. She did not want to be, as they said, scooped.

"Innis makes a lot of money, I think," I told her. "And likes the hours well enough."

"Here's hoping," she told me. "You really think that's all he's doing here? Seven Leagues Over what-fucking-ever?"

"If not," I said, "he is wasting a lot of money having me here, because I am photographing for a travel book and not a crime report."

"So you say," she said, but I thought she did believe me.

She was simply being a reporter, bound by an unspoken code that said she must never completely trust anyone.

"Why would he be asking about Al Harper?" she asked.

"I didn't know he was," I said. "But he did say… he found it odd that this one murder had remained in everyone's memory so long, in a city where there is that chart. The Bell Toll."

She made a face. "That's cheap. Bad journalism. Don't ask why. Don't look at the stories. Just print the numbers."

"But this police officer was different," I said. "Is it rare for police officers to die here?"

She smiled. "Are you grilling me, Mr. Roth?"

"No," I told her. "I'm curious."

"I'll say," she said. "I think this murder's something different. Aside from the fact that it was Al, and everyone liked Al. It's something big. It's only a feeling, but I've been doing this a long time. It means something. Do me a favour and don't say that to your boss."

"Do you expect me to tell him I spoke to you at all?" I asked. "Consider the circumstances."

She considered, then nodded. "Fair point. And why are you so interested in whatever Innis does?"

I opened my mouth and realised I had nothing to say.

"I—don't know," I admitted. "I saw some things, and I wondered. And it is worrisome, don't you think, if he is doing something and doesn't know it?"

A smile crept onto her face, so slowly that I did not think she noticed.

"You worried about what he might do?" she asked. "Or about him?"

How had she known to ask this? I did not believe I had done or said anything to suggest I would so much as hold open a door for the man. But I was a bit worried, yes, to see an agreeable person courting disaster. And it was always possible for someone to be a mind reader. Doubly possible in the Dominion. So she may have sensed this in me.

Nonetheless, I instructed my face not to blush and attempted to sound unbiased.

"Is it good for anyone?" I asked. "When someone is doing magic and doesn't know it? It would be similar to having no control. So… I suppose I am worried in general."

"Uh-huh," Donna said. "Well, you're right, it's the kind of thing that could get a guy and the people around him in trouble. And it wouldn't be the first time Innis overdrove his headlights." She stood. "You finish your coffee. Enjoy. And look out for Innis, will you? He never did have much sense."

"I'll do what I can," I told her honestly. I touched her arm as she passed me, and she stopped. "What about Jake?"

"Jake?" she said. "Don't worry. That guy can take care of himself."

Innis Stuart

ONCE WE were off the river and back in the car, it was around time for dinner. After all the exercise, my stomach was advocating for the idea.

Jake suggested steaks, regular beefsteaks, with baked potatoes and sautéed mushrooms and a side of totally normal. It wasn't why I'd come to the Dominion, and I should have protested, but I took his suggestion instead. With gratitude. I was getting overwhelmed, and obviously he could see it.

He took us south, into the Pines, where residents often tried to pretend that everything was normal and where entire blocks were fenced off because within them reality was too unstable to be tolerable to most people's minds. The space above those zones was cut off to flight, both personal and mechanical. Any of the Dominion's many public teleportals that had been placed near those unstable regions had been shut down or moved elsewhere.

Locals called the area the Changing Rooms.

"The PD has a search and rescue team," Jake said as we drove by one such zone, "that goes in after drunk university kids who figure the stories must be exaggerated. Hey, maybe the secret to life itself is being hidden in there, and no one has been brave enough to check. Until now. Fucking egotistical morons."

I looked out the window. The fencing was chain link, hung with warning signs like the fence outside a power station. Inside was the eerie sight of houses, row upon row of the small neat character homes that were no longer to be found anywhere else in the Pines. Everywhere else in the quarter, ranch houses and double garages had replaced them.

The lawns of those houses had been allowed to run wild. The trees and hedges were overgrown. But it was still a city block, not the deepest darkest wood, and I could understand a nineteen-year-old, drunk or not, thinking it couldn't be as scary as all that. From what I'd heard, they put the fences up a block or so outside the actual range of the weirdness so that no one driving by would accidentally see something they couldn't process.

"Isn't that hard on the search and rescue team?" I asked.

Jake shook his head.

"It's a special team. Some of them don't feel the effects. Some of them don't care. One lady, I'm pretty sure she likes it. I have a feeling she lets herself in there sometimes for fun."

"What about the kids?" I asked. "The ones who get rescued?"

"No real point in it," Jake said. "They pull them out, send them off to loony hatches, give them the full psychic treatment and a bucket of healing potions. Never heard of one of them getting any better. And they don't come out of there looking too pretty either. Lot of clawed-out eyes. Some missing digits. I don't know. I guess you can't leave them in there, because eventually somebody's buddies are going to go in to get old Steve out."

"I imagine," I said, "the Dominion wouldn't want people finding their own way out either. Wandering the Pines like that."

"That's a good point," Jake allowed. "I still don't see why we don't just send the team in to shoot the stupid bastards. Shoot 'em, douse 'em in anti-haunting juice so they don't walk the grounds, and get out. Put photos of the bodies on the fence as a warning to others."

"You've... ah... gotten to be kind of a hard man, Jake," I said cautiously. Jake huffed out air in what I took for derision and kept driving in silence.

I didn't find the rest of the Pines much more enticing. I've never been a fan of ranch houses with window treatments and vinyl siding. It occurred to me that the bear-hater lived out here somewhere, and I wondered if we were passing his house. Maybe he'd be arriving home as we passed, having finally gotten his hands on the last of the forms he would have to fill out. A lot of people had probably spent eight hours or more on the ground floor of City Hall. They'd missed the beautiful day the Dominion had bought for them.

After a bit I was cheered somewhat by the sight of the famous Ghost Bus of the Pines. Number 32. It was a retired city bus that often took up its old route, which wound through the northern part of the Pines, into the East Hills, and across to the Old Quarter. I was surprised to see riders gazing out the windows, wearing what appeared to be modern dress.

"Are there people on that bus?" I asked Jake. "I mean, live people?"

"Yeah," he said without looking. "Idiots. You never know where the bus is going to stop."

"Isn't the route known?" I asked.

Jake snickered. "Sure. But sometimes that bus doesn't make the whole route. Sometimes it just... stops. Dis. Ap. Pears." He snapped his fingers.

The bus was pulling away from us up the street, but I could still see people through the back window. They didn't seem nervous. Most seemed bored, as bus riders usually did.

"What happens if the bus stops when you're on it?"

"No one knows," Jake said. "People disappear. No one's ever come back to give a report."

"Can I ask," I said, "why in hell you'd get on it in the first place? Do people ride it on a dare?"

Jake glanced at the bus through the rearview mirror and scratched absently at the end of his nose. "Some do, probably. But there's a rumour going around that you don't age while you're on the bus. You ride it for an hour a day, maybe you save yourself a little time in the long run. Dangerous game if you ask me, but people get crazy about aging."

"There are better solutions for that, these days," I pointed out.

Jake laughed again. "Yeah. But the ghost bus is next to free. Here's the place," he added, pointing out a low redbrick building to our right. Helena's Grill, a sign said.

The restaurant was dark and comfortable in a blandly timeless way. The kind of place where businessmen went after work to drink expensive Scotch and where couples in their sixties went for a quiet dinner on a special night. It was exactly what would have been considered posh in Brandon, and I had to admit it had a certain charm for me. The air felt dense, and the sound of conversation fell to near silence in the spaces between Tiffany-lit tables.

Private, sedate, and unlikely to offer up any surprises. It was about perfect.

Chapter Eleven

Excerpt from *Seven Leagues Over North America: Pacific Northwest*

Run your fingers through the shifting sands
There are no madmen in the madlands.
—Kate Cillian, "Madlands"

NORA DALY grew up fae and proud of it. Her dream from a young age was to join Connor Avery's One Tir headquarters on the rapidly expanding island of Surtsey. She was excited when, at the age of fourteen, she learned that her family would be moving from Baltimore to the Dominion. It wasn't the fae homeland Avery was building, but it was as close as Nora could get until she was old enough to apply for residence in Surtsey. And spending so much time with magic of all kinds would only help her chances of being accepted at One Tir HQ.

At the age of twenty-three, after graduating from Rubedo with a bachelor's degree in Applied Magical Arts, Nora made her application to Surtsey and was overjoyed when she was accepted. She put her clothes on inside out, packed up, and was gone within two weeks. It seemed like short notice to her friends, but she told them she'd had a foot on that road since she first learned to walk.

That made it all the more surprising that when after half a year on Surtsey, Nora was caught replacing plumbing material in Connor Avery's home with cold iron. An assassination attempt. She's still in prison today.

Rudolf Barrie didn't wind up in prison, but he did spend some time in a Dominion hospital after voices told him the cure for his impotence lay in having intimate relations with a hedgehog, an animal poorly suited to intimacy.

Jodi Aspen was a gifted computer programmer who grew up in the Dominion and became convinced that computers could simplify magic. She developed a program that searched for the true names of demons and other spirits much as dictionary attacks search for passwords. Why spend months or years going through crumbling books in a dusty library when you could give the job to your computer and have the solution in hours? The day before Jodi was supposed to demonstrate her program for a local investment company, she brought home a powerful acid bath into which she dumped her computer's hard drive and all of her backups. Then she walked out of her house and was never seen again.

What do these three stories have in common? They're all about residents of the Pines.

Ask people in the Dominion about the Pines and they'll tell you it's boring. The 'burbs. Bungalows and minivans. Sure there are a few quirks, such as street and house numbers that don't go in order—a memento from a developer who was deeply into numerology. But overall there's nothing to see. If you didn't have to drive through the Pines to get to and from the airport, no one would ever visit.

This description is accurate, to a point, but it leaves out the Changing Rooms, the large pieces of land where reality is unreliable and the rapidly shifting perspectives and time perceptions drive most unprepared beings—as well as most humans, prepared or not—out of their minds. Permanently.

Still, folks in the hipper parts of the Dominion will say it's no different from a suburb with a few toxic waste sites. That doesn't make the place interesting.

Mental health professionals, however, are starting to find the Pines very interesting. And yes, they say, it is like a place full of toxic waste sites, in that it's hard to contain that much poison. Something always gets out.

Rates of mental illness in the Pines are double that of the rest of the Dominion and more than twenty times that of comparable locations in other North American cities. The residents may hide it well behind trellises and barbecues, but they're not well. And the longer they stay, the more likely they are to need medical intervention.

Nora Daly's prison is actually a hospital for the criminally insane. In theory she could be released at any time, upon proving herself well. In truth she's unlikely ever to leave. Nora has been diagnosed with a dangerous and persistent form of Capgras delusion, a disorder in which people believe that others around them have been replaced by imposters. It was this belief—that Connor Avery and his family had been replaced by shapeshifters or androids—that led to Nora's attempt on their lives. She has never explained how she had managed to handle the iron long enough to install it, let alone why she believed cold iron, which is most effective on fae, would harm a shapeshifter or android. She's not that coherent.

Rudolf Barrie, as mentioned, heard voices. He still does but now understands that they're not messages from spirits. He moved from the Dominion to Kelowna, in British Columbia's Okanagan Valley, and he's made his peace with the voices but does not expect they will ever leave him be.

As for Jodi Aspen, it's believed that she walked into a Changing Room and that her remains have simply not been located. Anyone or anything to have walked into those areas, including wildlife, can be classified as mad, bad, and probably deadly to know. If you don't kill yourself, chances are good that something else will do it for you.

In any other town, it's possible—even likely—that an area such as the Pines would be closed off and the residents relocated. But, nonspace aside, space isn't endless in the Dominion. What's more, as Kate Cillian sings, "It's tough to spot a madman in the madlands." You say you're hearing voices? In Baltimore, where Nora Daly spent her early years, you'd be assessed for both metaphysical and physical possibilities. In areas with low natural levels of magic, or high levels of magic restriction, you might be given treatment automatically. In the Dominion… heck, you probably are hearing voices. And what else is new?

Pretty much anyone in North America will tell you that the Dominion appeals to people who don't like meddling. They don't appreciate psychiatric testing or public health initiatives. They like to take their chances on their own.

But that's the cliché about residents of the Dominion, and however true it may be of many people, it leaves out those who live there because it's where their work took them or where their parents moved. Even the independent-minded deserve information they can use to make up their own minds.

Rudolf Barrie would have liked at the least to have been warned about the insidious dangers of the Pines before he made a painful and humiliating decision, and long before he acquired a mental illness that seems to be with him for life.

Nora Daly wanted to help fae around the world. She didn't want to end up as the villain in a horror story that's told to fae children at night.

As for Jodi Aspen, we'll never know what happened to her. All we know is that she was bright, inventive, and hard-working. But it was her bad fortune to live in the Pines, and that's how her story ends.

Karsten Roth

BACK IN my room at the Pickman, my phone's message light was on. I called the main desk and was told that someone named Zahia had left a message for me—about Innis. *No record. Lucky bastard.*

I thanked the clerk and hung up.

I wondered how Zahia had known where I was staying but shrugged that off. She was a police officer, and I was making no effort to hide. It would have been more unusual if she had not been able to find me.

I turned the haunted painting around to face the wall, then lay on the bed to think. Donna hadn't thought there had been anything special about Innis, or Jake, when she'd known them before. But had she been in a position to know? Had anyone, other than Innis and Jake themselves?

Perhaps it was impossible to find this out. Or perhaps I was simply a terrible detective. This was likely, in fact, as I had never tried to be a detective before. I had not even read many detective stories or watched them on television.

I shut my eyes and tried to remember why it had seemed so important to me that I discover Innis Stuart's secret. I remembered when I had first heard about him from other photographers at a mass haunting outside London. They'd talked about how something wasn't right about the silver tongue, and somewhere between one swallow of beer and the next, I had decided that I must uncover the truth.

Entirely unlike me. And yet I had not questioned it. I had followed that impulse for months and had let it take me all the way to the Dominion, without stopping to ask myself why I cared.

What's more, I felt it still. Not, as I had originally thought, from outrage that this man could be dancing across the planet, twisting people's minds and playing the great adventurer. Now it was that I did not understand. I had never seen anyone who did this sort of thing without knowing it. I didn't know what it meant. I didn't know what Jake knew or did not know. And above all, I did not trust Jake.

There was another thing. As I had refused to admit to Donna, I was worried about Innis. Of course it was possible I was naive and under his spell, but I did not think so. I liked him greatly, but he did not unfailingly charm me. He had his faults, and I did not believe I would so clearly see them were I unduly influenced by him.

I thought, rather, that I had come to the Dominion seeking a trickster and manipulator and had found instead a flawed but good man—much better than he pretended to be in his books. He was considerate and gentle with people, genuine in his interest about their beliefs and their lives. I did not think he knew what he was doing because I was almost certain he would hate what he was doing. If he knew, he would not allow it to happen.

Donna had called it overdriving his headlights. The expression was new to me, but I could guess at its meaning. Innis was racing forward, a man of great curiosity and energy, but could only see so far. If something dangerous should lie ahead, he would not see it until it was too late to stop. This was an excellent way to describe what worried me. He was going toward danger, as anyone did when using magic they did not control. He was in the dark about this danger and had no hope of seeing it in time.

No hope unless I found evidence to convince him he clouded minds so that he could find a way to make it stop.

The back of my neck felt stiff on the left side, and my thoughts began to skitter into dark corners instead of staying where I could see them. This again. It was part of my normal life, and so I almost welcomed it.

By the time I had found the liquid gels and codeine in my camera bag, pain had begun. It was as if cement were moving up my neck, over my head, and down to my left eye, heavy and bruising, and now burning as it set. None of the magical cures had worked on me, and so all I had were the pills and my phone, which contained a playlist of music that somehow helped.

I swallowed the pills, pulled a sleep mask over my eyes, placed earbuds in my ears, and got as comfortable as I could to wait the migraine out.

Evening, June 16
Innis Stuart

WE'D BOTH had our fill of good, substantial food, and Jake was telling stories, as relaxed and expansive as he'd been since I arrived.

"…turns out the guy was a seventh son," he was saying as I finished the last bite of an apple crisp. "If he wanted you to notice him, you did. If not, forget it. Nice talent for a detective. I understand he's in New York now, asking a couple hundred an hour and getting it."

"The trick to having a trick is to make it work for you," I agreed.

I paused, knowing there'd likely be no better time but not wild about ruining what had been a decent evening so far. Still, it had to be said. So I said it.

"Jake… is something wrong with you?"

Jake, who was lighting a cigar, offered one to me along with a scowl. "What the hell's that supposed to mean?"

"No thanks," I said.

He shrugged, tucking the cigar into the breast pocket of my shirt. "For later."

I didn't expect to want it later either, but I could always gift the night auditor with it on my way back to my room.

"It means what it sounds like," I said. "You don't seem like yourself. You're on edge, you don't have a lot of patience with people, and your sense of ha-ha is AWOL a lot of the time."

"Jesus," Jake snapped. "Where the fuck have you been for the past two days? How much ha-ha do you think you'd have, working in this town?"

"Then maybe you really should leave," I said. "You don't seem happy here. Whatever business you have, maybe you can leave it unsettled. Just go back to Manitoba. Or kick around with me for a while. I can always use a bodyguard."

Jake laughed in that way he had now that made me think nothing was funny to him anymore. "Yeah, for fighting off your adoring fans."

"Fuck off," I said, not aggressively. "I get into some iffy situations. You know that."

"You get out of them fine," Jake said. "Look. I told you I have business here, and that's the end of it."

"What?" I said. "Why? Even if you're into something you can't just walk away from… fuck, Jake, tell me. Tell me what's wrong. Maybe there's something I can do to help. Whatever it is, maybe we can get you out of it together."

Jake took the cigar out of his mouth and stared at the lit end for long enough that it made me uncomfortable.

"Jake?"

Suddenly, he smashed the end of the cigar into his empty plate, ignoring the ashtray in the center of the table. They let you smoke here, I thought stupidly. So many places didn't. Even as I watched Jake's face grow ugly with anger and saw his shoulders bunch up as if he were getting ready to hit me, part of my mind was thinking about the restaurants I'd been in since arriving, whether I had seen anyone smoke.

"Stay out of my business," Jake said. "Do not come to my city like you're some fucking Red Cross supply drop here to save my ragged ass. If I want help or

I need help, I can ask for help. Maybe from you and maybe not. Maybe you're not the all-fired big deal you think you are, Saint Innis. Maybe I have better people to turn to in my time of need."

I raised my hands, palms out. "Hey. Jake. I didn't mean that. I'm trying to be your friend here, man. We go back, right? That's all I'm saying. You don't want to talk to me, that's your call."

"I don't want to fucking look at you anymore tonight," Jake said. He pushed his chair back and stood. "You're such a big shot, dinner can be on you. And you're an adventurer, so you can find your own way back to the hotel."

He was a few steps away from the table before I'd recovered enough to speak. "Jake?"

"I'll be there in the morning," he said without turning around. "But I'm done for tonight."

It went against my instincts and was damned difficult, but I managed to follow my brain's instructions and let him go. He'd said he'd be there in the morning. I had to trust that he'd meant it.

And I really wasn't much of an adventurer if I couldn't get across town by myself.

Karsten Roth

I CAME out of it slowly, hours later, with my usual sense of logy pleasure. It was, I suspected, endorphins—something like the runner's high. I was tired but relaxed, and also hungry.

My watch told me the time in Berlin, and I was still too exhausted to work it out, so I checked the bedside clock.

"HEX," the digital screen read. This stupid haunted room. I hit the clock and the letters stuttered and became numbers. Nine at night. I looked up and saw that the painting was facing outward again, though I had not touched it. Not unless I had walked in my sleep.

I cleaned up a bit and considered dining alone at Hounfor. I would not have felt uncomfortable, but it was not Cajun food that I wanted. My stomach wanted to be coddled, not challenged. I decided to ask at the desk for a decent place nearby.

The young woman I had spoken with earlier was not there, and I was relieved because it gave me a chance to tell someone else about my painting. A blue-haired man with cat's eyes nodded and said it would be dealt with immediately. I smiled as if I believed him and tried to determine whether his eyes were contacts or real.

He directed me to a bar across the street, as most of the restaurants in the neighbourhood would be closing their kitchens soon. I thanked him and thought I saw little claws at the ends of his fingers as he waved me onward. More modifications? I was starting to become annoyed by such things. Was it not hard enough to tell what was real in this place without people deliberately creating illusions?

But of course they liked illusions, or they would live elsewhere. Pittsburgh, perhaps. I had been there once on an assignment for a magazine. It had seemed a place of few illusions.

I stepped out of the hotel into the street, looking for the bar he had mentioned. It was a welcoming street, still warm from the day, with small lights in the trees and people wandering happily from bar to bar. I wanted to join them, to be in the crowd and of the crowd and not think of anything, but I knew it was possible I might become one of the many tourists killed in the Dominion this year. One more name to be listed in the Bell Toll.

The prospect of that was somewhat disturbing. Far more disturbing was the prospect of Innis calling me up on a Ouija board to tell me what a fool I was.

The bar was called Oscar's, and there was no way to tell, from the single word spelled out in neon, whether I was to think this bar belonged to Oscar Wilde or a local entrepreneur by that name, or perhaps Oscar the Grouch. It might, from the outside, have been any kind of place.

Inside, it was brick and chrome with tables in the center and booths along the walls. The music was live piano and not so loud that one could not think. At several tables, people were playing some kind of game with Zener cards. Poker chips were stacked in front of the players. I suspected this to be a sucker's game, at least for those who were not magically inclined.

I chose a booth at the back, not far from the piano, and a small, neat waiter silently brought me menus for both food and drink.

Once I'd made decisions and carefully placed the menus at the edge of my table, I watched the pianist play. He was handsome but lanky, with large hands that effortlessly played wide chords. I realized slowly that his hands were stretching, fingers lengthening to reach a tenth or more and then sliding back to normal size. It was almost hypnotizing to watch, and so I was startled when the waiter took up the menus and set a glass of wine in front of me.

"I haven't ordered," I told him.

"It's from the man at the bar," the waiter said and pointed at Innis Stuart.

Innis Stuart

GOING BACK to my room and watching television hadn't held much appeal for me, so I'd decided to stop in at the bar across the street from the Pickman. I hadn't been there more than ten minutes when a familiar blond had walked in and selected, unsurprisingly, a booth at the back.

I'd thought about paying up and walking out. I'd told Karsten he was off the clock until morning, and I didn't much care to explain why I wasn't still out painting the town red with my old buddy Jake. But I really didn't want to go back to my room, and I couldn't think of anywhere else in the Dominion I did want to go. The only other person in town I knew was Donna, and she'd probably bring up Jake.

With that in mind, I'd opted to stay.

Sending over a glass of wine had seemed like the thing to do. If he wanted to be alone, which was his perfect right, he could drink it in peace or send it back or ask for a beer instead. If he wanted company, he could wave me over. I wouldn't have to suffer any more upfront rejection either way.

As it happened, he only hesitated for a second or two before laughing and crooking a finger at me. I wondered if the waiter had sussed out that we knew each other. He spoke with Karsten as I crossed the floor with my rye and Coke and was gone by the time I arrived.

"I've ordered food," Karsten told me. "Should I have waited for you?"

"No," I said. "God, no. If I eat again this month, it may be too soon."

"Do you recommend I drink this?" he asked, lifting the glass of red wine and peering at it. "Or did you not want to waste good wine on a joke?"

"Who's joking?" I asked.

He scanned my face like he was trying to read the fine print. I was nervous, suddenly, so I gave him a friendly grin and started talking.

"I thought it was traditional to send a glass of wine to someone if you wanted to talk with them."

"Oh? But to strange women, I'd have thought.".

His face said he wasn't complaining. He was teasing, of all things. In this town where anything was possible, I might even be seeing the blue moon miracle of Karsten Roth flirting back with me.

"It was amusing," he added.

"It's probably drinkable," I said. "If you like red wine."

"I prefer white," he said. "Very dry."

He drank some anyway and didn't seem displeased.

"So," I said. "Of all the gin joints in all the world…."

"Why did I wander into yours? I think geography holds the answer to that question. Is Jake here as well?"

I shook my head. "He had business," I said. "I didn't feel like going back to the hotel. How was your afternoon?"

"I tried to ignore it," he said. "I had a migraine."

"No shit," I said. "A lot of visual artists get those. Not to sound unsympathetic."

"Perish the thought," he said.

In comfortable silence, we listened to the piano player for a while. He was good—a little off-beat and not overdoing it with the frills. He played "Here Comes the Flood" and "Desperados Under the Eaves" and a few things I didn't recognize, but none of them was "Stardust," so it was okay with me.

The waiter brought Karsten a sandwich, along with a beer to replace his nearly finished wine. Once the waiter had gone, Karsten tilted his chin toward the piano player.

"Did you notice his hands?"

I hadn't. I'd been too busy looking around the room and across the booth. Mainly across the booth.

I watched now as the man's bones and skin pushed forward to easily span the octaves of "I Don't Like Mondays."

"Nice," I said. "I wonder if he could always stretch his hands like that and if it's why he went into piano, or if his hands got stretchy because he played a lot."

"You wonder strange things," Karsten told me.

"I make a living at it," I said. "So do you."

"Not me," Karsten protested. "Are you certain you want nothing to eat?"

"Dead certain," I said. "What do you mean, not you? You're a photographer of the weird, my friend. If you don't wonder about things, why would you be in this line of work?"

"I never meant to be," he said. "I only wanted to travel and take photographs. I can't be blamed for the appearance of sea serpents and ghosts."

"Maybe not," I said, motioning to the waiter for a refill on my drink. "But you chose to go to Tunguska. And you chose the Seven Shamans tour."

"I was invited," Karsten said. "I met one of the shamans when I was in Borneo. I told him I was no mountain climber, but he insisted I should come along."

"Shamans usually have reasons for that kind of thing," I pointed out.

"And their reasons are their own," Karsten said emphatically.

He took the remaining pickle slices from the side of his plate and tossed them onto my cocktail napkin.

"I thought Germans liked pickles," I said.

"They're sweet," he said, with a facial expression that would have better suited the words, "they've been poisoned."

"You are a picky little son of a bitch," I told him. "How do you get away with that when you're traveling?"

"I don't always," he said. "But I have the luxury of choice here. Why waste it?"

I couldn't argue that, so I ate a slice of pickle instead.

"You do any climbing?" I asked. "On that tour?"

"Not really," he said. "They teleported me to wherever they needed me to be, then set me down. Of course they did something to adjust for the altitude. I did climb Kilimanjaro. The Coca-Cola route."

I smiled. The route was so named because there were huts nearly all the way to the summit offering lodging and soft drinks to trepid explorers. I'd gone up a different way.

"You got some striking shots," I said. "Really beautiful and unusual."

"Thank you," he said. "I'm surprised you've seen them."

"Why?" I asked. "They got a lot of play. And I checked you out before hiring you. I've seen a lot of your work."

Our waiter dropped off my drink and another beer for Karsten. Purely on spec, as Karsten's first bottle had barely been touched.

"I don't know that I've caught anything so striking here yet," Karsten said once the waiter had gone.

I put a hand on his arm. He had donned a T-shirt, leaving his arms bare. His skin was cool and dry despite the warmth of the bar. He stared at me, right in the eyes, fully attentive. There was a force to that look.

"You've got some pretty good stuff already. If you get something amazing, great. If not, it's still solid work. What I've seen so far anyway."

He frowned. "You can't see it well, through the camera's viewscreen. Before we leave, I'll show you on the tablet. It's somewhat better, though the colours are not.... I will have to adjust them. You can tell me if you would like anything reshot. Or shot in black-and-white. I can desaturate, but I prefer—"

"Okay," I said, holding up my hands. "That's a deal. But I think you'll find I'm not that difficult to please."

He laughed. "I heard you made Charlie Wrenn cry with whatever you said about his photos. He does not say this. He says you fired him for no reason."

I met his wry smile with a shrug. "You think I did that? Fired him, I mean, not made him cry."

"I think Charlie Wrenn is overrated."

"Agreed," I said. "But you aren't. You're also too vain to slack off and too self-possessed to cry over anyone else's opinion of you."

Something bright and sharp was in his eyes for a moment. It wasn't anger.

"Thank you," he said, raising his wine glass.

"I didn't say it to flatter you," I said.

He gave me a look both fond and knowing, as if we had been friends since childhood and I'd done something that was just like me.

"I know."

Tension left my back. I knew why, though the reason was shameful. Most conversations I had, I felt as if I were speaking with children. Likeable children often. Even bright ones sometimes. But still kids who needed to be catered to in case the words got too big or the thoughts too fast or the ideas too upsetting. I was responsible, like a benevolent God, for not giving anyone more than they could handle.

Hell, even Jake had started to throw tantrums.

Karsten wasn't going to do that, and he was no kind of kid. The only person I needed to worry about in this conversation was me.

"You went to a lot of base camps," I said. "Doing the Seven Summits thing."

Without looking down, he had taken his sandwich apart. I wasn't sure he knew he'd done it.

"It was not a great deal of fun," he said. "Even Elbrus—there is the cable car, so that's simple enough, but then you are warned about all the places you must not go for fear of being shot. And Chomolungma… that is a graveyard."

"So I've been told. You got some good haunting shots out there," I said.

He pushed his plate away. "A child with a phone could have done the same. The ghosts are everywhere. And people are eager to join them."

"I bet your shamans weren't there to climb," I pointed out. "You can magic your way to any damned place these days."

"Yes," he said, "and they did, but it is not considered sporting. Probably that is correct—it is not sporting. But I do not see the point in being sporting. I would rather be breathing."

"I hear that," I said, tapping my glass against his. "I don't see the point in Everest, period. Been there, done that. All people are doing now is trying to prove they're better than the dead men."

Karsten smiled shrewdly. "This from a man who vacations in war zones."

"Well." I ate another pickle slice. Was I actually getting hungry again? "At the risk of sounding like an out-of-touch hypocrite, I think that's different. I'm there to get at some truth. I want to meet people and talk to them and see what they think is going on. At the ground level. There's nothing to learn on Everest, or Denali, or Aconguaga. You can talk to the ghosts, maybe, but what are they going to tell you? That they're cold?"

Karsten looked down. He was pale and seemed as haunted as if he were standing in the middle of those ghosts again.

"Any number of things," he said. "But nothing you want to hear."

"You sound like a guy who heard from them," I said cautiously. He gave me an honest but sad smile.

"They seemed to take a liking to me. They stood on line to tell me their stories, even when I placed my hands on my ears and closed my eyes. But the shamans say the mountains, not the ghosts, speak to them."

I coughed on the rye in my throat. "Oh, come on, Kar… what else are they gonna say? Maybe the mountains talk to them and maybe they don't, but you're not going to launch this huge seven summits thing, spend all the money, go to all that trouble, and come down saying, 'They're a bunch of fucking rocks.'"

"They never said these were not fucking rocks," Karsten said, smiling. "They merely said the fucking rocks spoke to them."

"Uh-huh. What did they say the rocks told them?"

He shook his head. "They wouldn't tell me. They would not even discuss it when I was nearby. Strange, don't you think?"

"And irritating, I would guess," I said. "But they paid you a lot of money to go to remote and photogenic places. All the airfare, gear, whatever—I'm assuming that was on their nickel. Provided you flew instead of teleporting. Not only that, but they had telekinetics and telepaths and healers along, so you weren't liable to get killed."

"Yes. This was my thinking. But I would not say the experience came for free."

"No, it never does," I agreed. "Anyway. You say you're not into the weird specifically, but you went to Tunguska. I heard you've been on some cryptocritter hunts. And you asked to come along on this."

"Not the Dominion," he said. "Not specifically."

"No, but you know what I do," I said. "You knew when you asked to work with me."

There was a flash in his eyes again, different from the one a few moments earlier. He had seemed interested then, engaged. Now he seemed startled.

"Something wrong?" I asked.

He shook his head. "No. Jake's partner, Zahia—she asked me these things too. I'm wondering lately if I know myself at all."

"Christ," I said. "Can anyone afford to? You need to have some illusions to get up in the morning."

"Is that why I get up?" he asked. "I've often wondered."

He sounded sincere about that, but he seemed happy enough now. Maybe it was as simple as being off the clock.

"What is it with people?" I said. "They hate what they're doing and won't stop doing it."

"I never said I hated what I was doing," he said, and he did actually seem huffy at the suggestion. "I just said I didn't know how I had come to do it in the first place."

"You were good at it," I said. "You're lucky you figured out what you're good at."

"And lucky not to hate it," he said.

"That," I said, swiping a piece of turkey meat from the remains of his sandwich, "is key."

Karsten Roth

FOR A man who was not hungry, Innis was quick to finish the sandwich I no longer wanted. He did have the good grace to stop after stealing a few pieces and ask if I was done, and he left the plate in front of me in the apparent hope that I would change my mind and have something more. When he had finished, he regarded me with seemingly genuine concern.

"Have you eaten anything since lunch?"

"I am hardly starving," I said.

"How about a dessert?" he asked. "I'll split something with you if you want. Whatever you like."

"I don't want anything," I insisted. Then I said, "You are a good employer."

He didn't seem pleased to be told this. He seemed to be what my British friends would call "gutted."

"You're off the clock," he said. "I mean it. You don't have to be here talking to me if you don't want to. Tell me to fuck off. Although in fairness, I was here first."

"That is understood," I said. "All of it. I do not feel obligated to speak with you."

He blinked a few times as he thought that through.

"Well," he said finally, "good. Okay. But I'm not just worrying about you because you're working for me. I like to think I'm a nicer guy than that."

"Do you?" I tried unsuccessfully not to laugh.

He smiled sheepishly, but I thought that I had stung him nonetheless. I touched his arm lightly. He looked up sharply to meet my eyes.

"You are not precisely a nice guy," I said. "Else you would likely be dead by now. But I have no issue with you."

His smile now was slow and not sheepish at all.

"I have no issue with you, either," he said. Then he breathed deep and pulled his arm back. "How many drinks have you had without eating?"

I left my hand where it was.

"Not so many," I told him.

He nodded. He was thinking. I could almost hear it, the hum of his thoughts.

"Probably shouldn't have any more, though," he said. He was speaking more slowly than usual.

"True," I said.

We let the piano player have the floor then. I could see from Innis's face that he did not know the song. I did. Barry Andrews, singing about veils of clouds and the things he did not love anymore. Innis had been in the wrong clubs all his life to have learned the dark songs.

He scanned my face again, looking for something, then took out his wallet and dropped money on the table.

"Off the clock," I reminded him.

"Writing it off," he said. Though he did not take the receipt.

We stood and crossed the room. He placed his hand, again, at the small of my back. The street was less busy than when I had entered the bar. It was darker, and I realized that the lights in the trees were going out as a tall and indistinct shape passed beneath them. The shape was growing quickly, nearly as tall now as the trees it passed. Drunken people, weaving, were still aware enough to move out of its way, some of them stumbling into the street. We hurried to the hotel, and I admit I was reassured by the pressure against my back.

He walked me to my room, and I wasn't certain, exactly, the intent. I chose not to think about it. Then I opened my room door and forgot what I was not thinking of, because the picture was still in place. I could see its breath from the doorway.

"Damn it," I said. "I've told two of them already to take that picture away. I'll have to go downstairs and tell the night clerk that I want it gone."

Innis reached past me and pulled my room door shut, so that I did not have to see the picture anymore. I turned to him. He was close, and I had to tilt my head far back to see his face. He placed a hand on my shoulder, his grasp firm but careful. He had never taken hold of me in a way that hurt.

"You could do that," he said. "Or you could stay in my room instead."

I thought by the look in his eyes that I understood his intention. However, it was important not to be wrong.

"I am," I told him, "unfamiliar with the customs of North Amer—"

"That was a pass," he confirmed with a smile.

I found myself smiling back. I was distracted by how good it felt to want to smile at someone and do so without thought. To enjoy staring into someone's eyes without purpose. I forgot to speak.

"It's like this," Innis said, seeming to feel that there was more he needed to say. "You're good-looking and funny and smart. You also seem to be a decent guy, and I am finding that incredibly attractive right now."

I felt for him again, sympathy for what I could see had been a painful day. He was not the kind, I thought, to walk easily away from troubles with a friend.

"Your dinner must have gone very badly," I said.

He smiled again. "There's an offer on the table," he said, without his usual undertone of vigorous geniality.

And why should he have taken that tone when it was just us? There was no need to put on a show.

I stood as tall as I could, with my head still craned back, and put a hand at the back of his neck to suggest he should meet me at least halfway. The look he gave me then, surprised and perhaps even grateful, would have made his case for him if I had held any last doubts. He did not try to be persuasive in the way he pulled me closer or the way he kissed me. He gave the sense that this was a thing he was quietly pleased to do, and he seemed at peace when he was done.

"Your room," I said, "will be fine."

Chapter Twelve

Morning, June 17
Innis Stuart

KARSTEN AND I didn't talk about whether we'd discuss the previous night's developments with Jake. I was pretty sure we were on the same page about it anyway. I didn't particularly want to get personal with Jake after the way we'd left things, and Karsten wasn't about to mistake him for a confidant. As far as Jake was concerned, everyone had slept in their usual rooms.

Provided, of course, that Jake showed up at all.

He did, though, walking into Hounfor as Karsten and I were finishing breakfast. He smiled at both of us, and I decided that maybe he needed a breather. He'd always liked his space. And maybe he'd used last night to take care of some of the mysterious business weighing on his mind.

"Finish up and let's go," he said in a nearly cheerful tone. "My contact says the Sasquatch have somewhere to be this morning, so we need to catch them before they head out."

"Sasquatch," I said to Karsten.

He nodded. "This will ease the pain of your unfound Yeti."

I laughed and reminded myself not to molest him in front of Jake. "I still think they're out there. I've smelled them. But I've always wanted to meet some Sasquatch."

"Then we need to head out," Jake reminded us.

We put the food on my tab and followed Jake out to the Land Rover.

The Sasquatch didn't live in the Dominion proper. They were a few miles north of the city in an area that was properly called Pedis Mountain. Dominion locals called it by other names, most frequently Stinktown or Sulfur City. Like their Yeti counterparts, the Bigfoot were said to have a distinctive, often overpowering smell. Residents of the Old Quarter said when the wind was strong and southerly, it made its way into town. Many said it was like the reek of a pulp mill.

We were stopped briefly at the edge of the Dominion's force field. It was an invisible barrier designed to impede the flow of goods from the city. After three months of moving to the Dominion, residents were given an implant that permitted free travel through the field at all points of the land or air. Visitors and new residents could only come and go through checkpoints and were often searched for contraband. Much of what was freely available in the Dominion was forbidden in the outside world.

Jake had obtained passes for me and Karsten—I could only imagine how much effort that had taken—and he vouched for our basic lack of perfidy.

The country was beautiful, as you could expect from the Pacific Northwest. Mountains, thick stands of pine, salt spray in the air. I felt my shoulders drop and realized for the first time that I'd been holding them tense since we'd arrived.

As we drove, the scent of saltwater and pine was infiltrated by that other smell. It was, as I'd been told it would be, similar to the smell of Yeti. If I hadn't known better, I would have thought the Abominable Snowmen were nearby. Jake flipped off the Land Rover's external air intake.

"Fucking filthy," he said under his breath.

That wasn't like him, either—Jake had always been laid back about discomfort and inconvenience. You had to be to spend so much time in the military. I'd never before heard him complain about any smell, and I knew for a fact he'd been subjected to much worse.

I didn't have much time to ruminate on Jake's mood and how long he'd been in it, because we soon came around a corner and down a hill into the heart of the Sasquatch community.

"It looks like a camp," Karsten said, and it did.

A series of small white buildings was grouped around a large fire pit. At the far end was a community hall.

"It was a Bible camp," Jake said. "Methodist. They sold it to the Sasquatch when the land started to go off in the fifties."

By the time we'd pulled in, a small woman with golden-brown skin and reddish-brown hair was waiting outside the vehicle.

"Hottest Sasquatch I've ever seen," I said to Jake.

He ignored me and got out. Karsten and I followed, trying to be discreet as we coughed the foul air into our coat sleeves.

"Mina. Thanks for arranging this," Jake said.

She smiled. "Not a problem. I like having company." She turned to me and Karsten. "Hi. I'm Mina Sibal. I'm doing an anthropological study of this Sasquatch community. Welcome to Pedis Mountain."

"Thank you," Karsten said and shook her hand. "I'm Karsten Roth."

She nodded. "I saw your photos from Borneo. Just amazing."

He smiled and gave her a thank you that was more than politeness. She turned to me.

"You must be Innis. I've read your material about the elusive Yeti. It's interesting work."

"Interesting is an interesting word," I said. "It's tough to know how it's intended."

She took my arm. "Walk with me, all of you. Everyone's behind the hall."

As we strolled past the fire pit, she said, "You seem to think of them as a tribal society."

I shrugged. "I don't have any strong opinions. But I have to admit, a group of nomadic hunter-gatherers does seem pretty tribal to me. Is that not the right word, scientifically?"

"It's not that," she said. "But I believe there's more here than people are seeing. Sasquatch, Yeti, the Mothman, Ontario's Old Yellow Top, the Cornish Owlman… I could go on and on. If this is a tribe, it has somehow managed to spread itself throughout the world and, in the case of the Mothman, to travel the world without detection. Eight feet tall and more, with… well, you can't miss the smell."

Karsten and I laughed. Jake looked irritated.

"I think they want us to think they're tribal. Some kind of offshoot from the great apes or a missing link for humanity. Whether they're going to show me anything more than that façade while I'm working here… that's difficult to say."

Karsten, who had been taking shots of the buildings, stopped and looked at her. "If they are not, as you say, this missing link… what do you think they might be?"

She smiled. "Would you believe…." And she pointed at the sky.

I laughed. "Oh, come on. That rumour has been around for as long as mankind has had rumours. No one takes it seriously."

"No one except a woman who's been living with them for coming on two years," Mina said without rancour. "But discount me if you want. It doesn't matter. You're here to rubberneck, and I'm sure you'll have opportunities for that."

We rounded the corner of the hall, and there they were, bigger than life and twice as rank. At least a dozen of the beings were standing around the splintered remains of what seemed to have been a tool shed. Tools were scattered across the grass. Mina went to stand beside one of the smaller Sasquatch, tapped it on the shoulder, and gestured with her hands.

Karsten frowned. "Is that sign?"

"ASL," Jake said.

"American Sign Language," I said for Karsten's benefit, since they probably used something else in Germany. "Now that's interesting."

"What is?" Karsten asked.

"They use ASL with apes because they don't have the physical structure needed to form human speech. It may be the same with the Sasquatch. And either they don't want to teach us their language or we're not capable—"

He stopped, as Mina had returned to us. "You're in luck. You see that shed over there?"

I nodded. "Seen better days."

"It saw those better days yesterday," Mina said. "Got trashed overnight. Something's been running rampant around here. They've had enough. They want to go out hunting for it."

"We're going hunting with Sasquatch?" I asked. It sounded like a once in a lifetime opportunity.

"Looks that way," she said. "As long as you're ready to leave right away."

"Born ready," I told her. "Should we take our own vehicle?"

"Was it a Land Rover? I guess that would be okay. I'll have to take my Jeep since my gear's in there, but you can follow me."

The Sasquatch were communicating in that same whistle and grunt language I'd either heard or dreamed a hundred times in the Himalayas. It sounded almost digital, like a fax machine's handshake, and I wondered if there might be something to Mina's theory about Bigfoot being more than just a hairy face.

Without warning—or at least without warning to anyone who couldn't understand their language—they ran past us. It was incredible. The power in their limbs, the easy lope that gave them a pace faster than my best sprint... the sheer size of them up close. This was what kept me searching for the Yeti no matter how many times I'd failed. Whether they were our relatives or not, I considered them some of the most compelling entities on an increasingly interesting Earth.

We followed Mina's Jeep, which followed a fleet of Jeeps that were missing their rag tops. Shaggy heads and torsos stuck out the tops of the vehicles. The dirt road that took us behind the hall and into the woods was rocky and rutted, but I'd been on a lot worse. I had reason to believe, for example, that this road was probably free of mines.

"*Scheiße,*" Karsten said. It was a curse of amazement, not anger.

I followed his eyes and saw something that made me blink.

"Is that a prank?" I asked as calmly as I could.

Jake's eyes flickered to the left of the road and back. "You could say that," he said. "The Rubedo students like to make animals and set them loose up here. We've got a fair number of jackalope in these hills."

"Hardly seems viable," Karsten said.

"Most things out here aren't viable," Jake said. "They're extinct."

As he said it, I saw movement at the left of the road and gripped the dashboard in surprise.

"Stop!" Karsten and I said at once. Karsten was already half out the window, camera aimed behind us.

"No," Jake said. "We're staying with the group. What did you see?"

"Thylacine," Karsten said.

"Tasmanian wolf," I said.

Jake didn't seem impressed. "Got more than a few of those too. Someone's got to be taking them inside for winter because they're not good in this climate. I don't know why anyone would bother. Fuckin' angry little things."

"I'd be angry too if I'd been hunted to extinction before the Turn," I said. "You've got to be a little mean to get by in some places."

"In all places," Jake grumbled. "Rumour is there are unicorn around here, but no one knows for sure. Hang on."

We took a hard left, and Karsten made a mewling sound that he would no doubt deny if confronted about it. We straightened, swooped onto a flat piece of land next to an intimidating drop-off, and stopped short to avoid driving right up the back of Mina's Jeep.

Once we thought we'd be steady on our feet, we left the Land Rover and joined Mina alongside the Sasquatch.

"What's happening?" I asked her.

She was signing frantically and gave me an impatient wave. Karsten was looking around the clearing, probably searching for more impossible animals.

"That sucks," she said.

"What sucks?" I inquired.

Finally she turned to me. "Some jackass—jackasses, more likely—made a tulpa bear up here and left it to run around. The Sasquatch have some kind of ritual they want to do. They think they can convince it to hibernate for a century or so."

"Delaying the problem," Karsten said.

Mina leaned against one of the Sasquatch Jeeps. "Agreed, but they don't like to destroy thoughtforms if they can avoid it. I don't know why."

Karsten turned to me. "I'd like to go hunting."

"He wants to see if he can get photos of some of the rare animals around here," I said. "Is that okay?"

"As long as he's back here by the time the ritual starts," she said. "I can hit my Jeep's horn to let him know. It's better if people aren't wandering around when they call out the tulpa."

"Thank you for speaking as if I were not here," Karsten told us. "Now I will not, in fact, be here." He marched off into the woods, and Mina watched with a grin.

"He's adorable," she said.

I nodded. "A little bit."

A few feet away, Jake watched the Sasquatch with a look of distaste. He didn't move. He said nothing. Whatever was bothering him had to be big. I wondered if I even wanted to know.

Afternoon, June 17
Karsten Roth

I HAD about half an hour in the woods before the horn blew and spent it kneeling before a dodo. It approached me with no fear, just as sailors said the dodos had behaved before they had died out. Of course this dodo would conform to those reports because those reports were the cloth it had been cut from—as much a thoughtform as the bear.

It was a thoughtform that liked to be scratched beneath the chin.

It tried to waddle behind me as I returned to the open space, but I deliberately left it behind so it would not ask for a chin scratch from a bear.

I went to stand beside Innis, who was leaning against a vehicle. Mina was signing with the Sasquatch. Jake was to one side, watching. His face never changed. I wondered if I could ride back to Pedis Mountain with Mina instead of with this stiff and disturbing man. Surely Innis would welcome a chance to privately mend fences with Jake.

The Sasquatch formed a half circle facing the woods. They had procured drums from somewhere. They also had long wooden pipes, like recorders, made from the limbs of trees. Mina left them and stood next to Innis.

"You can join them, if you want," she said. "Beat a drum. Would that be good for your book?"

"Hell yes," Innis said. "There's nothing like getting the authentic experience."

He went to the Sasquatch, who seemed to be expecting him. They cleared a space and handed him a drum. It was a one-handed drum for the Sasquatch; it rested on the palm of one hand and was beat with the other. Innis needed both hands to hold it and had to sit, the drum balanced on his knees. He looked as comfortable and natural in this place as he did at the hotel bar.

I moved out of the way. It was important in these situations always to be out of the way.

The Sasquatch began to sing. It was loud in a way that music from speakers could not be, a sound that seemed to be from everywhere and everything, coming up from the ground itself and pouring down like rain. It went through me sideways, like a sirocco. It was keening and deep at once. Mina was recording it, and I thought that might be the most pointless thing I had ever seen. No small microphone was going to capture a sound so large.

Innis was concentrating on keeping time with the other drummers. I think that he did not even notice, at first, when the shape of a great bear took form in the middle of the singers. The tulpa roared, and his voice filled an empty place in the sound that I did not until that moment know was there.

They sang to him. He roared to them. Mina held out steel and plastic as if either belonged here. I felt someone at my side.

Jake had come to stand next to me. "Are you getting your pictures?" he whispered in my ear.

"Of course not," I whispered back. Anyone knew you couldn't take photographs during a ritual of that kind. Pictures could disturb the balance.

"I know you're not used to this place, but things are different here," he told me. "Our spirits are worldly. You can get a shot."

The bear was a shifting fog, layers of grey tulle that became nothing, turned, became a bear, turned again. It would be a shot unlike anything I had seen captured before. I looked at Jake.

"Go ahead," he said. "What did Innis hire you for?"

I hadn't taken a shot yet that I thought was really worth the expense of taking me to the Dominion. I thought, Jake must know. He lives here. I raised my camera and took my shot.

The bear's roar became louder and broader, no longer fitting neatly in the space left by the Sasquatch song. It hurt to hear, and I backed away, not knowing what was behind me. The bear saw this and charged, leaping over Sasquatch as if they were small rises in the ground. I stumbled backward until there was no more land beneath me.

I fell.

Chapter Thirteen

Innis Stuart

I DIDN'T actually see Karsten go over the cliff. He and I both caught a break there, because my impulse would have been to jump after him, and that wouldn't have helped anyone.

What I did see was the bear charging, and I heard people yelling—some screaming. It took a moment before I realized where Karsten had gone. The bear was standing at the edge, spewing rage down the cliff's face. I climbed the Jeep nearest the cliff and, from its roof, could see Karsten a few feet down, clinging to a small outcropping. He didn't look as if he could stay there long.

"Jesus Christ," I said. I was cold clear through. My hands shook.

"He decided to take a picture," Jake said. "Like a goddamned amateur. That's why the bear charged him."

It seemed impossible. Karsten was anything but an amateur. But anyone could make a mistake. I didn't care. I was a little preoccupied by him hanging on to that cliff's edge, about to take a fall even a Sasquatch wouldn't be likely to survive.

"What can we do?" I demanded of Mina as I scrambled off the Jeep.

She shook her head. Her eyes were wide and shocky. "The ritual was interrupted," she said.

She didn't have to say any more. Interrupting a ritual was like using half a bottle of antibiotics. It empowered the thing you were trying to contain.

"Fuck," I said. A writer, gifted with a word for every situation. "Fuck. Fuck."

I was breathing so hard that the air felt like sandpaper on my lungs. I could charge the bear. It might go after me instead. I was on the ground and headed for it when I heard the sound.

I thought at first that it was just my heart in my ears, but then the light in the sky changed, and I saw birds, not hundreds but thousands, coming toward us from the east. As they came closer, I realized I was seeing something that hadn't been seen anywhere else on the continent for more than a century, though at one time it had been as common as dust storms on the plains. It was passenger pigeons, enough to turn the day to dusk.

I stopped because they were headed directly to where I was going, right at the bear.

They passed the trees opposite the cliff face and dropped low, nearly level with the ground on our side. The bear roared at them and stood on its hind legs. The birds kept coming. They reached the tulpa bear and kept on coming, driving right through him. I saw scraps of him, the swirling grey that shaped him, clinging to their beaks and falling from their backs and claws. In seconds, the bear was nothing more substantial than an old spiderweb on the forest floor. The birds angled up and over the trees until they were out of sight.

Before I could move, before the first wisps of the tulpa bear fell to the ground, a Sasquatch reached down with one massive arm and rescued Kar. The poor guy was so pale that his skin looked like milky quartz, and his widened pupils made his eyes seem black.

I rushed forward and put an arm around Karsten's shoulders as the Sasquatch let him go, pulling him close against my side. He was shaking, and two feverish blotches of red were spreading across his cheekbones. I guided him toward the Jeep, wanting to get him out of there as quickly as I could.

"I am sorry," he said, his voice so soft I could barely hear him.

"Es macht nicht," I said.

"He said it would be all right," Karsten said.

I looked at him. "What?"

"Jake told him to take the picture," Mina said.

She was standing a few feet away, glaring at Jake. Jake turned his head at the sound of his name.

"What? Did you say I told him to do that? Don't be ridiculous."

It was ridiculous. Jake knew better than most people what the protocol was for a ritual of that kind. But Karsten was nodding.

"He said it was different in the Dominion."

Jake narrowed his eyes. "I did not. Christ. Can't admit you fucked up, hey?"

Mina kept glaring at him even as she spoke to Karsten. "I'm sorry, Karsten. I didn't realize what was happening until it was too late to stop you."

"It is not your fault," Karsten said.

I leaned him against the side of the Jeep and, once I was sure his legs wouldn't give out, stepped toward Jake.

"Is this true?"

He screwed up his face. "Come on. You know me better than that."

"Not these days," I said. "Again. Did you tell him to take that picture?"

Jake raised his hands to the heavens. "It was a joke, okay? Who would have guessed the kid would be stupid enough to take me seriously?"

The next thing he said was "*Uggggh*," and he said it because my fist had in that moment made contact with his mouth. He staggered back and put a hand to the trickle of blood.

"What the shit?"

"Listen up," I said. "Karsten is here on my ticket. You pull that kind of stupid crap with him, you're pulling it with me. And incidentally, ever since we got to town, I've preferred him to you, old friend. I don't know what has crawled up your asshole and died, but you need to have it removed."

"No, you listen up," he snapped. "I only took this bullshit tour guide gig because you were the one who offered it to me. I have more important work to do. You don't like having me around? Not a problem. I quit."

He stormed past me to the Land Rover. I had no desire to go after him. Watching him without even knowing I was doing it, I took out my phone and asked it to find me the first security company in the book.

Karsten Roth

INNIS ARRANGED for someone from another security company to meet us at the border of the Dominion. He was pale and out of sorts, pacing as he spoke on the phone.

Mina let us borrow her Jeep to get there. I waited until we were in the Jeep and out of sight of the Sasquatch before I said it again. "I'm sorry."

"Don't even say that," Innis said. "That was not your damned fault. I'm sorry Jake is being such a complete asshole. I do not know what his problem is."

"Stress?" I said.

It was the only polite response I could think of. Innis looked at me. I could not read his expression.

"Maybe."

"Watch the road," I said.

He kept his eyes on the road as he said, "It was his mistake, not yours." Then he smiled and glanced at me. How soon he forgot about watching the road. "Anyway, anyone can screw up. Did you ever hear about the time I went to see Duha Noche in Argentina?"

"Not that I recall," I said.

"I'm not surprised," Innis mused, "considering how many people I've paid not to discuss it."

"I did hear she retired a few years ago."

"Uh-huh. See, I spent about a year, off and on, trying to talk my way into an audience with her. I'm not a big fan of prognosticators, but I figured a hundred world leaders can't be wrong. She had to have something. So I finally get the okay for an interview. I walk into her apartment and it's tiny. She's tiny—about four feet five. All her furniture is just... little. So I barge in and the first thing I do is knock over a table inside the door. Everything goes flying. I grab the first thing I see falling and it's her Tarot deck. The deck fucking screams, catches fire, my hands get burned, and as I'm running water over them, she tells me I've ruined everything and she'll never tell the future again. Picture it—I've cut the world's most powerful people off from their chosen fortune teller. I was running around town, firing out money like a defective ATM. I was never here. Tell no one. Forget we had this conversation. I never did decide whether it was more expensive than humiliating or the other way around."

I stared out my window, hoping to see more of the wildlife. It was merely for the sake of interest, because I couldn't bring myself to lift my camera.

"I was in Kashmir searching for the giant owl," I said.

Innis laughed. "Total snipe hunt."

"Perhaps," I said.

"Karsten. Everyone knows there's no giant owl in Kashmir. All those 'I spotted the giant owl at midnight' messages are intelligence code."

I shrugged. "Some say yes. Some say no. I thought, if I can get a picture of the owl, that will be the answer."

"I assume you didn't get a picture, since I would have heard about it otherwise."

I smiled. "I… how would you say it… downplayed my trip. I was standing at the hillside, and I thought I saw something in the trees. I was moving backward to get the shot, and I wasn't paying attention to where I was going, of course, as you now know I do.…"

He laughed and squeezed my leg, just above the knee. "I'm not likely to forget it."

"When I looked down, I saw I was standing in a field of Crocus sativus."

He put his hand back on the wheel. "You stepped in some crocus flowers? So?"

"I crushed several square feet of the world's finest saffron."

Even in profile, I could see Innis's eyes grow wider. "Fuuuuuck. What would that run a guy?"

"Nothing, if the guy runs," I said. "I felt bad, but I didn't know who to pay, and I wasn't certain I would be asked to pay in money alone."

Innis laughed. "That's not good."

"It's very bad," I agreed.

We drove in silence for a few minutes. Then Innis said, "Did I tell you about the time I met Roland the Headless Thompson Gunner?"

"I have only known you for a few days," I reminded him. "You have not yet told me most of your conspicuous bullshit."

Innis grinned. "You've known me long enough to have my number."

"I have closely read your work," I told him.

"Ah. It doesn't stand up, does it? I'm not saying none of that stuff happened, to me or someone else, but… Kar, I am in the business of telling a good yarn."

I looked at him. "Does it not concern you that others might take your advice?"

"You said you've read my work closely. Have you ever read anything with more disclaimers in it?"

"No," I admitted.

He nodded. "I think I'm okay. So. As long as we're being honest here… I have a question for you."

I watched the trees as we went by. It looked to me as if the trees instead were going by us, late for an appointment and in a rush.

"You can ask," I said.

"Tunguska. Seriously. How the hell did you get in there?"

"Seriously," I said, "I do not know. I walked in. No force of earth or man attempted to stop me. Everyone thinks there is some great secret, but there is no such thing."

"Must have been a heck of a thing to see," Innis said. He sounded jealous; not in a bitter way, but wistful.

"It was," I said. I wished I could describe it, but this was why I carried a camera. Innis nodded. It seemed he understood.

"Can you imagine seeing the explosion in 1908? What do you think caused it?" I shrugged. "Pointless to speculate."

"Pointless can be fun," Innis said. "Taiga, taiga, burning bright. I wish I could have been there."

"You do not," I told him. "You would have lost your eyebrows at the least, and I can tell you are fond of your face."

He laughed, his voice shaky. Thin and high. It was not simply laughter, but a release of something. He laughed that way for a long time, long enough that I had more than my fill. I placed a hand on his face for a moment and this brought silence to us again.

Innis Stuart

WE DID as Mina had asked and left her Jeep at the city limits, where we were met by the security guard I had ordered over the phone—a giant by the name of Filip Holger. He was an amiable enough guy, with an axe that looked considerably less friendly. He had gone to Oxford, it turned out, and he and Karsten spent most of the drive discussing the benefits and drawbacks of higher education in the UK.

Karsten and I decided to have dinner at Hounfor. It wasn't very creative or adventurous of us, but we liked the food, and we'd had more than enough adventure for the day.

As we walked in, we were greeted by the sound of a reedy voice assaying Dr. John's "I've Been Hoodooed." A quick peek around confirmed my worst fears— the place was, at least for the night, a karaoke bar.

"Wodu karaoke?" Karsten sounded as if he could not believe it.

"Makes sense," I said. "It's a highly participatory religion. Do you want to bug out?"

He shook his head. "Too tired. I'll suffer through."

If the look on the face of the karaoke hostess was any indication, our suffering would be nothing compared to hers. She seemed as if she would consider being menaced by the thoughtform of a bear to be an absolute treat compared with her current profession.

"Big hand for Neil," she said, taking the mic back and shaking off a coating of dark green slime. "Next time, go a little lighter on the swamp juice. Now, let's hear it for Jeremy—he'll be singing 'My John the Conqueror Root.'"

"Love ya, Lynnie!" someone shouted.

The hostess blew him a kiss.

We took what was fast becoming our usual table. Danny Wedo was at his table as well, just over my shoulder... upon which he tapped me as soon as I sat down.

"That's my wife up there," he said.

"How about that," I said. "You got yourself a keeper."

"You know it's true," he said and went back to his plate of white rice.

"I'm sorry you're fighting with Jake," Karsten said abruptly.

"Me too," I said. "But it wasn't my idea. I don't know. This city seems like a stressful place to work. Maybe it's time he moved on. Or took a vacation."

"He is not normally this way?" Karsten asked.

"He... no. I mean, he can be a hard case. He's ex-military. But he was always pretty even-keeled, and he's not basically a bad guy. I've been friends with him since we were kids, and I'm not about to be friends for that long with a complete dick. I don't have the patience."

Karsten smiled. "You seem very patient to me."

"You won't be saying that ten minutes from now when I punch some karaoke singer in the neck."

He picked up the drink menu and looked at it. I couldn't imagine why, unless he'd forgotten how to spell "rum."

"No," I said. "Then I will call you my hero."

We didn't talk much over dinner. We were talked out and played out. It wasn't awkward.

During her break, the karaoke hostess went to Danny's table and put a hand on his shoulder.

"How are you tonight, Mr. Wedo?"

"No need to be so formal, my dear," he said. "We've been married many years."

"You're a sweet man," she said, "and any wife of yours would be lucky. But I think you confuse me with someone else."

"It is possible," he said serenely, "that you have been confused."

"Okay, Mr. Wedo. Enjoy your meal."

When she'd gone off to the bar, Karsten raised his eyebrows at me.

"Do you think, if you tell someone you're married to them often enough, they'll eventually believe you?"

"They might," I said, "or they might take out a restraining order. People being what they are, I'd call it a fifty-fifty proposition."

I set my drink down and looked at Karsten. He probably needed a distraction, after the day he'd had. We were on good terms, maybe even better than the day before. He certainly hadn't gotten any less attractive in the last twenty-four hours. The obvious thing to do was to invite him to join me again.

Except that I was too damned exhausted to be interested in even the finest of opportunities. And too damned chicken to say so.

"So," I said.

"So you punched your friend today and are tired and miserable," Karsten said without preamble. "Tonight you should get some sleep."

I stood, took his face in my hands, and kissed his forehead as a good-night.

"For a surly bastard," I said, "you are goddamned easy to get along with sometimes."

Karsten Roth

THE ONLY thought on my mind as I approached my room was that I hoped the haunted painting had finally been removed while I was away. I was exhausted and completely unprepared when three men stepped from an alcove beside my room and surrounded me. One had white skin. Not Caucasian but white. His clothes, too, were white, an identical shade. There was another with bright red skin and clothing, and a third with everything the purest black.

All three were holding guns on me.

"You're coming with us," they told me.

I did not feel in a position to argue. They rushed me down the stairs and out the back of the hotel, into a waiting black car. One drove, while the others sat in the back on either side of me.

"Nothing to worry about," Red said. "Manya wants a word."

"As long as she does not want my last words," I said.

The three of them laughed.

"No, no," White said. "If she wanted you dead, we would have killed you already."

"Unless," Black said, "you had gravely offended her and she wanted to do it herself."

I could not think of anything I might have done to gravely offend a criminal with metal teeth, but I also could not think what might give offence to a person of that type. This speculation occupied my thoughts as we traveled into the Scree.

I thought it was a shame that Innis was missing the trip because here was the excitement he had been looking for. People were shooting at each other with everything they had—bullets, fire, lightning. Buildings already charred from previous nights were burning merrily now. Through the middle of it trudged zombies, so slow and addled with disease that they could not think to hide. When something hit them, they cried like injured birds.

"Another night in Fun Town," Red said.

We drove directly into Manya's building, through a wall that wasn't a wall and then was again. White got out and held the door for me. I stepped out, and Manya came from the shadows to greet me. I could not be certain, but I thought she might have formed from the shadows themselves.

"Karsten. I apologize for any distress. Please, come with me."

It was late for the pretence that any of this was an invitation, but it did not seem wise to say so. I followed her into a small room, no larger than the bedroom of my compact apartment in Berlin, and sat where she said I should.

The room was done in red, from the Turkish carpet and claret paint to the few pieces of art in narrow cabinets along the back wall. Unlike in the other space, there was no breath of green. Manya and I sat in dark wood chairs with crushed red upholstery, small tables to the left of us both. The wood of the furniture was carved into complicated scenes of forests and animals and hunters hidden behind the trees.

"I am," Manya said, "in an unusual position. I am finding something awkward."

"Is it something I've done?" I asked, hoping to God it was not. "I apologize if so."

She folded her hands, those talons, and leaned forward as if we had a secret between us. "Karsten. I will be blunt. Do I know you?"

"Before I came here?" I said. "I do not think so."

She nodded. "I don't either. And yet, and yet."

She shut her eyes, giving me a moment in which I could look away from her face. I saw, for the first time, a painting on the wall above her chair. It was of an explosion in endless Siberian woods, carving a bowl for a lake. The same lake that had, a century later, spilled itself out before me.

She spoke, and I thought from her words that she must have seen me staring at the painting, but I looked to her face and found her eyes still closed.

"I often dream of Tunguska," she was saying. "More since you visited me the other day."

I almost asked if she had been there. She might not have been insulted. She might have been that old.

"I think of it often," I said. It was not everything I might have said, but it was true.

"Yes. The place of your greatest success. I am going to presume upon the intimacy I feel we have. Even if neither of us recalls any reason I should feel it."

I tried not to think of intimacy in the usual sense, or the things that might happen to a poor soul who was with her in that way.

She said, "You stand very close to your friend Innis. Perhaps you should not stand so close. He is, I think, accident prone. I would not want to see you hurt."

This was tricky. I spoke slowly. "Pardon me," I said, "but what does that mean?"

"What I said," she told me. "More or less. I forgot to offer you anything when you arrived."

"It's late," I said. "No, thank you."

She nodded. "You seem tired."

"But about Innis," I persisted.

She shrugged. She had an elegance, even at her size.

"I have a feeling. I think you should go to bed. I'll have my men return you to your hotel."

She rose and left, and a minute later, they came for me and brought me back. We did not speak along the way. I was in my room half an hour later. I rang Innis in his room, but there was no answer. I assumed he was asleep.

The picture was still there, but I was somewhat relieved to see that it had, at least, been covered with a sheet and could not see me anymore. Whatever breath fogged the painting's mirror caused the sheet to waft up and float down again until dawn.

Innis Stuart

I SHOULDN'T have been surprised, I guess, to find Jake waiting for me inside my room. At least he didn't meet me with a punch in the face.

Instead he was sitting on the bed, looking stiff and uncomfortable.

"I'm sorry about earlier today," he said.

I hung up my coat and went to the kettle on the bureau.

"I'm sure you are," I said. "Tea?"

"Sure," he said. "Thanks."

I picked two bags of bloodroot tea from the basket and dropped them into two mugs. The kettle was one of the instant heat generators that were all the rage. Rumour had it there was some kind of spirit inside. I didn't care for the idea.

I poured the water into the mugs and turned to look Jake in the eye. "What is it with you?" I asked.

He stared at me. "What do you mean?"

"You're not yourself," I said. "Is it stress? This can't be an easy place to live."

He turned flat eyes on me. I didn't see much of Jake in them. "I don't need an easy place," he said.

"I never said you did," I told him, "but everyone needs vacations, at least. When's the last time you had one?"

"I'm fine," he said. "You have a thread loose."

It was so off-kilter that I didn't even understand the words. "What?"

"A thread," he said. "Let me get it."

He took out his pocket knife, the same one he'd had since he first joined the military. I'd been there when his dad gave it to him. He moved closer to me, and I felt uncomfortable. I pushed the feeling away. He reached for me, and at the last second I saw his feint, the flicker of his eyes, his true intention. The knife was coming for my gut.

I dodged him once but was immediately hit with the fact that I'd been lucky. With Jake's training, I didn't present any kind of challenge. It occurred to me I would likely die here at his hand, and the thought was so strange and horrible that I thought I might be dead already, going through mental torture in whatever passed for hell.

I looked up and saw Jake frozen, knife in hand, rage now livening his eyes.

"Son of a bitch," he forced through his teeth. I knew, somehow, he didn't mean me.

I reached into his coat, hoping he had his cuffs in there. To my intense relief, my hand closed around them almost immediately. His arms were stiff, but I managed to take one and bring it close enough to the bed that I could lock him in place. I took the knife away and threw it into the bathroom, then came back and stood a few feet from him.

"Jake!" I yelled, looking him in the eye. "Jake!"

He blinked once, twice. His free arm fell.

"My god," he said. "What did I do?"

"You snapped," I told him. "Did you want to tell me again that you're fine?"

"You're right," he said. His voice was thick, slow. "I need a vacation. I thought... I don't know what I thought. That you weren't you."

"I know the feeling," I said. "Jesus. I hate seeing you this way."

"I'm sorry," he murmured. "It's been... I've had a rough few years."

I put a hand on his shoulder, still wary, and squeezed. "Maybe you need to see someone."

He scowled. "Fuck that."

"I know you tough guys don't care for therapy," I said. "But you have to admit, you're not much good right now."

"Fuck that," he said again. "I'll take a vacation."

"Well," I told him, "it's a start."

I handed him his mug of tea and he took a sip, then snarled and spat it out.

I jumped back. "Mr. Manners," I said.

He was flicking his tongue in and out of his mouth, scraping the top of it against his teeth. "Too hot," he managed between tongue flicks. He set the cup down. "You can let me go."

I didn't know if that were true, but I wasn't prepared to keep him there all night. Cautiously I undid the cuff. Jake stood.

"Sorry again," he said. "Didn't you tell me you wanted to see the Merrows?"

"Yeah," I said, "but I can't talk anyone into letting me down there. You know sea people are cagey. Why? Do you have an in?"

"Maybe," he said. "I owe you. And that snarky little fuck you're working with. Let me see what I can do. I'll come by around ten tomorrow."

"Okay," I said. On any other night, I would have shaken his hand before he left. On a drunken night, I might have hugged him. That night I watched him leave and bolted the door behind him.

I picked up my mug of tea on the way to the bed, glancing at the package the bag had been in. "Purification," it said. "Banishment."

I was hoping for something to soothe my nerves. I took a sip, expecting it to burn me.

It had already gone cold.

Chapter Fourteen

Morning, June 18
Karsten Roth

BREAKFAST AT Hounfor was corn muffins and thyme honey. As we ate, I told Innis about my trip to Manya's house, including her assertion that he was soon to have an accident.

"Jesus. Are you okay?" he asked.

"Evidently," I said, gesturing at my intact form.

"Okay, fuck me for asking," he said.

He took my chin in his hand and ran his thumb across my lower lip as he searched my face for bruises and my expression for some sign of trauma. Whatever he saw seemed to satisfy him. He ran the back of his hand across my cheek lightly before returning to his breakfast.

After a few bites he looked to me thoughtfully and said, "What do you think she meant by accident?"

I stared at him. "I imagine she is frightened that you will trip on an untied shoelace. What do you think she meant, for God's sake?"

Innis rolled muffin crumbs off his fingertips. "I'm not that stupid, Karsten. I know it was a threat. I'm just wondering if she meant it as a direct threat from her to me, or if she was saying that someone else was gunning for me."

"She would give me no details."

He nodded. "Well, it's funny you say that because Jake tried to kill me last night."

My coffee cup dropped from my hand. It was a good thing my hand had been resting barely a centimetre above the table.

"He...?"

"Tried to kill me," Innis said patiently. "He snapped. He didn't think I was me. I think he's seeing things."

I shook my head. "This is what you offer as reassurance?"

Innis reached for another muffin.

"Good people can go a little loopy when you put them under enough stress," he said. "Did you ever hear about the security guard who worked for the nameless dictator in South America? It was on that island near the Galapagos, where no one uses names."

I nodded. I knew the place, though I had not gone there. There had been much talk of it while the shamans had climbed Aconcagua. There is power in names, they had said. Perhaps this silly, superstitious land of no name would one day be proven wise.

"And the fate of this real guy?" I asked.

Innis swallowed. There was honey on his chin. "He was a regular person when he went there. For a mercenary type, anyway. But the whole name thing got to him and he came to believe that bullets couldn't harm him unless they had his name on them. Literally written on them. He started taking guns from people and going through the bullets, threatening to have them arrested if he found his name. Actually since it's illegal to use names there, it wasn't that crazy—aside from the fact that no one had put his name on anything and he had no reason to think they had. He got pretty obsessive. The last I heard, he was locked up in a hospital in Guayaquil."

I dipped a napkin in water and gave it to Innis. "Your chin," I said. "That is an interesting story, but not so interesting as the one about Jake attempting to murder you."

Innis took the napkin and wiped the honey away. He was quick and impatient. "The point, Karsten, is that the kind of work Jake does, in this sort of environment... it can get to a person. I think it's only right that I cut the guy some slack. I'm going to encourage him to get help, obviously, but it can be a tough sell because guys like Jake don't like to show weakness."

"And this is it?" I asked him. "This is all you have to say on the matter?"

"I don't know what more you want to know. It's not much of a story. I've given away the ending by not being dead."

"Do you think this is funny?" I asked him.

He stopped smiling. "No. I think he's a mess. He needs to get out of this town."

"Perhaps after he has killed you, he can have your seat on the plane."

Innis rubbed his eyes. "I don't think he'll try to kill me again. He's picking us up at ten, by the way."

I shoved my chair back and stood. "Are you mad?"

"It's been alleged," Innis said as he hooked an arm around my waist. "Look, I wouldn't have taken his offer to make it up to us—" He paused while I choked on that. "—but he thinks he can get us into the Merrows. Do you have any idea how long I've been trying to talk my way into the Merrows? I can't make this happen by myself."

I stepped out of his grasp and took my seat again. "That is not credible."

He set down his coffee cup. "What do you mean?"

I should not have said it, but I was angry. "People are happy to do whatever you ask them to do. As you ought to know."

He seemed confused, perhaps hurt. "What are you talking about?"

"Do you honestly think," I asked, "you are so smooth-talking that you are convincing everyone to see the world your way?

"What are you suggesting?"

I slapped a hand on the counter. The bartender glanced up, saw we didn't want anything, and returned to wiping glasses. I would have thought in this place they would have used a glamour of some kind to keep the dust away.

"You are not so obtuse in any other respect. You have a knack, Innis. A gift. I have been watching you here, and I know something of your career, and it is indisputable."

"I dispute it," he said. "I'm just folks, Karsten. Nothing special about me."

"Horseshit," I said. "You have something."

He shook his head, his lips pressed tightly together. I thought he wanted to tell me to fuck myself and was half afraid that I would be compelled to do so.

"I've seen it," I told him. "Again and again since we arrived here."

"I don't do anything," Innis insisted. "I don't make people do things."

He seemed horrified, as if I and not-Jake had attempted to place a knife in his heart. A hand fell on my shoulder and I startled.

"All will be well," Danny Wedo said. He had icing sugar on his lips.

"Thank you," I said, though I had my doubts. He patted my shoulder and returned to his seat.

Innis Stuart

WHATEVER WAS wrong with Jake, he was still a man of his word. At ten on the nose he was in the lobby. I had thought Karsten would dig in his heels, but he had apparently decided that he needed to chaperone me. That or, like me, he couldn't resist a chance to see the Merrows.

Jake went so far as to nod at Karsten, which he probably thought amounted to an apology. Karsten did not hit him, which I thought amounted to an exceptional show of grace.

I tried to ignore what Karsten had said about me and this supposed quirk of mine. It was ridiculous and spoke more to the disorienting quality of the Dominion than to whatever he thought he had seen. Hell, I'd been with me all my life. If I had something special, I'd know. As for Kar, he'd get over it once we got clear of Crazytown.

Speaking of Crazytown, we were about to intersect with one of the Dominion's craziest quarters. The Merrows, known to locals as the Wet End, sprawled under the Pacific from about a half mile off the shore to several miles farther west. It was populated by the usual suspects—merpeople, selkies, and the merrows for which it was named. None of them, in my experience or anyone's experience that I knew of, were particularly friendly to landlubbers. They called us "dustheels" and other less flattering names.

As we drove to the shore, Jake explained that he hadn't received permission to take us to the underwater city.

"I have some contacts, though," he said, "and they're willing to meet us in the Talk Tank."

I'd heard of it. Most people had. The Tank had been built offshore during the early days of the Merrows' development so that officials from above and below the water could meet with relative convenience. It was half in and half out of the water, with couches for dustheels and tanks for the wet ones. Since underwater types were notoriously snooty about mixing with dustheels, the few conversations held in the Talk Tank amounted to a large percentage of the conversations anyone anywhere had had with mermen and their ilk.

"I'm happy with whatever I can get," I said honestly. "They won't even take my calls."

I looked at Karsten to see if he cared to express disbelief again, but he was eyeballing the back of Jake's head and had no time for me.

Jake had arranged for a small boat. That was another thing that hadn't changed about him. He was always well prepared.

The air was sharp with cold, and it only got worse as we headed offshore. The salt air, usually refreshing, now reminded me of the smell of Sasquatch. I was beginning to regret breakfast.

Karsten seemed in his element on the boat. No surprise. Germans, even the inland ones, were born to wear cable-knit sweaters and stare expressionlessly at the horizon. When they were blue-eyed, like Karsten was, their eyes matched the colour of northern seas.

Instead of just staring, though, Karsten was taking pictures of the Dominion skyline while he could. There was heavy fog, and by the time we reached the edge of the Merrows, it would likely be obscured.

"Feeling any better?" I asked Jake.

He nodded. "I didn't have much sleep the last few nights. I've been on a case. Got my eight hours last night."

"Good," I said and clapped his shoulder.

"Keep an eye out for Caddy," he advised Karsten.

"The Merrows has a golf course?" Karsten asked.

It was deadpan, but I was pretty sure he'd meant it as a joke. Jake didn't smile.

"He's our local serpent," he said.

Karsten didn't go so far as to smile at Jake, but his shoulders relaxed a bit under his borrowed slicker.

"I'll hope for good fortune," Karsten said.

He didn't say whether he was hoping Caddy would dance in front of his lens or hoping that Caddy wouldn't pop up beneath us and overturn the boat. Odds were he was wishing for both.

He seemed to have softened and I decided to see whether he was open to conversation.

"Friend of mine went looking for the Turtle Lake Monster," I said. "Years ago."

"I don't know of that one," Karsten told me.

"Yeah, it's obscure. Middle of Saskatchewan, not even that big of a lake. Some water dweller—I forget what kind—asked my friend for passage to the lake. Said he had to talk to the monster. Well, you know, he didn't say monster. But whatever. Anyway, my friend was a photog at the time, so he said sure, as long as he could take pictures."

"I sense a moral coming," Karsten said.

I grinned and looked at Jake. Jake was gazing at the ocean, seemingly deaf to us. Fair enough. He was responsible for getting us wherever we had to go, and that was probably more difficult than it looked.

"No one knows for sure what happened," I said. "The merguy or whatever, he rented a truck that could hold a fair-sized aquarium and that's how my friend took him across the country. Probably wasn't very comfortable, but you know water people and teleportation. Or maybe you don't."

"They will not use it," Karsten said. "One more reason we should all be wary of teleportation. Go on."

"Right, so they get to the lake, and the merguy hops in and my friend follows him by boat… and that's all anyone sees or hears of them for days. Then the merguy shows up at the main beach, dragging the boat. My friend's in it, but he's not talking to anyone. Flat-out catatonic. He still is. He's in his childhood bedroom with nurses looking after him, which he might once have considered a dream come true except I don't think this is how he would have wanted it. And the merguy, get this, insists that nothing happened. The monster never showed up. All he cared about was getting back to the ocean."

Karsten had watched me carefully through all of that. His camera was in his lap.

"Maybe I should speak to these people," he said, "in your stead."

I tried not to roll my eyes. Rolling my eyes was childish, and I needed to stop. "I'm a pro, Karsten. I don't particularly care for water dwellers, but that's no reason I can't interview them."

"How noble of you," he said, getting full value out of every word.

I did roll my eyes at that. He'd earned it.

"The day I meet one who isn't a prick," I said, "I will gladly change my mind."

I glanced at Jake, hoping he hadn't been listening. It seemed he hadn't. I took a deep breath in celebration of that small mercy. I had a feeling anything he added to the conversation would have been inflammatory, and the last thing I needed was Karsten and Jake getting into a scuffle on top of the Merrows in a small and tippable boat.

Karsten, calm and steady, went back to scanning the waters for the Dominion's pet serpent.

The Tank became visible as the Dominion disappeared behind us. It was a bright yellow box, about fifteen feet across, jutting bravely out of the waves. Jake pulled up beside it with expert skill, showing the years he'd spent guiding boats across Manitoba's endless lakes. He tied off, pushed the steel buttons of a lock, and shoved open a hatch. I pictured the Dominion's mayor and officials from Canada and the U.S. scrambling awkwardly out of their skiffs and into the narrow opening, because it was the only way the merpeople would deign to speak with them. I couldn't imagine something of the kind happening anywhere else.

Karsten Roth

IT WAS not easy to take photographs and keep my eyes always on Jake. I did my best. Whatever he said, I didn't have the faith that he had not meant Innis harm or that he was feeling much better after a good sleep. I only hoped we would make it back to the mainland.

I was surprised that the merpeople would not talk to Innis, but if anyone could resist charm of any kind, it would be them. I had spoken with them in Borneo. They had taken the bearing of adults who were being kept from an important task by a dull and irritating child.

Some people said the water dwellers were fighting a war at the bottom of the ocean, against kraken or worse. Some called them the defenders of Earth.

I was content to believe this and leave them to their work.

Jake was the last through the hatch. I did not like this. It was the only exit, and he stood beneath it.

Innis was laughing at the accommodations. Ratty plaid couches faced seawater tanks built of scratched Plexiglas. The floor was concrete, only half of it painted.

"I can't believe they use this place," he said. "Isn't it below their usual standards?"

Jake didn't say anything. He was watching Innis, whose back was turned. Carefully I turned to face the tanks, as if taking a photograph. I saw a fire extinguisher to my right. I watched Jake in the water's shifting reflection. I was not surprised, not at all, when he pulled a gun from the pocket of his coat.

Chapter Fifteen

Innis Stuart

"*VORSICHT*!"

By the time my imperfect German told me I had received a warning, it was over. Jake was on the floor, unconscious but breathing. A gun lay beside him. Karsten stood over him, a fire extinguisher in his hands.

"Jesus," I said.

Karsten looked away from Jake to glare at me. "I don't think he'll try to kill me again," he said in a broad Canadian accent.

"I do not sound like that," I said. "Jesus. He's worse off than I thought."

Karsten opened his mouth, then shook his head. "Never mind. Are there ropes in here, do you think?"

"Gotta think there would be," I said.

A quick search turned up ropes that were thin enough to easily tie but thick enough to hold. We had Jake trussed up less than a minute later. For good measure, I put Jake's gun into my jacket pocket. Then I stared at Jake until Karsten's voice distracted me.

"Hello? Who is this? Hello?"

I turned to see him holding his cell phone to his ear and looking confused.

"It's all voices," he said, holding the phone toward me.

A voice like a rasp running over gravel said, "Skiiiiiinbaaaaaag...."

"You need a better EVP filter," I said, showing him the attachment plugged into mine. "With that cheap thing, it's no wonder you're getting ghosts."

"Give me your phone," he said.

I pulled it back. "Why?"

"Because I am calling the police," he said.

"Nuh-uh."

He gaped at me. A real gape, with his jaw slack. "Do you still think your friend is merely cranky?"

"No," I said. "I don't know what I think. But I don't want to bring the police into this. We don't know if we can trust them."

"We don't know if we can trust *them*?" His voice went mouse-high on the last word.

"I need to think. Why would he try to kill me?"

"Here's a thought," Karsten offered. "Have you considered that he might not be himself?"

"I said he wasn't acting like himself. I said that days ago."

"I don't mean not acting like himself." Karsten sat on one of the couches. Dust rose from it as he landed. "I mean, what if Jake is not Jake? He could be possessed or a doppelganger or shapeshifter. Any number of things."

I shook my head. "He remembers things. He knows our past."

"Are you certain? Has he said things only you and he would know? What exactly has he said to you?"

"Nothing much," Jake said from the corner. "As little as possible."

We turned to look at him.

"What did I do, Jake?" I said. I heard my voice shaking. The part of me that made my worst decisions told me to try for a joke. "Is this about me giving your bike a flat tire in the fifth grade?"

Jake didn't smile. To be fair it wasn't much of a joke.

"Wasn't my bike," he said. "I have some bad news for you, Innis."

I sat on the edge of the couch. I was probably blocking Karsten's view, but I didn't care. "What would that be?"

"I'm not Jake."

"Really," Karsten muttered.

I held up a hand for silence. "Go on."

"Jake's pretty well eaten up. This body's coming apart, and I've been knitting it together with what's left of him. He and I had a good run, though. Almost twenty years."

"What the hell are you talking about?" I demanded. "Jake and I were teenagers twenty years ago."

"So was I. You and me and Jake."

The penny dropped, and I slouched against the back of that filthy couch. It moved as Karsten leaned forward to look past me at Jake. Not-Jake.

Carl.

"What is he talking about?" Karsten asked.

"We went to high school," I said, "with a kid named Carl Levon."

"The boy who vanished?" Karsten asked. "And you were all grounded?"

I was surprised enough to turn to at him. He was staring at Jake. Or not-Jake.

"How the hell do you know about that?" I asked Kar.

He looked at me. His pupils were blown, far larger than they should have been even in the dim grey light of the Tank.

"Is that right?" he asked. "Was it Carl who disappeared?"

I wanted to yell at him, shake him, demand to know how he knew enough to ask me that. But he was terrified, and I couldn't stand to make it worse. I couldn't even raise my hand.

"Yeah," I said.

"Have a cigar," Carl said.

I remembered the cigar Jake had put in my pocket in the restaurant, and my stomach lurched. Had that been Jake? Had I seen Jake here at all?

"It was Donna," Karsten said. "I spoke to Donna."

"What?" I said. "Why? How did you—"

Karsten shook his head. He now seemed both terrified and miserable. Had I done that? Either way it was hard to watch. I turned to Jake. Carl.

"Carl wanted to be a magician," I told Karsten, my eyes steady on Carl. "I think he figured he'd get into Rubedo."

"I would have made it," Carl said.

Suddenly, I was more angry than afraid.

How long had he been toying with Jake—and by proxy with me? What had he done back in Brandon? None of us had thought…. Carl's magic, it had never worked out. I chanced another look at Karsten. He was breathing deep and steady, trying to calm himself. I started to explain.

"Carl invited us over one night to help him with some spell he was working on. Neither of us really liked magic, but Carl was a pretty convincing guy, and he talked us into it."

"You don't say," Karsten said.

I eyed him. What the hell was that supposed to mean? Was that a dig about me, what Karsten claimed I could do?

"You're a born peanut gallery," I told him.

"Tell me the rest," he said.

"We never found out what he was trying to do, but we were both pretty sure something went wrong because, like Donna told you, Carl vanished. Puff of smoke, just like the cliché."

"Clichés are clichés for a reason," Carl said. "I didn't go far."

"Apparently not," I said.

"I was inside Jake for a long time," he said, "Watching. I enjoyed seeing you cover up the evidence that we'd been doing magic… getting your stories straight… telling everyone in town that you had no idea what had happened to me."

Karsten put his hands on his knees and his face in his hands, as if that would cover up for me somehow.

"We were scared," I said. "You have to have known that if you were inside him."

"You're both cowards. Doesn't matter. I started getting my turn at the wheel about seven years ago. I moved us here because I thought someone in town might be able to help me step up permanently."

"Manya," Karsten muttered.

Carl looked at him, surprised. "Why would you say that?"

"She warned me. She knew you were trying to kill Innis."

"Fair enough," Carl said. "Yeah… I've been bringing her pieces and parts for a while now. Werewolf change purse. Cop pipe. I don't know what she's got in mind, but she's a smart lady. She thinks she can fix this body up right and hand me the reins."

"It's not your body," I said. "It was your idea to do that spell in the first place, whatever it was. It was you who bitched it up. It needs to go back to Jake."

"There's no Jake for it go back to," Carl said. "I told you. I've been burning that fuel for a long time."

"You're a liar," I said, "Or you're wrong. Take your pick."

Carl raised Jake's dark brows. "Oh?"

"If there were no Jake in there, I'd have been stabbed last night."

No one said anything for heartbeat after heartbeat. I heard the soft thud of something landing ungracefully on the roof of the Tank. I peered through the skylight, which was stained with guano, and saw an albatross watching us with keen interest. Maybe it thought we were giant fish. Maybe it wanted a word with Jake—or Carl—about yesterday's lunch. I turned to Karsten. He had raised his face from his hands.

"You still want to go to the police?"

"I would like that," Karsten said. "Yes."

"Then let's go."

Karsten Roth

AS SOON as Innis put a hand on Jake to move him toward the boat, Jake—or, I supposed, Carl—started to pitch and roll. It was plain that he would not be suitable cargo for our small boat, not even for as long as it would take to reach the Dominion's shore.

"I could take the boat back," I said, "and you could watch him."

Innis shook his head. "I don't believe in splitting up when things get ugly. Watch a horror movie sometime. The results are never good."

I couldn't help smiling, even in those circumstances.

"I bow to your experience and education," I said.

"Yeah, do that," Innis said. "But I'm not seeing another solution."

I wanted to say that Innis had a gun—the gun Carl had aimed at him, in fact—and could use it. But it would have been unfair to ask Innis to do such a thing, and it was possible that he was right. There might be a good man in front of us, waiting to be saved.

I saw the fire extinguisher from the corner of my eye. It was bright red, and so I could not tell if there was blood on it.

"I could hit him again," I suggested.

I did not mean it. Innis smiled a little to show he understood and agreed. It was a chancy thing, to hit someone in the head that way. You never knew what damage you might do. And to do it twice was far more than twice as bad.

"Now that you say that, though…." Innis said.

He did not finish that thought, but instead began to rifle through Jake's—or Carl's—pockets.

"Getting your rocks off?" Carl asked. "You like the ropes, Innis? You like that?"

Innis ignored Carl and continued his search as Carl attempted to twist away from him. As Innis slipped long fingers into the inside breast pocket of Carl's coat, he smiled.

"Ha!"

He pulled out a small foil packet and held it up for me to see. It was red and gold, with writing on it in runes I did not recognize.

"Jake always used to carry sleep dust," Innis said. "Even in the army. He said it came in handy sometimes."

"That is creepy," I said.

I could feel Carl's eyes on me as I said it. Innis looked hurt, and I realized I had said this not about Carl, but about Jake.

"I'm sorry," I said.

"No," Innis said. "I always thought it was a little seedy. But it turns out he was right. There are times when it comes in handy."

"Why don't you just shoot me?" Carl asked as Innis knelt beside him. "Isn't that what you want to do? One shot to the head and dump me over the side? Your little friend there would do it, if you weren't here."

"No," Innis said calmly. "He wouldn't. But I can see where you'd have trouble imagining how a decent person might act. Karsten, cover your mouth and nose and face away from us."

I did as instructed. I then heard some thrashing and assumed it was Carl, trying to avoid the dust. This went on for what seemed an impossibly long time. I imagined Innis must be holding his breath through it all. Finally I heard Innis stand, and turned around. Carl was on his side near the door, unconscious. Innis looked exhausted, and his hands were shaking.

"I've never seen sleep dust given to someone with a concussion," I said. "He probably has a concussion."

"I know," Innis said. "It was a risk. But we'll get him to the cops and they can call a healer or take him to the hospital."

I would have given Innis a moment to catch his breath, but he wanted to move quickly. With difficulty, we rolled Carl into the boat, then climbed in ourselves.

"Goddamn," Innis said softly.

He had said it to himself, I thought. I unhooked us from the Tank and started the boat's small engine. Innis watched Carl as I turned us around, toward the shore.

Innis Stuart

KARSTEN WAS composed and certain steering the boat, eyes on the fog-wrapped coast of the Dominion. He might have fooled me into thinking he was doing all right if he hadn't been so pale. Even the bite of the sea air did nothing to put colour in his face.

I probably didn't look any better.

"Karsten," I said.

He glanced at me. "Yes?"

"I'm sorry."

He snorted. "Yes. This was all in your plans, I'm sure."

"I mean it," I said.

He sighed and gave me a longer look. "I know you do."

"I shouldn't have let things with Jake... you know... go this far."

"He's your friend," Karsten said. And turned to the shore.

"After yesterday, what he did to you—I should have told him to fuck off. Merrows or no Merrows."

"It's just as well," Karsten said. Water droplets were starting to collect on his face and eyelashes, making his ghostly skin look like ice. "He can be helped now."

"I hope so," I said.

I reached over and put my hand over Karsten's free hand, the one that wasn't steering the boat. It was so cold that it almost hurt to touch.

He glanced down at our hands. I thought about letting go for long enough to shrug off my coat and put it around his shoulders. As if he sensed it, he turned his hand over to grasp mine. Then he looked for the shore again. Reliable and conscientious. That was what one of his references had said about him.

"Why were you talking to Donna?" I asked.

He breathed deep. "Zahia told me Donna had grown up with you and Jake. Because I asked Zahia if she knew anyone who knew you."

I couldn't look at him, or at Jake taking shallow breaths on the bottom of the boat. I watched the ocean, steely and unending.

"Why did you ask her that, Kar?"

"Because I believed you had a talent. As I told you at breakfast. I know you don't know what you are doing. But I don't know how you don't see it."

He turned to me and cut the engine of the boat. It rocked steadily beneath us. The water seemed louder, somehow, than the engine had.

"These reservations and appointments," he said, "that are kept only for you. This paperwork that disappears at the wave of your hand. The night we arrived, customs sending us through. Innis. You are a man of considerable charm, but this is more than that. And going through your life this way, changing minds without even knowing you've done it... this is not safe."

I still had his hand in mine and felt no desire to let go, no matter what he'd said. Because it was understandable that he'd think what he thought about me.

Because it was understandable.

Because it explained so much.

Because I was a man of considerable charm. But maybe it took something more than that to make the whole world spin my way.

And Carl... he had been a very convincing guy.

I did let go of his hand, then. I saw a flash of hurt feelings, but it wasn't what he thought. It was nothing to do with him.

"What did Donna tell you?" I asked. My voice was weak. I hated the sound of it.

"She said she saw nothing unusual when she knew you before," he said. He was watching the ocean now, as I had a moment earlier. "But she said that she could believe it now."

Even Donna believed it. Karsten was right. There was no excuse for me not to have known.

"Karsten." He turned to me. I met his eyes. My vision blurred. "I am so sorry."

He seemed puzzled for a moment. Then, oddly, he smiled.

"Are you? I'm not."

"I'm not sure you're following me," I said.

"No? I think I am," he said. "Just as I followed you to your room the other night."

I shut my eyes. He put a hand on my leg. I opened my eyes to see it resting there because I couldn't believe he was willing to touch me after what I'd done. What I had, apparently, made him do.

"Now," he said, his voice gentle but firm, "you follow me. Innis, you are often annoying. I disagree with many things you say and do. Think back. Since we met, have I been tractable?"

I did follow him, then, and I found myself smiling back at him.

"God no," I said. "You can be a righteous pain in the ass. And surly."

"People often complain," Karsten said, "that I won't do anything I don't want to do. And I won't. Since we arrived here, I swear to you—I haven't."

"Yeah," I said. With my hands free, I was able to take off my coat and wrap it around him. "You're a bastard."

He started the engine again. "If you don't like it, you can fire me."

Afternoon, June 18
Karsten Roth

INNIS STILL looked ill, but less so than he had moments earlier.

"I fight with a lot of people," he said. "Don't I? People argue with me."

"More than you'd expect," I agreed. "Considering."

I had to watch where I was going for fear of hitting flotsam or a sea monster, but I could see Innis nodding from the corner of my eye.

"I must only do it sometimes," he said, sounding as if the words were large rocks he had to roll forward and force from his mouth.

"I believe so," I told him.

I could see the shore now and was pleased by that. It was better than going on faith.

"I'm worried about the police," Innis said, "for a few reasons."

I glanced at him. "I thought we had an agreement."

"We do," he told me. "But I want you to know this."

I looked at Jake, or Carl, or both. Still asleep, from what I could tell. "Yes?"

"You saw how other cops treated him. Did Zahia say anything to you?"

I thought about that.

"She said he was temperamental and did not get on well with people. She said that he was a poor choice of guide because of this. And she said that you had no criminal record."

Innis gave a weak laugh. "Excuse me?"

I did not look at him. "I asked her if you had ever been in jail, anywhere. Because I had heard that you had not and thought this was odd in your line of work. She left a message for me at the hotel yesterday."

"Jesus, Karsten."

Other boats were passing us now as we placed more distance between ourselves and the Tank. I wondered if it was forbidden to go too close to the Tank. There had been very few boats near us on the trip there.

"I'm sorry I asked her," I said. "She dislikes Jake, and so she dislikes you. I am concerned that she will make—what is the expression? Hay?"

"Yeah, that's it," Innis said. "Well. No such thing as bad publicity, right?"

"Wrong, I think," I said.

"Let's pretend otherwise. Anyway, yeah—the DCPD has no love for Jake. Maybe they know... I mean, did I hear him right back there? Did he say... did Carl kill that cop?"

"He didn't say the name," I said. "But he said 'cop pipe.' Is that not the one part of Harper that was never found? The windpipe?"

"Jesus," Innis said again. "They must not know, or he wouldn't be walking around loose. But they might suspect him."

"Donna thinks you are here about that cop," I told him.

Innis smiled briefly. "I know."

"She should have been talking to Jake," I said.

Innis looked ill again and shivered.

"Probably lucky for her that she didn't."

"So he is a cop killer," I said.

Beside the boat, a gull swooped down and took a fish I had not noticed. How did their small eyes see so well? Before I could ask, it flew away.

"Yeah. Cops don't love that. So I'm concerned about whether he's going to get a fair shake."

"Also," I said, "there is corruption. As you said."

"Yeah. I think that's mostly in the Scree. Jake always said they were a decent enough bunch in the rest of the town. But hell… was that even Jake I was talking to?"

I wanted to cut the engine again and talk with Innis about this, but it would be better for Jake to get him to land and into a healer's care.

"You said you know Jake is in there," I said.

Innis said nothing. We neared the shore, and I glanced at him. He was watching Jake.

"I want to drive him to the police station," he said. "I don't want to just call them. I want to take him downtown, where he worked. So we know we've got good cops."

"All right," I said.

"And we'll see how it goes," he said. "We'll see what they can do to get Carl out of him."

I nodded. I could see the Land Rover, now.

"And if it works," Innis said, "I'll ask them to get Carl out of me."

Chapter Sixteen

Innis Stuart

I FELT better once I'd said it. I'd thought it would be terrifying to hear the words, but I felt safer instead. It was as if I'd moved Carl into one of those shift boxes zoos put in the cages of venomous snakes to pen the snakes up while they cleaned.

I didn't think he'd had the influence on me he'd had on Jake. I couldn't think of any missing time, any mysteries in my life. I'd felt no urge to move to the Dominion or to do anything else in particular. Maybe I was kidding myself, but I thought I'd gotten a much smaller piece of Carl than Jake had.

I was still unclear on how Carl had wound up inside us in the first place, but he really had been a terrible magician. It had probably been an accident. Lord knew what he'd actually been trying to do.

Karsten and I said little as we moved Jake, still asleep, from the boat to the Land Rover. It was heavy, awkward work. Karsten was in good shape, but he was small, and I wound up doing most of the lifting.

We put Jake into the far back of the Rover, the cargo area. We didn't discuss it, just did it. Obviously we both thought it would be good to have some extra space between us and Carl in case he woke up and somehow got free of the ropes.

We were walking forward to get into the vehicle when a black SUV screeched down the road and stopped in front of the Rover. Before we could react, three men got out.

I recognized them from Karsten's description. All in red. All in black. All in white. Karsten said something quiet and rude in German. I saw guns on us and stayed very still. Whatever Manya was, she could probably have killed us with a snap of her talons if she'd wanted us dead.

"Mr. Stuart, we are here for you and Mr. Adler," Red told us. "Mr. Roth can go."

I tried to think my way around that. What did Manya want with Jake, or Carl… and with me? She must have figured out that I had some of Carl in me. Maybe he'd told her that. But what did she want with Carl?

If I went to them, they'd let Karsten go. Or so they said. We did have some reason to think that Manya didn't want to hurt Karsten.

I could go with them. Bad news for me and Jake, but odds were Karsten would be okay. I eyed him across the hood of the Rover. He looked frightened, but determined. He glanced at the keys in my hand, deliberately, then met my eyes.

"*Wir laufen*," he said. Simple words, aimed at a simple guy without a lot of German. I processed it.

We run.

He'd take the risk, for me and for Jake. More for me probably. But he did consider Jake an innocent now. And I had that to consider too. Giving myself up meant handing him over. And it meant letting Manya get away with whatever she meant to do.

Could we run?

We'd have to get to the cops before Manya's guys caught up with us, but they were away from their SUV, circling around the back of the Land Rover to get Jake. Whereas Karsten and I were right next to the Rover's front doors.

I nodded once, and we moved.

Karsten Roth

INNIS DROVE both madly and expertly, as I had hoped he would. It was the sort of skill a person would need to do the work he did. The surprised faces of Manya's henchmen had been almost comical as we'd pulled away.

"There is," Innis said as he swerved half onto the shoulder to pass an oncoming car, "a gun in my pocket."

Not having time for jokes, I nodded and took the pistol. I hoped I would not have to fire out the window on crowded streets, but it was best to have it ready.

It was Jake's gun, I realized. Innis had taken it from the floor of the Tank. And now I might use it in Jake's defence.

But it was, it seemed, no more Jake's fault that he had turned his gun on Innis than it was Innis's fault that he had a way with words. And so turning either of them over would have been wrong. Unfair.

As we reached the end of the narrow road leading to the ocean, I saw another black SUV coming toward us from the north.

"Nine o'clock," I said.

"I see it," he said, and turned a hard right.

My hand tightened automatically, and I was glad I had left the safety on the gun.

Now we had two SUVs behind us. Red and White and Black were in the closest vehicle, and the other had fallen in behind them so I could not see who was driving that one. More of Manya's goons, obviously, but I didn't know whether they were another matching set.

We were being forced south, away from the police station and, worse, toward the Scree. I saw a road coming up on our left. What was to the left of us, this close to the river?

"Roserood," I said, remembering. "The park."

Innis glanced at me, then grinned. "What the hell," he said and turned.

Theoretically all three of the vehicles in this chase were made to drive off-road. However, I suspected the sleek new SUVs behind us were only nominally equipped for such things. Whereas Innis and I had a Land Rover that Jake claimed had never let him down.

We surprised our pursuers when we veered south of the entrance ramp leading to the bridge to East Hills and instead took a dirt road to Roserood. They had to slow and correct their turns.

The day had become somewhat chilly, and it was a work day as well, so I saw no people in the park. I rolled down my window and took a shot at the first SUV.

"Any luck?" Innis asked.

"I think I hit them."

"Hot damn," Innis cried, and slapped the steering wheel.

"No," I said. "I think it because the bullet was stopped by a force field."

"Shit," he said.

"Yes," I said.

"Good aim, though," he added and then turned for the uneven ground leading to the heart of the park, where the Dominion's two rivers met.

"Jake said there was a curse," I reminded him, though I should have known he would not care. Not with his contempt for curses.

"You think we can be in much more trouble?" he asked.

"The police—they said no one came out of the Heart alive."

And then, from the corner of my eye, I saw one of the warning signs the police had said were there. Dire warning signs, the sort that guarded nuclear plants and avalanche zones.

"We're in serious shit here, Kar," Innis pointed out. "This isn't optional. Tell me about the layout—do you know anything?"

"There's an island," I said, trying to recall everything Jake had said and what I had seen on maps of the Dominion.

"Where did Jake say the bridge was?" he asked.

I shut my eyes and tried to ignore everything but my memory. The rivers had moved. They had learned the island was cursed. But before... I recalled old photos, black-and-white. Rose bushes everywhere, and enough cut down to make a dirt road and lay wooden planks.

"Ahead, I think" I said. "But, Innis...."

"What?"

"It will not have been touched in over fifty years."

Innis Stuart

AHEAD OF us, I could see a line of rose bushes, as wild as the ones guarding Sleeping Beauty in the fairy tale. I had a feeling we weren't going to find a princess on the other side. Still, we were in the strangely freeing position of having no choice.

"There," Karsten said and pointed to a place in the roses that, to me, looked no different from the rest. But he had a photographer's eyes.

At the last second, Karsten thought to roll up his window. We had momentum, and the Rover was high and solid. We pushed through the thicket.

I saw the river ahead of us, and it was a relief to see anything after plunging into the roses on a wing and a prayer. Petals and thorns still littered the windshield and the hood. The sight of the bridge, though, wasn't cheering. Karsten had been right to be concerned.

Beam bridges require attention from time to time, and this one had been left to rot. Some planks were missing, others suspiciously dark. Our best bet was to move across at a high enough speed that, if the bridge fell away beneath us, we might still make it the rest of the way.

At least the tiny island was clear. No roses. No trees. Just a bed of silvery plants close to the ground. I could see where two other bridges had fallen away—and one remaining bridge to the southwest.

I breathed deep and went.

Karsten was watching behind us as we crossed, possibly because he didn't want to see the bridge.

"One SUV has turned away," he said, and his voice shook as we crossed the uneven planks.

"Chickens," I said.

And then it was over, and we were on solid, if rocky, ground. Just like that. The forbidden island was beneath us, and nothing had happened. Some curse.

Karsten gasped, and, a half-second later, I saw it, too—a golden eagle flying low, coming from behind us and down past the windshield, almost touching the hood before it shot back up into the sky. It was flying faster than we were driving. I couldn't spare the time to check our speed, but it seemed impossible.

It went toward the other bridge, at the southwest. I did the same. It was the only way off the island apart from the way we'd come. I tried to keep our speed up, since the other bridge wasn't likely to be in any better shape than the first one.

I heard a crashing sound behind us.

"The second SUV," Karsten said. "The bridge fell."

"They make it?" I asked.

"Yes."

So we still had someone on our tail. It was, at the moment, the least of my concerns.

"Hang on," I said needlessly. If Karsten hadn't been hanging on, he would have gone through a window already.

He looked back again as we took the second bridge. I made it a single piece in my mind: the bridge and the rose bushes beyond. Over one and through the other. It probably didn't matter what I thought, how I framed it, but it kept me from losing my nerve.

I heard a rumbling, almost gurgling, and I flashed back to lying on the couch with my mother when I was a small boy, my head on her stomach, watching TV.

Then the vehicle began to shake, more than it had from the speed and the rocky ground, and I gritted my teeth. Whatever was happening, the only solution was to move. Hope for luck and keep moving.

The bridge held us, barely, pieces flying as the tires hit. The rumbling noise grew louder, and I thought of rockslides in the mountains. I ignored it. Nothing I could do about it.

The roses—it had to be an illusion, but I could have sworn they tried to bow down as we approached. It seemed as if, had we been going slower, we wouldn't have hit them at all. But we did, hard, and came out the other side with even more foliage attached to the Rover.

We were intact, though. I was going to make a smartass comment, brag it up a little, but Karsten beat me to it with something I hadn't heard out of him yet. A scream.

I looked back then, over the flattened roses. It was more than a glance in spite of our speed and the uneven ground beneath us. But it only took a moment to see more than I could stand.

The second SUV was still on the island, no longer moving. It was caught in rocks that now rose up like teeth, made eerily white by the silvery plants that had covered the ground. The island was folding inward, toward itself. It was chewing, tearing, and grinding the SUV and everything inside it. Eating it. Making a paste it could swallow. I saw someone trying to climb out, his legs left behind, and I saw him fall back inside.

As I turned to face the front again, I could see tears on Karsten's face. He was crying silently. I gripped the wheel hard, much too hard, and kept going. Out of the park. Away.

Karsten Roth

I HAD managed to stop crying like an infant by the time we reached the edge of the park. I was ashamed but told myself that Innis did not look much better than I felt. What we had seen would unsettle anyone.

As we left the park and found paved road again, a black-and-white police car flashed its lights lazily at us and sounded its siren for a moment. I sighed, and Innis's shoulders dropped. Finally. The police.

Innis pulled over and stepped out of the car. I got out and went to stand beside him.

"We've been trying to get to a police station," he told a tall blond officer as he left his car. "We have a few things to tell you."

"You can tell them to Manya instead," a redheaded female cop said from the other side of the car.

"Goddamn it," Innis groaned. I realized it too as he spoke. We'd gone to the heart of the city, then taken a bridge to the southwest. "We're in the fucking Scree."

The cops trained their guns on us, and I thought of Jake's pistol, lying where I had left it on the seat of the Rover. No matter, I supposed. I wouldn't have been able to outshoot the cops, anyway.

"Hey, you don't need to—" Innis began.

"Shut up," the redhead said.

She had apparently heard about him.

They frisked us, finding the empty packet of sleep dust and our Swiss Army knives. My camera was checked over and returned to me.

Then they ushered us silently into the back of the car. No handcuffs, for which I was grateful. The doors locked, and we were behind thick soundproof glass and plastic. I could feel the dull pressure of wards. Innis put his hand on my leg, and we watched as the cops took Jake from the Rover and put him in the trunk of their car. Undignified, to be certain, but at least they did not murder him on the spot.

We could still hope that Manya, for whatever reason, wanted us all alive.

"So much for my lack of arrest record," Innis said.

I regarded him. "I don't believe this will be in a record of any kind."

"True," he agreed.

We waited, calm and still, as the police officers got into the car and began driving us to Manya's home.

"I'm sorry I got you into this," Innis said after a few blocks.

I shrugged. He was sitting close enough that this moved his shoulder as well.

"I came here because I was investigating you," I said. "I thought I might then speak to a reporter in Germany, a friend of mine, about whatever I had learned…. I didn't just get the idea here that you did magic and had a secret. I've thought it for a long time."

Innis considered that, then started to laugh.

"Good call," he said, and then I laughed with him.

The cops seemed a bit afraid of us as we were clearly mad.

It was not a long drive. I was both impatient to arrive and aware that I might be wishing away some of the last minutes I had remaining to me. Finally we drove through the same brick wall I had been through the night before and pulled up in the center of the building.

The lady cop stood beside the back door of the car, on my side. Her tall partner went to the trunk and lifted Jake out by himself. He set the body on the ground. We waited inside the car. I looked sideways at the table and chairs where I had seen the carved taimen. The tray was still there, its seven-pointed pattern clearer with the cups and teapot taken away.

I felt suddenly as if something were crawling along the base of my spine. Something was wrong. I picked up my camera and began flipping through photos. Innis peered at the viewscreen with me, curious. I stopped on a shot of the mayor's office, one I had taken as I sat. The lens of the camera had been forced upward, and I had caught, by accident, the white moulded ceiling with the symbol I had somehow recognized.

"Holy shit," Innis said softly. He looked from the mayor's ceiling to the tray and back. "What do you think that means?"

"Seven points," I said.

He stared at me. "What?"

"Seven points in the design," I said. "Seven points in the city. Seven parts of Aloysius Harper, found in seven places."

"Fuck," Innis said. "What does that mean?"

I shook my head. There was movement to the right of the car, and we turned our heads to see Manya walking toward us. She ignored the car and the police officers and knelt beside Jake, who was blinking now. Waking up.

"Carl," she said.

"It's good to see you," he told her.

His voice was rough.

She tilted her head. "Are you sure?"

She stood and gestured for the cops to release us from the car. They did so without delay. They seemed ill at ease.

"Karsten—I apologize to you once again for the way you were brought here. No harm will come to you," she said. "You are safer here than any place on Earth. Except perhaps Tunguska."

I was so surprised that I barely noticed when Innis stepped forward to confront her.

"Look, I don't know what kind of deal you have going on with Carl, but he's not the rightful owner of that body. What would it take to get you to restore Jake Adler and remove Carl? I'm guessing that's a thing you can do."

She smiled. "Are you offering me money?"

"I don't think you're short on that," Innis said, glancing around. "I'm asking what you would want."

"Oh," she said. "It's sweet how you boys all come to me with proposals. Carl told me he wanted full possession of this body, and I had him kill a cop for me. Then he said he needed a little piece of him taken from someone else, and I said yes, bring him to me and I'll do this too, but of course the price will be higher. So he placed the pieces of cop at the seven points of power. Now all I have to do is sacrifice Carl, and I'll have the power of office. I honestly can't think what I would like more than that, but you are welcome to make an offer."

"The power of office?" I said.

She turned to me with a smile. I would have much preferred she not smile at me.

"The seven points of the Dominion are represented in the ceiling of the mayor's office, and this confers the mayoral power. The ceiling did not burn when City Hall was destroyed. Did you know that? It was the only thing to survive. To the disappointment of a certain dragon, to be sure. He wanted to know what would happen if the mayoral power were freed."

Innis stared at her. "You want to be mayor? Couldn't you just hire a good campaign manager?"

Manya laughed, and this was much worse than her smile. I shivered. Innis put a hand to the small of my back.

"I don't want to be mayor. I want the mayor to do as I say and the Dominion to do the same. I have investments in the north end of the Scree. I won't have an earthquake disrupting my buildings. Or if I wish, I will have a earthquake removing a slum. And of course the permits to gentrify the Spree will come only to me."

"You would do all of this over land?" I said.

"Karsten," she said, "what are wars fought over?"

"Ego," I said. She laughed again.

"Your people would know," she said. I felt Innis tense. She may have sensed this too, as she turned to him.

"I merely need to remove Carl's essense from you, and then I can continue with my business," she said. "It will be painful, but you will likely survive. If you do, you may leave with Karsten."

"Likely survive," Innis said. "Gee, you make it sound great."

"If it were me," she said, "I would prefer it to housing a man who wished to destroy me and take my place. Which he will, you see, once Jake's body is no longer available. You have been spared only because you have the least of him."

"What do you mean, Jake's body won't be available?" Innis said. "You can do the same for him as for me. Remove Carl and let him go."

"I wish it were that simple," Manya said. "The ritual has no end of stipulations. You would think it had been written by the Dominion City Council. Carl must be whole and in control of a living person when I sacrifice him. This will be easiest by far with Jake, as most of Carl is already present and is already in control."

Jake, or Carl, had begun to stir. Innis had a strange look to him. He gave Manya a smile that was too big, too false. He said,

"You don't want to hurt any of us, do you?"

Innis Stuart

I KNEW I might be trying too hard. Hell, I'd never tried at all before. But my "gift," that little drop of Carl, was all I had, and I didn't think I'd get a second chance to use it. I imagined shoving my will toward her, even leaned forward a little to move it along. She blinked and her expression softened.

"No," she said, uncertainly. "It isn't that I want to hurt you…."

"You don't have to," I said. "You could let us go."

"But I have plans," she said. She sounded dazed now. I touched her arm, in case it would help.

"There are other ways," I told her. "You don't need us."

"I don't?" she asked.

"No," I said. "You'll let us go."

"Yes." Manya nodded. "Yes, of course. I will let you go."

My heart was beating so hard I thought it might break my ribs. I had her! All I had to do was keep her convinced while Jake woke up and we could steal away. We could figure out how to deal with Carl once we were gone. I turned to Karsten and instead of relief on his face, saw horror. I thought for a second that it was because I'd used my power so roughly, but then I realized he was looking at Manya. I did the same and saw her sharp, predatory expression back in place. She saw my confusion and laughed.

"Did you really think such a small thing would work on me? Do you think I would be where I am and who I am if that were so?"

I said nothing. I moved closer to Karsten. I had my hand against his back, and I pressed lightly to turn him toward me. He looked at me, seemingly unruffled, as if I were drawing his attention to something on a restaurant menu. I would never be that cool.

"You should go," I told him. "All the way out of town and don't come back. Monomyth will get you out. Or Donna will, if you tell her I asked."

He considered that. The moment drew long. He shook his head. "I would have to live with myself, so it would not work out for me in the end." He turned to Manya. "I have a question for you."

"Of course," she said. Always gracious to him. What was it that made her react this way?

"Are you the daughter of Lake Cheko?"

The only word for Manya's face, and one I never thought I'd have had occasion to use for her, was this: flabbergasted. Her jaw actually dropped, at least a centimeter, and her eyes were huge.

"Who... why... what... brings you to say that?"

"I had a dream," he said. "About Tunguska. The lake told me its daughter owed me a boon."

Was that true? He'd never mentioned it to me. Of course there was no telling from his face.

"Impossible," she said. Her metal teeth snapped off the end of the word. I flinched. Karsten did not even blink.

"Are you her?"

She was breathing in quick, hard bursts. Finally she drew a deep breath and looked him in the eye.

"I have that name."

"Then you owe me, I think," he said. "I think this is the intimacy you said you felt. I don't know why, but does it matter? What's owed is owed."

Her lip curled in a sneer. I didn't think she knew it.

"I could not say," she said. "You would have to ask Her."

Karsten glanced at me as if I might know who She was. As if I had any idea what was going on. I shook my head, and he looked at Manya again.

"Her?" he asked politely.

"The old woman. You can call her, but it won't be pleasant. You have to meet her at her heart and it is a terrible place. Fatal for some."

"Where is this?" he asked, like he was going to go there as soon as he got a map. I turned him toward me again.

"Kar. You can leave. You don't have to do any of this. This is my problem, remember?"

He put a hand on my face. "Danke," he said. "But I am an adult and I will choose."

Before I could think of a response, he had turned to Manya. "Where do I go?"

"Nowhere," she said. "You will travel where you stand." Her eyes flicked to me. "Alone."

"That's not how we do things," I said, like we'd been working together for decades. Karsten smiled a little but otherwise ignored me.

He said, "How do I begin?"

She reached with one talon and nicked his forehead, drawing a drop of blood. "You already have."

I counted ten heartbeats, though they were quick ones, before something shook him. His head went back, and his eyes closed. He trembled, like a seizure but more like someone buffeted by a hurricane. His skin began to glow, deeper and deeper red, as if burned. She watched, impassive. I put my arms around him and lowered him to the ground before he fell. Stayed with him there, half sitting, holding him against my chest. He gasped, and his skin rippled, and he was boiling with fever. I looked for water, something to cool him, and she gave me a warning glare.

"Do not interfere. For his sake. Anything you do will make it worse."

So I held on, pressed my face to his shoulder, and waited.

Karsten Roth

I WAS at first in a larch forest. It was morning—by the dew and the birds singing everywhere. So many birds. They were loud in a way that reached my bones, like standing before the amplifiers at a rock show.

It was spring or summer—by the green on the trees. The air was the freshest I'd ever breathed. I raised my face to the sky, and a wind shook everything around me. Like a desert wind, hot and dry. Everything shook and bent. Larch snapped around me. I could not understand how I was still on my feet.

And then it all started to burn.

How do I describe this? There was a smell like roasting meat for a moment, and then all I could breathe was fire. The heat was more than I had ever known, more than anyone could feel, and I stood and felt it, and I did not know that it would ever end. I should have been dead. Anyone else who knew this feeling would be dead. And it was still more. The sense of myself peeling away, charring, snapping off. Everything inside me boiling and rupturing. I did not know what was up or down or even what these things were. And still I stood there and the heat grew and there was white light, much brighter than the sun.

I had a moment of understanding, a sense that something was rushing into this space from far, far outside. It did not belong here. It did not fit. But it was sending what had been here away and taking its place. The push and pull, the bending of things where they could not go, was more than could be borne.

It is difficult for me to remember, now, exactly how this next moment was. I think that every cell burst and spilled out steam, burning the shards of itself, trillions of times over and all at once. And still I stood there. I could no longer feel or see or hear, but I knew I had my feet on the burning, steaming ground. It was not possible to move or scream or, most of all, to die. To end it. How did one suffer anything without the idea that there could be an end? I thought this might be forever, and I am certain if I had spent another second there, I would be mad.

But I did not. I was suddenly in Manya's house. On the floor in Innis's arms, gasping for the air that was sweet and cool as ice cream, if not as thick.

"Kar?"

I could feel his hand on my hair. It did not hurt. Nothing hurt, aside from the normal small aches of existence. I was not burning. I could not think what to say.

"It's okay," he said. "You're okay."

I could see again and looked for Manya. She was in the centre of the room, and I thought at first that my eyes were wrong because she seemed to shimmer like a mirage. The motion quickened, and Innis said, "Oh my God," and then I knew it was not my eyes.

She seemed as if she might scream, but nothing came. She ballooned, becoming round and large in all directions. Then her body began to reshape itself. It folded and squeezed down. It was making something human, but smaller than Manya by far. Things did not go where they should. Her face was stretched around the new form's back, one eye bulging from its side. The taloned fingers were poking out from the short round body like the feet of a penguin.

Innis held me tighter, and I felt him swallow hard. I hoped neither of us would be sick.

A face formed in the cloth that had been Manya's dress. Stitches moved to draw eyes, a mouth, small pupils. Wrinkles. An old woman, as Manya had said.

The cloth mouth opened and a voice, thick and dry as cotton wool, said, "Hello again, Karsten."

Chapter Seventeen

Innis Stuart

IT WAS probably a good thing I was holding on to Karsten, because that made it difficult to get up and run away. That was my first instinct when the thing puppeting Manya's body spoke to Karsten. My second and third impulses, to soil myself or throw up my last few meals, were also quashed by the fact that they would have been unpleasant for him. Really, hadn't he had enough?

The light changed in the room. I don't know why I noticed that with the… thing… standing before me. But I did, and I looked up, and the skylight was dark with birds.

"Do you remember me?" the shape said. Of course he didn't. If Kar had ever seen something like this before, I was pretty sure he'd have said so already. Hell, he'd have a picture of it.

But damned if he wasn't tilting his head like one of those skylight birds.

"I think… I may," he said. "But, excuse me… I cannot think from where."

"You had taken the train to Siberia," she said. "You came on instinct, before the others. You were alone at the station."

Then she smiled, showing a few button teeth. I thought I saw mischief in her cloth eyes, but to this day I couldn't tell you how.

"Almost alone."

He sat up so quickly that it was either let him go or move with him. I chose the latter.

"You were there," he said. "You were… human."

"Never that," she said. "But I was there. I was thirsty. Even I thirst."

He nodded. "I had a few cans of cola. I gave one to you."

"You showed kindness," she said. "I tell you now what you have not known before: I know you and I watch and call to you. This is outside of matters of hospitality. You are of my line. I can and will aid you. I can and will presume upon you. You have been called to Siberia and to Vinson Massif and here, with these men. You do my will unknowing. But for today there is the matter of the cola. Daughter, you are to give this man a boon."

I swear I saw Manya's bulging eye blink, like she'd heard and understood. I told myself again to keep my food down.

The body ballooned and twisted again, like a clown was making a Manya for a kid at the fair. Karsten was very still. I wouldn't have blamed him if he'd never moved again. We stayed there on the floor and watched until Manya stood before us again.

She moved her neck to each side, and it cracked twice, like a cap gun going off. Karsten, who had been so calm until now, started. I rubbed my thumb against his arm. His skin was smooth and cool again, as if nothing had happened to him.

"Ah," Manya said. Her voice was rough but better than her mother's. "Karsten. Right you are. Tell me what I can do for you."

It has occurred to me since that he could have asked for anything. He didn't have to save me or Jake. He could have asked for the moon and stars, and she'd have sent some goons to get them. But I honestly don't know whether that has ever, even for a second, occurred to him.

"Free them from Carl," he told her. "Innis and Jake. If they want that. Don't harm them. And let them go."

She breathed deep, through her nose.

"The process will hurt," she said. "They will likely survive, but there is a small chance it will not go well."

"Is there anyone better for this job?" he asked her. "Here or anywhere?"

"Do you appeal to my vanity?" she asked, then smiled. "No, I don't imagine you do. I say without ego, you could do no better."

He twisted in my arms to look at me. "Do you want this?"

I thought of what Manya had said about housing a being that wanted me destroyed.

"Yes."

I stood, pulling him to his feet beside me, and we went to Jake. He was awake, but he was Carl, so there was no point asking what he thought.

He told us anyway, or I should say he told Manya.

"Don't you do this, you fucking bitch. You and I had a deal."

She crossed the room to stand over him. "Yes, yes, a deal. Do you remember what I said to you about Karsten?"

He pulled at the ropes we'd put on him a few centuries ago, or so it seemed.

"I don't give a shit about him. This is about our deal."

"Mmm. It is. I told you not to hurt him. And what did you do the very next day? You told him to photograph a tulpa, or so I hear."

Carl scowled, turning Jake's face far uglier than it had ever been.

"It's not my fault he's a goddamned idiot."

Manya sighed and straightened. More cap gun sounds as her back stretched.

"I am disappointed. I had plans. I put a great deal of work into all of this. But, Carl, the one thing that is not objectionable is that I am still able to destroy you."

She waved a hand and men appeared, pushing a pair of antique gurneys. She always seemed to have more goons. Another two arrived to move Jake to one of the gurneys.

"Right here?" I said. "Is this sterile?"

She threw back her head and laughed. "You are delightfully ridiculous," she told me. "Please, if you would. The gurney."

I had climbed mountains with far less fear than assailed me climbing onto that gurney. Karsten steadied it with one hand so it wouldn't roll away. He looked about as sick as I felt.

"Only the blink of an eye," Manya said.

She pushed up the butterfly sleeve of her green silk coat.

"You notice she didn't say it wouldn't hurt a bit," I said.

Karsten put a hand on my shoulder. "I do her will unknowing. What do you think is her will?"

"I think it's impossible to have the first fucking idea," I said. He leaned down and kissed me.

I heard Manya's heels clatter on her way to Jake. Carl.

"Bitch," he said once she stood over him again.

"Asshole," she said and plunged her talons into his stomach.

He didn't scream. It would have been easier if he had. He made a soft choking sound, and his eyes flew open, wide with terror. She was fishing around in there, blood spilling from the sides like water sloshing out of a bowl. She whistled, something fast and Slavic.

I could smell the blood and something sour. Bile. I swallowed hard to keep my own bile inside. Karsten's grip tightened, and I welcomed the mild pain. It was like ice water or cold fresh air.

"There you are," she said and held her hand aloft.

She was gripping a pale white body, tiny and twisted, like an infant gone wrong. There was nothing above the eyes but empty space, and the eyes were slanted and bulging like the eyes of a frog. Manya waved her other hand and fire burned in midair. She threw the body into the flame.

It cried like a real baby as it died.

Manya shook blood from her arm to the floor and gave me her broadest glinting smile.

"Nothing to be afraid of," she said.

I could see Jake's stomach mending itself already, the sides pulling to the center and fusing there, even the blood and bile vanishing.

"Piece of cake," I said.

And remembered nothing more.

Excerpt from *Seven Leagues Over the Dominion*

For everything there is a reason.
Except the Turn.
—Gratian Camilo, Parliamentary Poet Laureate, 2002

THERE ARE those who say the reason for the elitist attitude in the Merrows and other underwater communities is not simply snobbery. Rumours abound, as they do about anything that still carries an air of mystery in a world where most mysteries have dropped their cloaks and daggers and walked out into the daylight. Most people seem to think there's a battle underway between the water dwellers and some threat in the deeps. An army of aliens. The kraken. A demon or a god. Some say the Turn was caused by this threat, or that it was caused by the water dwellers.

Either way, this theory assumes that the water dwellers—who have been down there since the planet was young—have been fighting their war for a very long time.

It also assumes that the Turn happened for a reason. That it was part of a struggle and it meant something.

Other theorists link the Turn to World War II, which immediately preceded it. Or to the birth of the atomic age, which was of profound importance to the world in the brief time before it became irrelevant. We can't even imagine today the difference a potentially planet-destroying weapon made at the time. It was a sense of threat that people had not experienced before. Now we live with thousands, possibly hundreds of thousands, of things and people at least that dangerous, and the A-bomb seems almost quaint.

There are people even now who don't believe there is such a thing as magic. It's technology, they say, advanced beyond our capacity for understanding. From another world or another dimension or our own future.

Most of us don't bother much with these esoteric subjects. The origin of the Turn is sought by dogged scientists, magicians, and even philosophers, but most of us consider it the greatest of the world's remaining mysteries, and one that may be destined to remain undeciphered. We prefer to spend our time living with magic, living with what we call the supernatural, and doing our best to come to peace with our world as it is.

As of this writing, roughly one million sentient beings reside—walk, fly, and swim—in the area demarcated as the Dominion. Theorizing about how a place like the Dominion can exist, where the magic came from, what it means... this is not a popular pastime for the million. They're too busy trying to negotiate the maze of fly and no-fly zones, picking up forms at City Hall, and keeping their heads down on the nights of full moons. They live complicated lives. They're busy. If you told them their city had an open mouth where its heart was supposed to be, they would shrug. What difference does it make?

The true history of the Turn is nothing but trivia to them. Even if it were uncovered and made available to them as simply as placing an internet search or picking up a newspaper, most would consider it a detail they did not particularly want or need. What happened, happened. What is, is. And life goes on.

The truth is that the truth about the Turn could destroy the uneasy peace the world had come to in relation to magic. If we don't know what happened, who did it, how, or why, then we can't attach value to it one way or another. It's not good or evil. It's not dangerous or safe. It just is. People who do magic and supernatural beings also just are, and we can attach judgement to some of them, maybe, by their actions, but we can't say that magic taints or elevates them. This is, for the sake of all of us and our lives together, probably for the best.

I believe this, and yet if someone approached me with the secret to the Turn and said they would tell me, but they would also have to tell the rest of the world… I would take the deal. Maybe that's because I'm naturally curious. I can't help it.

Or maybe it's because I believe there could be something to those theories about aliens or kraken or gods. That maybe the water dwellers really are a front line in a war we can't see, or maybe there's something even more mysterious going on. Either way, I wonder about our innocence—naiveté—in the face of all this newly accessible power. We think we're learning to use it. We think we know what we're doing. But the truth is that we don't even know what we're dealing with, let alone how to deal with it. We don't know what any of this means.

And I'm enough of a pessimist to think that's going to bite us all in the ass someday.

Karsten Roth

"IT WAS a bit like a baby," I said, "but it wasn't as ugly." I looked at Jake. "Not so ugly as yours."

"Didn't see mine," Jake said.

He was hunched over the table, hands on his stomach. He'd said it didn't hurt anymore but that he still felt the urge to protect it.

"Yours was pretty ugly," Innis said, and the three of us laughed.

It wasn't healthy laughter. It was, however, better than screaming.

"Goddamn, you guys, I know I keep saying this, but I am so sorry."

"Why couldn't you just tell us you were possessed?" Innis asked. "Did you think I wouldn't understand? Come on."

"I didn't know," Jake said. "I know that sounds stupid, but everyone gets missing time in the Dominion. It's that kind of town. I thought I was having a lot of bad dreams. I thought I was being ridden sometimes, maybe, but I didn't think… I never thought of Carl."

"That should be the title of our joint autobiography," Innis said. He sounded disgusted with himself. "*We Never Thought of Carl.*"

"Don't play any violins for him," Jake said. "He got himself into this situation. And when he started to express, he could have marched right into the hospital and asked for help. Instead of making my coworkers look at me for the murder of a damned good cop."

"So they did suspect you," Innis said. "I was thinking, after I woke up, maybe that was why you quit."

"I was invited to quit," Jake sighed. "I didn't understand why."

Muddy Waters's voice was pulsing from the speakers about the Hounfor's bar. I knew that because Innis had identified the singer. He said he liked the blues.

The karaoke hostess was at a table with Danny Wedo, each leaning so far forward they nearly met in the middle. They were holding hands.

"You remember nothing?" I asked. "Nothing about the murder?"

Jake frowned at his beer. "I don't know what I remember. I had some strange dreams. Were they dreams? Or was that shit Carl got up to?" He straightened and looked at me. "I dreamt that I figured out the commune murder, and I blackmailed Syd into selling me a kind of ward—a mask. If I put it on, no one would recognize me."

"Did it make you look like a blur?" Innis asked. Jake blinked in confusion, and Innis waved it away. "Never mind. Maybe you should go through your apartment."

Jake swallowed his beer. "I searched it before you got to town. Here's a fucking laugh—I felt like something was watching me. I turned the place inside out. Didn't find anything."

"Search it again," Innis recommended.

"Yeah," Jake said, nodding.

The song changed. Voices sang in the odd island French I could not follow.

"So," Innis said to Jake, "what now? You could tell the cops you've been possessed. It's probably a bad idea to rat Manya out, but you could tell them just enough. Maybe get your job back."

"Not in this town," Jake said. "I may not look guilty, exactly, but I sure as hell do not look smart."

"Also," I pointed out, "you do not know where you've been."

Jake did something odd. He smiled at me with sincerity. He had never done so before.

"Damn straight. I got no clue what I've done, who's gunning for me. I don't even have my quirk anymore. I'm a sitting duck around here."

Innis was rubbing his hands together. Lady MacBeth.

"Your ability… maybe it protected you. I get how seeing through illusions could be handy. I don't know, though. Maybe you're better off without it."

"Funny comment from a guy who lost his own little quirk," Jake commented.

Innis nodded. He did not seem concerned. "I know. Sour grapes. But having a quirk, it's like carrying a gun. Sometimes it protects you. Sometimes it makes you a combatant."

It may have been an illusion I could not see through, but Jake appeared to think about that.

"I don't care," he said at last. "I don't need my quirk, and I don't need the Dominion. It's time to move on."

"Good," Innis said. "I can always use a security person. Where do you want to go?"

Jake tossed back the last of his beer. "Nowhere you're going."

Innis seemed hurt, and I thought about stabbing Jake with a fork. Jake saw Innis's face and sat up straight.

"No, no, not like that. I mean, I've had enough adventure. I'm thinking I'll go back to Manitoba, maybe get a cabin by a lake. If I sell my house in the Dominion, I should have enough to live on for a while."

"You need a vacation," Innis agreed, though he appeared disappointed. He smiled at me. "As for you, how are you at underwater photography? Specifically I'm thinking of the Strait of Gibraltar. Around there anyway."

"I have not had much practice in general," I said. "Why?"

He was interrupted by the arrival of the karaoke hostess, who slid into the booth beside him. She looked subtly different from the way she had the night before. Her skin was making colours from the light, like mother of pearl.

"How are you all today?"

"Much improved," Innis said. "Thank you for asking. How is your husband?"

"A good man," she said.

She was wearing gold hoop earrings with crosses through them, the way the rivers crossed in the middle of the Dominion. As they spun, I thought I could see something through them that was not her neck or hair or the bar behind her. I stared until I could make it out. It was another place, with dark blue waves under more stars than I had ever seen before.

"Did I hear you say you would be visiting the ocean north of Africa?" she asked. Innis was running his fingers up and down his glass of beer, dragging the beads of condensation into lines.

"We might. Do you know the place?"

"Better than you can imagine," she said. "Sing me a song before you slip inside."

She stood and went back to her table.

Jake raised his brows at Innis. "All the strange ones want to talk to you."

"Hence," Innis said, "my entire career."

"Excuse me for a sec," Jake said. "I have to think there's a bathroom in this place somewhere."

Innis Stuart

I WATCHED Jake leave the table, tall, strong, and broad. A perfect protector, or a perfect monster. He'd always seemed outsized to me, always larger than I was as we grew up.

John Lee Hooker was telling us that things were gonna change. Maybe they even were. I leaned toward Karsten until my mouth was next to his ear.

"The people of Gibraltar say," I whispered, "there was an island near there that sank in the last days of the Second World War."

He stared at me. Fascinated despite himself.

"Did something magical sink it?"

"I don't know," I said.

"You want to go looking for it," he said. Not a question.

I grinned. "Don't you?"

He hesitated, then raised his glass of rum in acknowledgement. He seemed intrigued by the idea. He might also have been, as I was, reluctant to say goodbye.

"It would make a good story," he said after taking a drink. "Even if we find nothing."

"A good story," I said. "Right."

I rolled my fingertips on the table, trying to put a voice to what was bothering me. Had been since shortly after we'd arrived.

"Do you realize," I said, "that you almost got killed by a thought?"

He frowned. Like I said, he was a little bit drunk.

"I almost got killed a few times," he said. "Can you be more specific?"

"The bear," I said. "The tulpa. That thing was an idea, Kar. Someone put some magic behind it, but it wasn't real."

He cocked an eyebrow and stared into his drink as if he'd lost something in there. "Real enough."

"I know," I said. "This place is crazy, Kar. People die because of shit other people just… thought."

Karsten laughed. I couldn't see what that could possibly be about. He looked at my face and reined his amusement in.

"Innis… first, yes, this place is crazy. But the things people think have always killed other people. Someone thought of chipping rocks into arrows. Someone thought of gunpowder. Someone thought of the atomic bomb."

"At least you had to chip the rock," I said. "Think of that as a cooling-off period. And if you wanted to kill a bunch of people, you needed enough people to chip rocks, and enough of the right kind of rocks…. Thinking up something lethal and boom, it happens—it's too easy. And it would have been a stupid, horrible waste for you to have died because of it."

Karsten set his drink down and smiled. I was going to ask what he was smiling about now when he put his hands on my shoulders and leaned in to give me a kiss. He was still smiling when he pulled away.

"Thank you," he said, "for thinking it would be a waste if I died. But it would have been no less ridiculous for me to have fallen under a bus. That bear being the product of magic is not important."

I put my hand on his. "I see what you're saying. But I think it's too easy to think up a bear. Or… maybe it's too easy to do it without knowing what you're doing, or without knowing how to control it. Like…."

"What you did."

I pressed his hand.

"What I did. Maybe it's that, or maybe it's spending time in this place, but I'm starting to see where Syd is coming from with that stupid commune of his. Except that Syd is an idiot."

"Also a liar," Karsten added.

"Yeah, that too. But we—I mean, all of us, everywhere—we're in bed with magic in this huge way, and we don't know what the hell we're doing. Or where it came from. Or what powers it."

"Or when it might go away," Karsten said. "Overnight, as it arrived."

Now I smiled. "You get it."

"Yes," he said, "but I am at a loss as to what anyone can do about it."

"Sometimes I think we're all doing... it. Yeah, something changed at the Turn, but since then... look, we all know magic can be shaped and directed. That's how we use it. And I'm Exhibit A that you can shape magic without knowing you're doing it."

"And?" he said, though not as if he doubted I had a point.

Instead he wanted to hear more.

"And maybe," I said, "we're all directing it. Maybe that's why after we got magic, everything from our fairy tales and movies and nightmares showed up, acting pretty much the way we expected it to. Maybe the mayor is onto something with all this bureaucracy—but not because it balances out the magic. Because of the other thing they said, about the rules making it possible for people to have expectations. Maybe if people here didn't truly believe their houses would stay in one place or, Christ, even that the sky would stay up... I don't know. Without people expecting a certain degree of order, even in the Dominion, maybe there would be no order. This whole place would be like the unstable regions in the Pines. It would be uninhabitable."

"You think the people who live here are subconsciously controlling the magic? And shaping the Dominion?"

It was amazing how sober Karsten was suddenly, sitting up straight and staring me in the eye.

"I'm saying maybe we're all doing it. Everywhere, not just here. Without even knowing." I sighed. "Hell, Kar, I don't know. We're both sort of drunk, and it's been a fucked-up week. I'm running my mouth, which I know is strange for me."

He laughed. "I can't imagine what you would do if you were suddenly unable to speak."

"Learn ASL," I told him. "Look... Kar, if you're serious about coming with me to Gibraltar—and I really hope you are—"

"I am," he said.

I picked up his hand and kissed it. He ducked his head when I did it, blushing adorably.

"Then you should know that I'm not thinking about what a good story it'll be. I mean, it will be, and it'll sell books, and that's why my publisher will support the idea… but I have another agenda. I really want to know what happened at the Turn. After all this… I want to know what's going on."

Karsten picked up his empty drink glass with his free hand and rang it off my empty beer bottle.

"Then we should leave this town," he said, "and go find out."

Coming Soon

Seven Leagues Over Seven Cities

Seven Cites: Book Two

The Isle of Seven Cities isn't where it's supposed to be, it doesn't have seven cities except when it does, and it's disorienting even to those who live there. But it's also the best lead to how magic came back to the world, so journalists Innis Stuart and Karsten Roth are en route to Seven Cities to dig up the biggest story of their lives.

Preorder Now

GAYLEEN FROESE is an LGBTQ writer of detective fiction living in Edmonton, Canada. Her novels include *The Girl Whose Luck Ran Out*, *Touch*, and *Grayling Cross*. Her chapter book for adults, *What the Cat Dragged In*, was short-listed in the International 3-Day Novel Contest and is published by The Asp, an authors' collective based in western Canada.

Gayleen has appeared on Canadian Learning Television's *A Total Write-Off*, won the second season of the *Three Day Novel Contest* on BookTelevision, and as a singer-songwriter, showcased at festivals across Canada. She has worked as a radio writer and talk-show host, an advertising creative director, and a communications officer.

A past resident of Saskatoon, Toronto, and northern Saskatchewan, Gayleen now lives in Edmonton with novelist Laird Ryan States in a home that includes dogs, geckos, snakes, monitor lizards, and Marlowe the tegu. When not writing, she can be found kayaking, photographing unsuspecting wildlife, and playing cooperative board games, viciously competitive card games, and tabletop RPGs.

Gayleen can be found on:
Twitter @gayleenfroese
Facebook @GayleenFroeseWriting
And www.gayleenfroese.com